The Young Man Who Perfected Love

The Young Man Who Perfected Love

by

Dennis J. Reader

www.sempervirensbooks.com

*For my wife, Karen, and
our long loving journey together*

--Contents--

The Young Man
Who Perfected Love

PROLOGUE

"Geronimo from San Francisco"

Geronimo from San Francisco

1.

"What's in a name?" asks a famous question. During those violent years of World War II his fellow soldiers called him "Geronimo from San Francisco," because they witnessed his secret wild solo raids against the German enemy in the North African night, and they had heard that his duffle bag might be full of severed German trophy ears. But he was not a renegade Chiricahua Apache and he killed, if he must, only out of love for a charming petite German girl. Her name—as he would explain to the Army psychiatrist—was Silke Wolke, who lived at 122 Adlersweg, Augsburg, Germany. In point of fact, he himself was not even from San Francisco, instead from Redwood City, which is nearby, close enough to ignore and not spoil a good rhyme.

His first nickname had been "GMC" for General Medals Corporation, an affectionate term since the soldiers pined for the Chevy, Buick or Oldsmobile built by General Motors Corporation that they drove at home not long ago, before 1942. This thumbs-up acronym was due to his quick rush of combat medals and promotion to sergeant. Yet after a time when repeated mad bravery seemed more just ordinary madness, and after a time when the sergeant showed more appetite for dangerous deeds than for his food in the mess tent, to the uneasy soldiers the highly decorated sergeant became, in the end, a friendless Geronimo.

"This is *not* your *private* battlefield, Sergeant," an upset, or confused, officer once informed him, without raising his voice much. No one cared to threaten the sergeant directly. While this Geronimo without fail acted calm and civil, nevertheless here stood a man, at polite attention, said to slit throats by moonlight.

No surprise that eventually an order arrived for the sergeant to attend a mandatory evaluation session with Major Seymour Fiedelmann, M.D., an hour's bumpy ride rearward from the combat zone. The major held office in a large canvas tent with red medical crosses on its rooftop, and furnished inside, somehow, with genuine civilian wooden desk and chairs. Upon the desk rested several very fat file folders with the sergeant's serial number stenciled across the front. The two occupants in the privacy of the tent presented many contrasts: the major immaculate, slight, pallid, bespectacled, hunched forward in his seat, and standing there the sergeant, rangy, rough at the edges, his brown eyes and uncut brown hair blending with desert-browned skin. What the two had in equal measure was certainty of purpose. The little major felt no fear of Geronimo.

"Sit, Sergeant Lemay, sit. I read in here"—tapping the files on the desk—"that I could call you Sarge Starlight or Captain Midnight or how about The Grim Reaper. Have you heard the men using those names before?"

"Along with Kilroy Killed Here."

"That one missed making the reports. Otherwise I know your story quite well. Quite well." The major did know the story, *quite well*, and to prove it immediately began reciting the particulars of how a new soldier, private first class, arrived at the battle front, an interrogation/translator specialist in German, who had cooked up excuses to hitch rides with the HQ couriers collecting field reports from the company commanders, and while overnighting there had outright lied his way into tagging along with squads doing picket duty on the perimeters, and later with the sentinels perched at the edge of no-man's land, and finally he was wandering off by himself beyond where only snipers went. One thick dissolving dawn this Geronimo had surfaced, luckily with the correct American password, his Colt M1911 .45 pistol herding a pair of German sentries, their mouths stuffed full of sand to guarantee silence. The Army decided to award the private with his first promotion and first medal.

To create a legend or a scandal, a story repeats itself beyond reason. On many more nights the new corporal disappeared alone somewhere into the unnerving bareness of the Tunisian plains, helmet off, dabbed with his own home brew of camouflage paint, toting an extra (unauthorized) revolver and compact binoculars. Before darkness fell he always informed the closest lieutenant of his departure, without asking for permission, his tersely given logic more than once recorded in field notes as "The corporal stated that a family relative was an expert bowhunter who had taught him a big bag of stalking tricks." His subsequent rise in rank to sergeant and his recommendations for medals often had in their citations—too often had—such feeble nonsense as "Lost when seeking to find a latrine, the sergeant engaged the enemy, whereby he . . ." followed here by an enumeration of stolen German weapons, the precise location of German positions, and the occasional befuddled actual German soldier.

"No more citations can come your way," said Major Fiedelmann, "no more promotions. Do you understand *why*?"

"Yes, sir."

"Does that disappoint you?"

"No, sir."

"I thought not. Sit back, Sergeant, lean back and relax. Okay, I see that you *are* relaxed. Sergeant, you possess a high education, two university degrees, and I intend speaking directly, without any of the usual psychotherapy stratagems or maneuvers. You comprehend why we're together today. You know already that your nightly adventures are abnormal, counter not only to military regulations, but a deadly threat to your own safety."

"Yes, sir."

"And so I need to determine why you do it, and if you intend continuing to do it. Please be honest with me. This is a difficult war and we can't waste time. All right. Let's jump straight in. Do you enjoy danger, Sergeant, or feel a craving or desire for intense excitement. To put it simpler, do you like being scared shitless. Is it—remember I said be frank—sexual for you in any sort of way. For example, do you ever masturbate when out there by yourself?"

"No on all counts, sir."

"No on all counts. All right. Let's go to the main issue then. Can you imagine changing your pattern, tomorrow or next week, changing your motives, whatever they might be, and stopping these strange outings of yours?"

"No, sir."

"All right. I asked for honesty, and I received it, which is appreciated. A lesser man would have lied his way out of this hole we're in here. All right. Sergeant, if I use the term 'freelance berserker' would you understand me?"

"I think so, sir."

"While it doesn't happen often in our army—rare in fact—we do have our case studies, where war is a fun party for homicidal deviates, a perhaps once-in-a-lifetime license to murder with free heavy weapons provided by our own USA. And I look at you, Sergeant, and I ask myself, is that *you*. Are you a real Grim

Reaper that your buddies talk about?"

"I probably don't have any buddies, sir."

"Are you a killer?"

"Sir, I can't answer."

Major Fiedelmann studied his oversized steel-rimmed wristwatch, oversized at least on his spindled wrist, using the protracted squint to shuffle his mental cards. "I have another appointment due," he informed himself and the sergeant, "plus I was scheduled to submit, today, my recommendation on whether or not to send you back homeside, to the States." But in no apparent hurry the major began thumbing the sheets inside those folders on his desk, not reading them, merely riffling the pages with a monotonous flip-flip-flip noise. "I noticed your academic honors," said the major, "and I noticed you refused the Army's request to attend Officer Candidate School, making a little stink over the issue."

"Yes, sir. I chose to be a shooting soldier right away at the front, sir."

"Your great wish to be a shooting soldier is the puzzle, is it not. And your assignment as translator has been a disappointment no doubt, although you found other solutions, shall we say. Tell me, Sergeant, do you have a special animosity against German people?"

"No, sir."

"Is your own family of German heritage?"

"Swiss and British more or less, sir."

"You have those two degrees—bachelor's, master's—in German language and literature from Stanford University. Your German is officially rated as *native speaker*."

"An academic specialty, sir."

"But *native speaker*?"

"I was a motivated student, sir," said the sergeant. "More specifically, I found myself in love with a German girl, a foreign student on campus."

"Sergeant?" The major removed his glasses, although the blinking soft focus of his eyes indicated that he could not see well without them.

"By graduation we were engaged, sir. At the moment, sir, she still lives in Germany."

"Hold the horses. Put on the brakes. Let me count to ten. Better, I need to count to a hundred. What the devil are you telling me. That you do your nighttime stage show in order to get to Germany? Faster? Quicker? Because what, you what, you love a girl there?"

"Yes, sir."

Now the major did check his watch with a more practical intent. "All right. Waiting outside my tent is an eighteen-year-old infantryman from Tallahassee who shot himself in the foot, on purpose. Quite a different tale from yours, we might judge, except the boy was married shortly before sailing over here. All right. All right, all right, all right. I'll be requesting one more meeting with you before my decision. Please get out so my head can stop spinning."

"Yes, sir."

2.

A dusty wind slapped and scratched against the tent's walls, a miserable morning, identical to most mornings in this tortured land. Absent from Major Fiedelmann's desktop was the bother of any file folders and in their place steamed a mug of coffee, reeking its bitterness to the heavens. The major projected a figure ready for stern duty: clean-shaven, damp hair freshly combed, uniform pressed and exemplary. He stated the rules for their session. "Today, Sergeant, you will do the talking. You will elaborate about this lady, your fianceé. No more of these one- or two-word sentences from you. Sergeant, you will begin at the beginning and end only at the end. Sergeant, you will spill your guts out today."

The sergeant need not stretch far to retrieve the details for the major. No, the opposite of far. Of course he will deliver Dr. Fiedelmann only a cautious protected monochrome version of his story, while the sergeant's own simultaneous memories blossom with a rainbow palette. Rainbow palette? To him there could be no possible hyperbole about Silke Wolke.

Even at the first, back at the absolute first, when she entered a crowded Stanford lecture hall, circled anxiously about, finally locating an empty seat next to his, even then everything he saw and felt about her registered at an outer limit. "Have I here the proper class of Mr. Professor Fitch?" she asked, her English spiced with numerous sweet missteps and struggling to Americanize its British imitation. She waited for an answer, looking up, not a stroke of cosmetics on her face, nothing to distract him from the gray-with-green eyes or green-with-gray, whichever the ceiling lights chose to reflect at any instant. There was no mistaking her for an American girl. Her midnight-color hair swept forward along the sides into what people call a pixie cut, yet with sufficient length to touch her temples, resembling, in his agitated mind in those initial moments, a crown of feathered ebony. Trimly tailored black tweed slacks met up with strapped wooden sandals. And that burgundy sweater hugging her, expensive cashmere it was, and worth every cent. "The correct room," he reassured her, lacking the gumption to continue with "and I beg you to come back, to sit beside me every single day." As she did, Major Fiedelmann, as she certainly did.

Fräulein Wolke was nineteen when she walked into that classroom. By the end of their first week he had bought a German dictionary, to help her over the language potholes. By the end of their first year he had switched his study program to German. After three years of days and nights together he knew that she would be coming to sit by him for the rest of their lives. When he started his graduate work they rented adjacent studio apartments, preserving the appearance of propriety. Naturally that lone wall never separated them and they examined one another as much as they read their books. Once he stood behind her as she sat at a desk, reaching down with the fingers of each hand to press against each fluted side of her throat, telling her to read the Rilke poems aloud, and he felt with fingertips those sensuous German gutturals, those teased umlaut vowels, those lavish sibilants. "Go on," he would say, then and often, "keep speaking in German." She would laugh and consent with a mock groan, "So I'll never learn English, but anyhow my German is improving." When he told her that he intended to master her language, by this fingertip osmosis preferably, she reminded him, "Who should care. You're already the master of *me*."

With her delicate figure and features, her cheeks and lips rose-tinged without makeup, Silke could be misjudged as childlike. Beware, beware, because that slim body and that intellect both packed a potent wallop. And although her complexion, especially without clothes, shone nearly a China Doll alabaster, Silke was not some dolly plaything of accommodating emotions. Her full name, Silke Wolke—by combining faulty English spelling with correct German—can be translated as "silky cloud." He elucidated this linguistic magic, as they lay on a bed, by running his hand down her naked supple back, over the rise of a hip, down again along a *silky* thigh. Her skin was the color of a pearl cumulus *cloud* that appears in the sunlit sky on warm summer afternoons. He so described to her why she was by name a bilingual beauty, and she responded by twisting his nose, hard, and labeling him "a silly guy in love."

He agreed. "Not much to argue with there. Let's admit though that my translation skills are a stairstep higher than yours, and I'm sticking by the truth of my rhetoric."

"And I love you for loving me that much. But you're still a goofy boy."

Together, in August of 1941, they visited the Wolke home in Augsburg, where her father is a successful banker of importance. The substantial house at 122 Adlersweg commanded a fine downslope view of the city. Her parents were courteous and respectful. Her only, and younger, brother turned out to be a male copy of his sister—slight and refined of build, a handsome kid, almost pretty, friendly as blazes to the American, an all-around excellent candidate for a brother-in-law. His name was Stefan and in an aside he whispered, "Mom and Dad had an affection for names beginning with *s*, no?" "Just consider," he had whispered back to Stefan, "since my name's *S*-pencer, we form a perfect trio." Soon—if not already—Stefan would be old enough to wear a military uniform, a troubling thought. But on these August 1941 days, as a family group, they enjoyed the late summer weather, ignored the war bulletins, went picnicking on the greens along the Lech River, wicker baskets heaped with fresh bakery goods.

On December 1, 1941, Silke made a return trip for the Christmas holidays in Germany. On December 7, 1941, as the radio in California reported the Japanese war attack in Hawaii, he forgot to breathe and wondered what this news meant for him. It meant the worst of possibilities. And it meant that this sergeant was now on the coastline of Tunisia, only the Mediterranean Sea away from Europe, in a hospital tent with a major who was about to send him back to America.

That major was peering down into his coffee mug, musing. "Well. All right. That has to be a compelling history of yours, because I forgot to drink this java juice." Slowly he raised his usual sloped shoulders upward into their authority position, the posture of a Major Seymour Fiedelmann, M.D. "All right. Let's settle up now. I admit to conditional sympathies with you. I can appreciate your compulsion to be in action, that is, to feel yourself in command of a destiny, putting yourself in *motion* toward an important goal. I do appreciate that. Yet I remind myself that I am the doctor and you are the patient, and you *are* a patient, Sergeant Lemay, howsoever much we may dislike that reference. Bluntly—as we must be now with each other—you are what we medically consider 'a danger to yourself.' In other words, Sergeant, if I don't send you home immediately, the Army will ship you back to California sooner or later in a box, likely sooner. Then you'll never meet up again with your fianceé, will you. Don't worry, don't worry, this won't be a Section Eight mental disability discharge, not with those medals and citations of yours. The report will recommend a simple honorable transfer to stateside duties. I only hope you respect and grant me my requirement to be a good doctor."

"Major, I ask another requirement of you."

"You do?"

"Yes, sir."

"A requirement for me?"

"I do, sir. I ask that you be a better Jew than you are a good doctor. Anyway for this single time, sir. From your silence I believe you want me to explain. I will, sir. To begin, I've read *Mein Kampf.* Twice. I read the German newspapers. I visited Germany. Major, let's please not pretend we two don't know what's up there. Major, you might sit behind your desk during this war and save my skin or you can allow this sick-headed sergeant to be a sword in your hand. I can't express it in any other words. If for my own selfishly foolish purpose I put myself in Germany three hours faster than otherwise would happen, then the Army arrives three hours earlier. Sorry, sir. We did agree on honesty, sir."

The major took a long reflexive suck of his coffee and spat it back into the mug. "Awful," he said, "cold and awful. Excuse the splatter." In a desk drawer he found a tissue and blotted his chin. "You're a crafty smart-ass fellow." The wadded tissue got sent like an angry bullet into a wastebasket. "Come back tomorrow, late. After five o'clock."

The third and final meeting with Major Fiedelmann was grim and swift. "Do not give me anything resembling a thank-you," instructed the major, "and that's an order. Do *not* put a smile of any type on your lips."

"Yes, sir."

"I know about a young combat officer, a West Pointer, just

made captain, an ambitious guy who sticks his nose into the middle of the fight. He agrees to take you for a scout as your sole duty, day or night, no hassles, no interrogation work, *if* you promise a genuine commitment to stay alive."

"May I meet the captain tomorrow?"

"He's waiting for you outside with his jeep."

3.

The captain, Captain Donald Delaney from the Chicago shore, walked with the sergeant to the seclusion of his jeep, parked under a camouflage tarp. "Welcome to my personal garage," he indicated. The captain was youthful yet matured by a taut intensity, his body fidgeting from some habitual preoccupation or other, his blue eyes bright and sharp, his cropped blonde hair already receding. Settled with the sergeant into the jeep's front seats, he said without prelude, "Sure, Geronimo, I know what the men call you. And the brass suspect you have only one oar in the water. I looked over your medico dope sheet, the spiel about compulsion *this*, delusional *that*, destructive *whatever.*"

"Destructive narcissism."

"A swell mouthful. Is it on the mark?"

"Maybe halfway, sir."

"So you're crazy, Sarge?"

"But only halfway, sir."

"Ahh." The captain rapped a thumb knuckle thoughtfully

against his front teeth, viewing the sergeant impatiently. "It's obvious that you're taller and bigger than I am. You're a goddamn tougher soldier. And you're older than I am and kinda better looking. I graduated 14th in my class at West Point, but you're smarter and more educated. If you *are* crazy, who the hell am I to figure that out, or care, and I don't. This is business between us, yes, Sarge? In awhile we'll sail for Sicily, move on to the Italian mainland, with lots and lots of business to handle, and you and I can do each other some good."

"I like our arrangement. Incidentally, sir, could you pick me up one of those new Winchester M2 auto carbines, that paratrooper's version with the folding skeleton stock, pistol grip, 30-round clip?"

"Incidentally?" The captain had to unloosen, letting out a positively boyish grin. "Oh, Sarge, you sound like a *winner*. Okay, sure, incidentally I'll try. What I can't give you are recommendations for any medals or promotions, and that's goddamn unfair."

"I never wanted medals."

"I believe you. I believe that, without having a clue about what does make you tick."

"I'm in a real hurry to reach Germany, sir."

Captain Delaney brushed away the pesky inevitable Tunisian gnats. "Yeah, right. We want to get this goddamn war finished and over."

"Let me lay it all on the table. My fianceé is waiting for me in

Augsburg, Germany."

"Your? Say again. Did I hear what I heard?"

"A German girl, waiting for me in Augsburg."

"Seriously?"

"Yes, Captain, seriously."

"God*damn*. Weird enough, but fair enough. Let's go then."

4.

They were drunk or close to it, the sergeant and the captain, having reached the bottom of a gallon of local wine, a pulpy drink that could be chewed a little before swallowing. Their jeep was parked in a dry creek bed, near the decrepit Italian hamlet Bellsignana, out of sight in case they got too drunk, and since their partnership months before had been planned in the seclusion of a jeep, so it continued. The captain, betrayed by a relaxed state of loopiness, was slipping into forbidden questions he had never wanted answered before. "Hey there, tell me. Tell me how you ever picked up those German field maps."

"Not important," said the sergeant.

"But I want to hear about it for once."

"I bring back crap all the time."

"Crap? This wine is crap. German field maps are a *treasure*. Losing them is a *disaster*. You didn't find these things waiting by themselves under a tree somewhere."

"Under a tree."

"Under a tree. Hogwash. Look at me. Are you seeing straight? Jesus, I can't tell 'cause I'm not seeing straight either. But hogwash."

"Well, the maps were under a tree."

"How *dangerous* was this? How goddamn dangerous was that goddamn tree?"

"I can't say how dangerous."

"You can't?" The captain tipped back a final swig, the sergeant the same, their lips and tongues stained a crude purple, and the jug was empty. "You can't. Why not, you can't?"

"Seems like at sometime, somehow, at someplace, or other, I lost the feeling for whatever danger is. Just lost it."

The view far to the northwest was of a mountain known in Italian as Mount Felicity, where lately sorrow had reigned instead. Captain Delaney at this instant felt in his bones why the other men, when eating in the mess tent, sat apart from the sergeant after nodding respectful hellos, their distance an instinct for a safety zone. The soldiers did prize their Geronimo, whose reconnaissance miracles brought fame to his military family, and yet, few men can sit easy around a spectre who prowls after sundown like a hungry vampire, and who will end up with a silver bullet in his own heart. "The jug's finished, right?" said the captain. "The goddamn jug. Listen, you can hear me. If I use a *please*, will you tell what went on that night. With the goddamn maps?"

"My same old routine. Same whoop-de-do. Wait for night,

smudge up my face, wiggle though woods, slide-slide-slide past both front positions, way beyond."

"Risky," said the captain. "Very very risky."

"Once you reach the rear zone, it's easier. Nobody expects trouble from behind. Nobody checks backward. At daylight I hole up in the brush, eat my rations, nap."

"Risky. Very."

"Check around any battlefield and you find mostly blank space with plenty of hiding nooks, some comfortable. At nightfall here I come again, in reverse, directly up their backs."

"Craziness. You *are* crazy. Stop. You're scaring me sober. No, no, I mean go on, finish it. Go-go-go ahead, finish."

"I wait until two o'clock in the morning about, until it's blackest and coldest, when the Germans want to stay asleep, the same as our men do. Sometimes I think a tired soldier would rather die than wake up. Sometimes he does die. If I locate the shape of a map case, or anything special, I crawl in to snag it, and by crawling I mean slow as, say, twenty meters in an hour. That's the trick, being slower than the shadows. If a voice speaks out, I might answer. That's the best emergency trick, the mother tongue, the mother tongue that coaxes the fussy baby to close its eyes. I've had many conversations with voices from the dark, half in German, the other half in English when I meet our sentries. Of the two, green GI's worry me the most."

Captain Delaney rolled his head back, neck blocked against the seat top. "I'm trying to picture this. I'm concentrating, sort of.

You go creeping in. You might chat a bit. You take the goddamn maps. *Auf Wiedersehen*."

"It was black as sin. No moon."

"No moon. Easy as pie."

"A rainy night with no moon is absolutely tops. I could steal their underwear."

With a clatter the captain rolled the jug over the jeep's door cutout, onto the gravelly ground. He scolded himself, "I'm another American litterbug in Europe. Empty shell casings and empty wine jugs covering a continent. Sarge, don't make me send back home the wrong kind of letter. Our business together isn't so much fun for me, nowadays, you should know. Whenever you vanish for a day, or *three* days, I think, goodbye, that's it, finally."

"Their underwear while they still had the underwear on, if that part wasn't clear."

"You have a mother and a kid brother or someone waiting back in California. They write. I saw the letters."

"No living mother or father. But there's a mothering older sister, who dotes on me, her son, my brainy kid nephew, both in California, her husband, a decent guy fighting out in the Pacific, Silke Wolke in Germany, a captain and sergeant stuck in Italy without any wine in a jeep with a white star on the hood. That's my summary."

"Silke Wolke. Huh? Oh, she's the one. Goddamn that wine for letting me ask about those maps and goddamn you for telling. That's my summary."

* * * *

Seasons shifted, locations to hide a jeep changed. On this Sunday afternoon, with the jeep's fabric top and panels in place, its windshield raised, a rain by itself created sufficient privacy. As window droplets congealed they turned into abrupt downward trails on glass, their unpredictability a silent entertainment. Today's superb vintage *Chianti Riserva* had to be commandeered by Major Delaney, whose excuse for the theft was celebrating an advancement in rank and his reassignment to France as tactical liaison officer with a regimental HQ staff. The new major was considered a super-duper prospect, he told the sergeant, "the most successful young officer in this sinkhole Italian campaign." The major handed over authentic crystal stemware for the wine. "But we both know I owe my brilliance, and my career, to you."

"Don't puff it up."

"I'm not. Puffing it up I'm not, my good friend. What grates on me is how to give you credit without pitching both of us into hot water. Anyhow I'll guess that you've a reward suggestion from me. Whoosh, this ambrosia goes down quick, eh? Listen to this crystal ring." He pinged his empty goblet rim before refilling.

The sergeant, after his own refill, said, "And you guessed right about my reward. Take me along to France. Put me and keep me in a spearhead unit. Advise my company commander that I'm strictly recon and will report to Major Delaney through him. Congratulations, Major, by the way. A shiny gold oak leaf suits you. Lovely foliage."

The new major finished his glass. "Wait, what am I doing, gulping this expensive wine." He poured his glass full again. "I'm sipping now. Oops, not sipping."

"With these mountains in Italy," said the sergeant, "and the Alps up ahead, we won't make it into Germany before the war ends. In my opinion, the big push will roll across the flatlands of France and Belgium."

"With armor and air cover."

"Let's drink to a fast dash to German dirt."

"You and me."

"The sergeant and the major. Congratulations again."

"How do I pull off your transfer?"

"The smartest young officer in Italy has only a minor request. You West Pointers always chum together. The brotherhood of the best. Terrific wine."

Major Delaney was already refilling both glasses. "Goddamn terrific wine." Looking through a crack around the jeep's side curtain, he checked the soggy grass below, the mud in the field, inhaling its smell, imagining the sticky goo back at camp, and not forgetting that the sergeant had previously announced he was scouting tonight because of this weather. "Sarge, don't be offended. But I wonder if I can handle the responsibility of you anymore—to spell out my worries in capital letters. This week I discovered three or four white hairs, at my age, and I don't own that much hair in the first place."

"Fill us up. Then drink up."

"Don't go out tonight, Sarge. Let's take a break. We can coast for a while."

"Drink up. I'm headed to France."

"Why do I do this, letting you go out again in the night. I can break a promise. Why don't I order you to stay?"

"Because you know why *I* do it, and besides, the major intends to be a light colonel before we reach the Rhine and a full bird colonel before we leave Europe altogether."

Major Delaney did drink up. "God*damn* it. You turned me into a genuine drunk."

"Goddamn it."

"Goddamn me especially. If you let yourself be killed, I'll fry in hell, and deserve it. Stay alive. Stay alive at least until I make lieutenant colonel, which could ease my sins a little. What's this burbling in your Chianti. Am I such a joke?"

"Negative. I laugh when the major is good, when the wine is good, and when Geronimo gets an overnight slog in a rain poncho."

* * * *

While Major Delaney always had expected this day, he felt a blow, and an unprofessional pain, when their last private meeting happened, late 1944 with their American units in grimy snow on the pastured fields of Belgium, waiting for suitable weather and the assault into Germany. Instead of sitting in a jeep, the major and sergeant sat in the heated kitchen of a stone farmhouse. Instead of stealing a select wine to celebrate the major's approval for another promotion, they smoked expensive cigars and cozied up to the stove. "Passing out cigars," said Major Delaney, "is the honored custom for announcing new babies or new lieutenant colonels, I forget which."

"Make it then for a baby lieutenant colonel. I don't notice any other colonels your age around here."

Through their twin streamers of cigar smoke the major, observing across the table, already experienced a sinking of spirits. Possibly the bleak icy sky behind the windows on this cheerless Sunday had its effect, but the sergeant himself showed a bleakness. He fit the standard storybook illustration of a Wild West frontier hunter gone feral: too gaunt, too unwashed, quiet from too much solitude. The top half of an ear was missing. A grizzly could have chewed it off in a tussle, although another sort of beast did the job, a Mauser MG42, recognizable by its deep coughing growl at 1200 bites a minute. "Goddamn it," Major Delaney had bellowed out from afar when he saw the bandage and softer, much later, when touching the curled scar tissue. "Close, close, close. Like I said before, you deserve another medal, but goddamn it, why the Purple Heart?"

They snacked on fresh baguettes and potent cheese, an acquisition equal to the cigars. "You never fail to be an A-1 provider of treats," said the sergeant. "And of favors. New boots, new transfers. And now your last favor for me. Please."

The major lurched, mistakenly set his cigar down on the wrong plate, dusting the baguettes with ashes. "Sure. I think."

"I need to be put into the best possible combat position for Augsburg, Germany."

"So soon. Has that time come already? Lord, can I even find Augsburg on a map?"

"Here's my best condensed schoolhouse lecture. Ready for it? Augsburg is located near Munich at the confluence of the Wertach and Lech rivers, founded 15 B.C. by Roman emperor Augustus, population 185,000, Mozart's father born there, Silke also born there. Today she still lives there, along with its fabric mills, acetylene producers, machine factories, and unfortunately the Messerschmitt aircraft works. The Huns destroyed Augsburg in the 5th century, Charlemagne in the 8th, the kingdom of Bavaria in the 11th, now American and Brit bombs in the 20th. Reassign me to the end of our southern flank, the 3rd or 7th Army, or whoever will lead into Bavaria. Check with the big brass and pull all your strings for me, will you?"

"Goddamn. Is my head nodding? I feel my head nodding *yes*, even though you're a habit I'd prefer not to break. And you just spoiled my celebration party, incidentally."

"No, no," said the sergeant. "For that I'm sorry."

"Hey, old friend. I look at you and don't like what I'm seeing. I see a beat-up soldier who's lost maybe twenty pounds, has dirt under his fingernails, and in general looks like a pile of barnyard fertilizer."

"This dirt and I are very good buddies. We travel everywhere together, have for months."

"I intend to ask you to do *me* a last favor. Allow me to arrange a two-week furlough in Paris, or London . . . better London, if I can manage London. Spend two weeks soaking your fingernails and the whole rest of you in a hot soapy bathtub. Don't wag your head NO."

"Am I wagging my head?"

"You wag your head without wagging your head. Two short weeks. A favor to me?"

"Anything else and I would. Anything else. But thanks. And thanks for the booze you bought and stole and shared. Thanks for letting me roam far and wide. Thanks for not asking questions. Thanks most for all those worried *goddamns*—they were goddamn authentic, I know."

"Here's my hand. Let's shake. I want you to find whatever you want to find, if that makes sense. Where's that booze when we need some?"

The soon-to-be colonel and the sergeant leaned across the table for their handshake, avoiding the dishonesty of saying, "We'll get soused together again after the war."

5.

Today in Germany is, and feels, like springtime, with a cheery April sun and warmth by mid-morning, more green on the ground than mud for once, birds everywhere on the wing. Germany wants the hard winter to stay away and never come again. Four

American soldiers move through the sylvan landscape on an advance probe into unknown territory, across wooded slopes above Swabian valleys, in the direction of Munich. In the lead is the sergeant. Behind him come the other three, each age twenty, one from Texas, one from Utah, one from New Hampshire, each on tiptoes like trespassing hikers. Nobody intends to die and ruin such a lovely postcard day when the war is already good as won.

Whenever a farm building or house appears, the reconnaissance team edges to higher terrain and scans below with binoculars. Other than an abandoned *Kugelwagen* jeep the *Wehrmacht* has left no trace, and the fighting apparently will resume farther ahead, at Ulm or Augsburg and the buffer strip around Munich. Now the American scouts are scheduled to turn back, and the soldier from Utah calls softly, "Whatcha think, Sarge?" The one from Texas adds, "Past 11 hunnert hours, Sarge." And the sergeant halts until they bunch together, the private from New Hampshire unpeeling a chocolate bar, everyone waiting for instructions.

The sergeant reviews their return route because he will stay behind as usual. He says, "Tell the captain not to wait for me, and I'll turn up when I turn up, and if I don't turn up, put me down as MIA. Tell him under no condition to stop and search for me. Who knows, maybe I'll meet you boys later in Berlin for the victory party." The soldiers have anticipated this sort of briefing, given the extra fullness of the sergeant's pack, just as they expect their captain once again to cuss before tossing up his hands in resignation. The boy from Texas, an unspoken admirer, would join the sergeant, almost, but lacks the nerve to go along, let alone the nerve to ask. None of them wishes the sergeant good luck. General Medals Corporation, drinker of German blood since North Africa, needs no luck: sneak a peek at those metallic eyes, at his skin weathered into a piece of animal hide, at that ear torn away—bitten off by an SS sniper he had choked to death the scuttlebutt was.

Instead of a goodbye the men share their food snacks with the sergeant. In the middle of this social pause he disappears, blending into forest patterns with his camouflaged paratrooper pants, olive wool cap snug over his hair. On their return trip, Utah, Texas, and New Hampshire hurry along, nagged by a confidence slump without Geronimo from San Francisco nearby in the lead.

* * * *

By himself the sergeant moves faster, winding through screens of Black Forest pines and firs, orienting his memorized map toward 122 Adlersweg. Late in the afternoon at a musical mountain rill split by a thrust of boulders, and sent splashing down into separate ravines, he hides himself, uses his pack as a pillow, and falls asleep listening to the free lullaby. With darkness he is on his feet again. Despite all the splendid stars, under the forest canopy the night has contracted into syrupy black, allowing him safe passage on a wide hillside path abandoned by anything human, or at least by sensible people afraid to be caught at dark where the brothers Grimm found witches and wolves on the loose. The sergeant lets a few of their folktales occupy his mind, and the miles pass by.

At dawn, into the daylight, he remains on the open path, parallel to a road in the valley below. This exposure could be risky, but Germany seems deserted. The sergeant calculates that two more days at this rapid pace will find him closer to Augsburg than to his own American troops, and that city, broken apart, was ripe for his invasion, with or without the U.S. Army. Throughout the day he does not stop or leave the path until his afternoon rest. During the next long night he hurries over the foot trail, taking out a poncho when a chill shower hits, and he walks faster yet, in defiance of the wet, eating on the go. The rising sun at dawn scatters the nighttime clouds into salmon-and-soot colors, finally with the passing hours chasing them altogether away, leaving behind the bluest sky and warmest day of the season.

At noon the sergeant notices in the distance a collection of roofs—a village surrounded by plots of farm fields—and shifting into the forest cover as he approaches, he uses this opportunity to sit, concealed, and finish a meal of K-rations. He tries to count the number of cows being herded by a farmer through a gate. The total is either eight or nine. Finding a dry cloth in the pack he wipes down his M2 and cleans the ammo clip, inserting it back into the rifle. The smell of fresh metal, as part of a customary routine, reminds him to brush his teeth, rinsing his mouth afterward from the hip canteen filled with brook water. Deciding to count those cows exactly he hauls out the binoculars. Eight cows. There are eight cows, and tucked behind the barn's corner, under a ramshackle lean-to, is a *Schützenpanzerwagen* 251 armored half-track, painted German field gray, complete with a 20mm *Flak* mounted on its anti-aircraft pedestal. Removing his pack the sergeant angles in a serpentine drift down toward the village. Binoculars out again he locates several more *SdKfz* 251's squirreled away in ambush positions, these equipped with 37mm *Pak* cannons. Over there, under camouflage netting beside a rustic cottage where somebody's grandmother was presently hanging out her laundry to dry, stands a short row of 75mm light artillery pieces. All the gear, all the visible soldiers in their matched uniforms, display a legitimate fighting *Wehrmacht* unit, not a nest of stragglers, and the sergeant decides they have orders to delay his own advance column of Americans—metaphorically, a frantic strike by a cornered snake just as a boot stomps down to crush its head.

Uphill at his pack again, he sits, gathering up his equipment and his thoughts before he pulls out of here for Augsburg. The sergeant has no desire to reverse his direction and make the trek back for a military report. Let the U.S. Army end the war without him. Let him clear his mind of this war—he never liked it anyway—and leave room inside only for images of 122 Adlersweg and a happy August filled with days also bright and warm, as this April day is.

So potent are his activated visions of 1941 they invent a

deception. Because the sergeant hears Silke's voice speaking aloud, her actual voice, or a female German voice that could have been heard at a picnic on the grassy banks of the Lech River. And it is a real voice. He aims himself at the sound, leaving behind the pack to burrow quietly through the tightest thickets, ending at the edge of a small open circle near the pathway. Brush arching overhead, the sergeant lies there flat on his stomach in the spongy rot of last year's leaves, his chin resting on the sideways M2.

Out in the cleared space, on a blanket, a young couple in an appropriate coincidence is finishing a picnic, marmalade and rolls, a modest imitation of the Wolke family feast. The girl wears a traditional dirndl frock that seems out of place in a forest, with flared sleeves and full skirt, pale in color, decorated by pink embroidery down the bodice. Her companion has on a baggy militia uniform, the pants held up by a civilian belt, and street shoes instead of regulation boots. Speaking in an ardent mush of Swabian diphthongs, the boy is praising the girl's hair. "Gretel" he calls her, proving that the Grimm brothers knew their business hereabouts. Her hair does deserve approval, with a rich maple sheen from the wavering sunbeams, its single heavy braid, meticulously woven and laid forward over a shoulder, falling under its own weight to lodge into the focus line between her breasts. The embroidery there at the bodice depicts pink flowers on green vines. She approximates the age of Silke Wolke back when Silke first walked into the lecture hall at Stanford, but unlike that sylph from Augsburg, this girl's image suits her dirndl dress. Her face has a healthy, buttermilk-fed, country maiden's complexion, her lips and the entire fulsome body voluptuous at this early stage before it soon passes into comfortable plumpness. The boy wishes to kiss those lips, he says. She permits it without showing excitement. "I think about you always," the boy tells her, "and that makes me feel very good." He places an awkward arm around her shoulders. Somberly, she lectures him, "Whenever the shooting starts, duck down and stay down, if you can. Dieter, keeping out of it is the best idea."

They continue talking, with interference from an occasional kiss, the girl channeling the topic into further cautionary advice. To concentrate the sergeant closes his eyes, following the complex musical score of her German cadences. He knows it has been a lifetime since he last pressed his fingertips against Silke's throat, registering there her words and her heartbeat, a mixture he could never forget, but which feels in April 1945 more and more like only touching a dream about a dream. Her last words to him had been written, not spoken. In 1942 came a letter from Augsburg to California, via Lisbon, Portugal, when such a contact was still possible, and the letter rushed him that same day to an Army recruiting office. Silke's precisely chiseled handwriting, a calligraphy nearly, he had recognized with hurtful delight. The intent of her letter he had not recognized. "The big world has left our tiny world behind," she wrote, a storm of ambiguity hanging over that sentence, and this from a mind that by choice always insisted on clarity. She did not include the important word "love" above her signature. Unavoidable, how much the letter had frightened him, threatened him, with its demand for answers. Here was Silke Wolke seeking to protect him in some sacrificial way. Or here was Silke Wolke the pragmatic banker's daughter dealing out cold final facts.

* * * *

"Grüß Gott, grüß euch," intrudes a series of hellos from out front in the clearing, as a German patrol enters in its tactical file, 1, 2, 3, 4, 5, 6, 7, 8 soldiers appearing, one for each of the farmer's cows. All are armed with front-line weapons, the *Gewehr* 43, an *Obergefreiter* even carrying a *Sturmgewehr* MP 44, the best attack rifle in the world and a gun the sergeant would be using himself had he collected enough German ammunition. These soldiers, hardly older than the boy, appear a generation beyond, from the grime deepening their facial creases, from that fatigue, that surrendered fatalism in their body stance. The sergeant is familiar with these dangerous hallmarks and he carefully rotates his M2, safety off, from under his chin toward the crowded meadow.

The group chats about the nice weather, makes introductions, the soldiers identifying their unit, as does the boy, who offers how he got lucky with a two-day home pass for his mother's birthday. A soldier extends a pack of cigarettes, clipped into halves. "Thanks, no," says the boy. Another soldier unwraps a square of marzipan for the girl, which the boy also declines on her behalf. The soldier insists, "I want her to have it. Here, my last piece of sweets." "No—" begins the boy, but the girl, wiser, steps up and takes a bite, performing a conciliatory "Mmmm . . ." She switches her braid from the breasts to down her back, prompting a soldier to announce, "Such a pretty girl," more a rash observation than compliment. The boy declares, "She's my fiancée."

A significant quiet settles over the clearing, suspending movement, and talk, until a soldier breaks in with his troubled calendar calculations. "The last German girl I kissed was . . . a year ago, April, 1944." Another soldier recalls summer 1943 as his last kiss in Germany, and since then only Polish or French whores. "Wait now," complains the boy, "no foul language, for the sake of my fiancée" and the girl tells him, "Dieter, never mind about that." The soldier in command, a *Feldwebel*, a rank identical to the sergeant's, comments without malice, "Your fiancée, my ass. Your two-day pass, my ass. Nobody gets passes anymore. Germany has a rope around its neck and we're all choking, or didn't your mother explain that at her birthday party?"

"My dear young lady," suggests the soldier with the marzipan chunk, "all my candy, every crumb of it, for a kiss on your palm. I ask as a gentleman."

The boy eyes the exit routes, reciting aloud the hours and minutes the girl is already overdue at home, when someone instructs him, again calmly, to stop lying. "We know what you're after here in the weeds with her, Dieter. We're men, too." A new soldier proposes, probably as a joke, "All the candy, all our cigarettes, all our cash—worthless these days but take it—and what we ask is for some German soldiers to smell a German girl's hair." The boy demands, "I won't permit more talk like this. Won't."

"Dieter*chen*, close your trap," says the *Feldwebel*, his voice at a level now below even calmness, down to indifference, and he bows to the girl with weary reasonableness. "You're a patriot, aren't you? Of course. Shouldn't a countrywoman permit her brave countrymen to smell her clean hair? So little would mean so much. The day after tomorrow the Americans arrive, or the next day, or the next at the latest—"

The boy shouts. His vocal pitch cracks like the youth he is, losing its male timbre. "You pigs! You'll be reported for these filthy threats!"

Instinctively the soldiers react to this abrupt noise, checking around in their survival habit, over their shoulders, into the woods, at the sergeant. But shortly they are chuckling when the boy repeats, "I'll report you myself!" The soldiers say, "Will you tattle to Field Marshal Kesselring or go direct to Berlin and Mr. Hitler? Please tell him how you went AWOL to bang this girl."

Holding her fingers out the girl hushes her friend, and he makes use of this gesture by gripping her hand, leading the two of them away. A quick expert stab with a rifle butt breaks the boy's nose, sinking him to his knees. "Ouch, too bad for the kid," says a soldier, apparently meaning it, with another soldier wondering, "Christ, is this all leading somewhere?" The girl aids the boy to a seat against a tree. Blood gushes desperately, those pink flowers on the girl's bodice lost in spreading stains of red and she staunches the bleeding with her skirt hem. Meanwhile violence has awakened the soldiers from their lethargy and the sight of the girl's soiled dress plainly disturbs them. "The thing is ruined. What a helluva day. We should soak the dress to save it, yes? Steinhauer, your family runs a laundry."

When the soldier, apologizing, makes to examine the bloody fabric the girl shrinks aside, and up struggles the boy, flailing about like a circus clown with a ruptured tomato for a head. A mere shove flattens him again. Most sorry, say the soldiers to the girl, please forgive us, forgive such a terrible embarrassment to you, but the dress must come off. She undoes the hooks, fingers trembling, the halting progress of her slow fumbles, perversely, an allure. Pulling the dress up and over, the girl presents it to the two soldiers who have their canteens ready, and she stands in a muslin chemise, also bloodied, refusing to remove it. But a soldier respectfully inches off the undergarment. The clothing is twice saturated and wrung out, and draped with fussy precision over a limb to dry by the former laundryman. What remains in her nakedness is the blood on her hands, arms, chest, shins, feet, which she washes by herself from a canteen. "Okay, okay," declares someone, "we're finished."

No, there are soldiers with something left to solve. They behave in the manner of certain visitors in an art museum, those novices who squint, perplexed, at a sculpture they might understand if they should step closer or change the angle of their heads or think harder. One of them asks the girl to unfasten her braid. She hesitates, before scooping the braid forward to unlock each knot, letting the hair fan out in rippled kinks as a partial cover for her breasts. This common bedroom action amounts to a revelation. Now the soldiers remember who this statue is and now the girl has eight different names besides Gretel.

"Dortmeier," calls out the *Feldwebel*. "Dorti, you can be the first to touch the girl's hair." The soldier instead politely requests, please *Herr Feldwebel*, if he might be excused to return early to camp. Permission is granted. After the departure, the *Feldwebel* feels obligated to inform the girl, "In February, Dortmeier's wife was firebombed in Dresden. On Valentine's Day, funny enough."

The soldier who last kissed a German girl in 1943 volunteers to kiss a German girl again. Another soldier says, "Hold on. What are we then, a gang of Ivans out raping helpless German women? Wake up. The *Wehrmacht* punishment for raping even a Polish woman is execution by firing squad. And I had to line up and watch that happen in 1940." The first soldier answers, "Who claims a kiss is raping," and another soldier, the *Obergefreiter* with the *Sturmgewehr*, slaps its stock. "Stop at kissing, will we? What an afternoon. I don't want any piece of this, none." He walks away, crouches down, hunched against his thighs. Another soldier says, "The point is, in a couple of weeks the Yanks and the Reds are going to take what we're only yakking about. The

Reds will just hop on her and the Yanks will buy her with a pair of nylons and a big toothy grin." Another soldier says, "Naw, you blockheads. Think why our unit got dumped behind. Think about eating six feet of dirt. That's the real point. Tell me, what'll we put in our empty fuel tanks to escape, our piss?" Another says, "Fuel or not, with these clear skies, the Mustangs will be strafing the meat off our bones."

A silent soldier is picked by the *Feldwebel*, "Because you, Joachim, are always patient and obedient, and because your home is in Königsberg, where your German family has been chased out and will never live again."

The soldier accepts his selection, its command imperative, and lays down his rifle, stepping in front of the girl, saying, "Look how clean she is. I got road crud on me." For all to notice, he is quaking as much as the girl, and under his tree the boy shakes the most. "I'll get her dirty, won't I?" An irritated voice speaks up, "Kiss her, Joachim, you moron. Grab her or something. We can't wait forever until our turn, you know."

The *Obergefreiter* hits the ammunition magazine of his MP44 with a slam of his hand. "Joachim, I'm prepared to shoot you."

"Point your weapon away, Corporal," orders the *Feldwebel*.

The *Sturmgewehr* stays on target. "I believe, yes, I'll plug any sonofabitch who touches her tits."

"Turn that weapon away," demands the *Feldwebel*.

"Joachim," says the *Obergefreiter*, "I like you a lot, but I'll put a round right into your scrawny rump and report it as a weapon malfunction. Joachim, I'm clicking off the safety."

"Horseshit," says the *Feldwebel* and instructs the soldier, "Go on with it," and the soldier takes a pinch of the girl's hair, samples its softness, and kisses that tiny bunch caught between his fingers. The pinch becomes a handful, the handful easily becomes two fistfuls, the kissing becomes tasting the hair as much as kissing, and the soldier's lips follow the flow of her hair down to the shoulders, down to her nipples.

The girl wails, "No shooting! No more blood! Nobody shoot!"

* * * *

This miniature German tragedy in the clearing could not turn any more dramatic, but it does. Out of nowhere and into the open appears the sergeant, his M2 unlocked and level at his hip, an explosive voice at top strength, deliberately putting back the American accent he had labored for years to erase: *"Halt! Keine Bewegung! KEINE! Passt ganz gut auf, meine Jungs,* here's an American soldier who'll gut-shoot you all unless those weapons drop to the ground—slowly, slowly, *schön langsam, schön langsam!"*

Slow they have to be, because the seven of them, the nine, are a tableau of utter shock. What in God's world was *this*, standing there, threatening in German, muck and leaves stuck to his front, outfitted like a forest bandit instead of a soldier, or like a raggedy scarecrow that walked itself up here from a farmer's field down below. But the scarecrow holds a real American rife, a deadly real Winchester automatic buzz gun, and the scarecrow does really scare. The German soldiers let their weapons fall, except for the *Obergefreiter*, who quickly swings around his *Sturmgewehr*, and the sergeant squeezes off a burst that kills him.

The Winchester's sharp chatter rings forth with an unmistakable alarm bell, bouncing copies of itself from mountainside against opposite mountainside, across the distance. Down in the valley bottom everything, and everyone, now knows there is trouble up in those woods, and raise their heads to search: the cows, the grandmother, the *Wehrmacht*.

Using the barrel of his M2 the sergeant directs the soldiers into a cluster, ordering them to strip down and "get as bare as the girl." When the scowling *Feldwebel* hesitates, up snaps the Winchester and the uniforms with underwear fly off in a flurry. "Now, friends," says the sergeant, "you have a choice. Either I shoot you anyway, or you can go, take the boy with you, and promise to have your medic fix his nose. Can you repeat *promise?* Louder. Good, my friends, good. Your clothes stay here. The girl stays here."

Left behind together in their little meadow the sergeant and the girl exchange a stare of mutual puzzlement and suspicion. With the return of stillness to the sunny afternoon the birds, knowing no better, start to sing again.

"Don't be afraid," he tries to reassure the girl, "I won't repeat what they were doing to you." The sergeant retrieves the girl's undergarment and dress, advising, "clammy still," and she accepts assistance fitting into the clingy corners. "Well, Gretel," he says, "an ugly day in an ugly war. May I sit by you?" Her wordless astonishment he takes as consent. "Since I overheard your name already, I'll introduce myself. Sergeant Geronimo. Too bad I'm not Hansel, that would make a fine pair of us, wouldn't it?" He tells her she is free to leave although he wishes her to stay, for a few minutes at least. First, the sergeant explains, he must examine the soldier he just killed. "Gretel, the *Obergefreiter* was the one I most hoped wouldn't make a move at me, but the one I thought who most would."

The *Obergefreiter* is a broken slumped pile of knees and elbows, and the sergeant rolls the pile over, face up, because this skinny kid resembles Stefan Wolke. It is not. At the chest a sodden circle of crimson indicates where a skilled Sergeant Geronimo, under extreme pressure, had placed a tight pattern of four bullets. The sergeant debates why he killed this youngster, why he did not keep himself hidden and safe in the brush, as he had two hundred times before. Was it to protect the girl, or hurt her, yes hurt her, with a bloody sight after she had shrieked out "No more blood!" Both questions made sense to him. Any answer made equal sense.

The girl is likely even more surprised than the sergeant that she sits there, waiting for him. He thanks her for the surprise. He joins her, alongside, and shows no interest whatsoever in hurrying away from danger. "Believe it or not, Gretel, I once *memorized* more German poetry than you probably *read* in school." The sergeant recites several stanzas of Schiller, from some of Silke's favorite lines. "In France I lifted a copy of Schiller from a dead German lieutenant, who wore eyeglasses with one lens missing. I attempted to tack together a political symbolism about that lieutenant and his glasses . . . without any success."

The girl half listens to this opaque rambling while her wide eyes stray over to the tree trunks, where she may have seen shifting shapes already.

"Gretel, about my namesake, did your author Karl May ever put Geronimo in any of those ersatz American westerns of his about the Indians? Geronimo was a kind of nuisance guy, also an Apache. For punishment, the Mexican soldiers executed Geronimo's mother, wife, and young children, and for revenge he struck back, and for revenge the Mexicans struck back, and for revenge, *et cetera.* So am I the Apache or the Mexicans? Take a guess."

The girl points to the trees. "They'll shoot you."

"And I've been shot before." The sergeant tugs his partial ear. "This poor boy, Dieter. He's not your fiancé although he wants to be. No offense to him but you can do better is my judgment, after spending an hour viewing you. A spunky fellow anyhow. The strangest thing is, Gretel, I have a fiancée practically a stone's throw from here, in Augsburg. *Augsburg,* how's that for a joke. We never had an engagement ring or any of the usual rigmarole.

We just had what we had."

"I'm afraid," says the girl. "Please run, sir."

The birds, in their eternal innocence, continue singing. The sergeant looks at her closely. "You're young, I suppose, but getting older by the minute. Gretel, you'll fit your country perfectly after this war."

"Please," says the girl, "please run. I can't stop them, never."

He agrees. "When they see that body behind me they won't stop. How can we blame them in the end."

"Please," she says.

"I'm sorry."

"Please don't make me watch, sir."

"I apologize. I do."

"Don't make me see it."

"You can go, Gretel."

"I'll shout at them."

"You'll shout. You'll cry. You're almost crying now."

"*Please*, sir."

"Forgive me. This is cruel. Forgive me that you have to be the one. *Tut mir schrecklich leid.* But I need a German girl's tears right now, immediately, no more waiting."

The birds stop singing and Gretel obliges Spencer Lemay.

Part I

"I really am lying."

<u>One</u>

Her eyes: contentment brown. His eyes: disconcerted blue. Brown caresses blue. Her body is next to his in a car moving through December rain, while warm familiarity heats the captive space inside.

"Missed you today," she says, eliminating the commonplace from those words.

"I missed you," he responds quickly.

"I missed you more."

"I missed you saying you missed me more."

When she laughs she gleams. Everyone—friend or outsider—thinks of her as a kind of jewel, so polished and compact is she. This spangle, furthermore, emanates from her decent nature, as unmarred within as her lucky complexion. She might be the only child of a wealthy man, but nobody has ever tagged her with the "little rich bitch" dismissal. Now her head rests, briefly, against his shoulder. In that scant moment she presses there, expresses there, a tactile speech of commitment.

Although the car travels in rain, she feels only a sunshine, and assumes her safety, not accepting how dangerous the world might become. Nor does he suspect it, with his blue eyes responsibly watching the slick road. Neither one imagines that a strange girl waits for him a mere mile away. When they meet, she will be undressed, this stranger, this girl, yet not move a hand to cover herself, hiding nothing. She waits. Soon he will take the first stumble of a fall (fall-fall-fall) in love. Falling by definition is an accident, and an accident, as is known, can be serious. Sometimes the mysterious occurs in a heartbeat, even in a modest California town with a utilitarian name ending in "ville."

__Two__

The year was December 1954, almost 1955, and they rode in a lacquered maroon '51 Ford coupe, its rear lowered, wheel skirts added, with the mellow rap of twin glaspak mufflers underneath. The couple in the car are at home for the holidays during their final year at nearby universities.

The girl, Marlee Stalich, wore a pullover, fawn in tone, with a straight heavy skirt of mottled tans that cut across the shins, and white saddle shoes with white socks folded down at the ankles. "Five-foot two" the song goes, "eyes of blue, but *oh!* what those five feet can do"—the old tune's tempo, exuberance, literal sense, all appropriate to Marlee, except for those dark Adriatic eyes that had originated a continent's full breadth away from blue. Her finely combed hair, with flipped tips at the shoulder, was likewise a deep brown, only seen not to be black when next to her friends Mary Takamoto or Alice Kawata, two paradigms of Christian names and Nipponese physiology. She had a smile that "could charm the socks off the devil" as her own father put it. So persuasive was the smile that few people noticed the minor defect in her teeth, the result at age ten of thumping her bicycle into a concrete abutment, damaging a new Schwinn and her upper right incisor, now carefully filed square again if a fraction short.

The legal name on his birth certificate—Lemay Scott Bakkan— is a clerical error, the first two names having been reversed. Once the family meant to correct this but the years slipped by. Marlee Stalich and Scotty Bakken. With hardly a fudge in pronunciation their given names could be rhymed. "Hear how they fit together?" friends have been eager to point out. The complement to her energy was his athletic intensity, his runner's image—lanky, lean, wide from the front and narrow as a board in profile, looking in his jeans like a cowboy made tough on the trail, plenty of bone and muscle but underfed. In fact he was exactly a runner, nearly a famous one. On a floodlit wall in a gymnasium hung bronze plaques of his school's track records: **440 YARD RUN,** *S. Bakkan*; **880 YARD RUN,** *S. Bakkan*; **MILE RUN,** *S. Bakkan*. Lots of *S. Bakkan*. And already, with the calendar turning into 1955, this town of Watsonville, California, County of Santa Cruz, anticipated more of him. Talk was, the local burg could claim the fastest new horse in the United States of America.

* * * *

The Ford followed along the curved streets and open spaces of an expensive neighborhood. Marlee's house stood crowning the crest of a slope, an impressive sprawl of brick at the end of a lengthy driveway. Her father owned controlling shares of two local banks. Scott shuts off the engine and behind the privacy of rain on the windows they fold into one another, without preliminaries, moving with the practiced skills of good dance partners. She does not flinch when he cups her breasts, unlike that first time when she was fourteen, on a May afternoon, a Sunday, in her bedroom in this same house. Now Marlee snuggles against him as satisfied and possessive as a purring young cat. He moves his hand over her leg where invisible stubble only emphasized the compelling slickness, continues up her inner thigh, its flesh a female paradox: yielding yet resilient, water yet wave.

Sex and sports, both predictable enough for a young man—nothing here out of the ordinary. The car radio, for its part, plays a song with the most predictable topic of all:

> *Do you love me*
> *And do you love me right?*
>
> *Baby maybe I do and maybe I don't*
> *But baby I won't say I won't.*

They chat along a string of trivia before Marlee finally asks him—hardly recognizable as a complaint—why not come in the house for half an hour, the way he always does?

Scott could answer with the simple truth, how he wants to visit the city library, alone. Instead he lies, some blather about a "conflict," and is appalled to find the lie in his mouth. "Wait. I don't know why I said that," he tells her. "I'm lying."

Her giggle is muffled into the hollow under his right jawbone.

"I really am lying."

She is not interested. There are other words she wants, more important subjects. At their daily farewell, Scott without fail presents her with a verbal bouquet, a phrase or few sentences that, however indirect, she translates into his equivalent of (what else?) I-love-you. Marlee is willingly addicted to this Final Word. Since originality usually requires effort, the Final Word stamped each day with the proper seal for her.

He begins searching for the qualifying goodbye, and because no one wants to disappoint Marlee, and because he is downright gifted at it, Scott assembles the text in less than ninety seconds. It was an artful, cheerier variant of "I won't say I won't," actually sung on key.

<u>Three</u>

Fate is exceptionally patient, and chance equally so. Whichever it is, his unknown girl, the naked one, still waits for him.

Off to the city library went the Ford, tires slishing on wet roads, windshield wipers devising a sullen tempo, side windows crawling with webs of blown water beads. Houses, a playground, small shops and stores, many of humble architecture, showed their smeared geometry in the rain. Twilight joined the clouds to diminish further the day.

He has been off balance lately, he admits, almost as if the earth itself were rotating beneath his feet, the literal physical globe. And why not claim that this new year, 1955, was in the act of teetering off the equipoise of midcentury. This place, Santa Cruz County, middle coast of California, itself tipped between the geographical extremes of the elongated state, mixing northern redwoods forests and southern mild beaches, while being split, longitudinally, by the notorious San Andreas earthquake fault. His past was defined by a hot war—with an uncle, who was more an older brother, probably killed in Germany's Schwäbische Alb exactly a decade ago—and his future by a nuclear cold war. Currently his grandfather is by him at home routinely dying. The latter had to do with his purpose at the library.

Scott Lemay Bakkan. He appears a normal guy, fondling his girlfriend, cruising in his Ford, doing sports, staying up too late. Unfortunately, regrettably, he is not normal at all. Even as a twelve-year-old he had already accused his parents, in youthful despair, "Nobody else in the world talks the way *I* do." This was because Scott had been trained from the cradle to be a human parrot, reciting a mishmash of elaborate literary quotations.

In the trunk of his '51 Ford, right now, are two fat hardback books, stashed there, out of sight. Not university textbooks, he owned them, had bought them new, and worn the pages with his own fingers. Scott understands that no one else his age in California, or the solar system for that matter, is carrying around this two-volume set—called *The Complete Poetry and Prose of Walt Whitman*—written by an American who died way back in the last century. Scott can regurgitate dozens of lines from those rambling stanzas of Whitman's *Leaves of Grass*. Considered from a sports viewpoint, *S. Bakkan* already holds the 1955 world recitation record in the subject of this Water Whitman, Jr., and also likely in Donne, Dickinson, Rilke, Baudelaire, and other masters of the poetry pen. Naturally no appropriate brass plaque dangled, proudly, in the school gymnasium, since too few others gave a dry spit about any poet.

In Scott's own family neither mother or father recognizes any responsibility for creating his parrot life. He had invented two outlandish tales to reveal the parrot process to his parents—and to reprimand them—but has not yet spoken the tales aloud, and might never. After all, he does respect his mother and father a great deal.

Looney Tunes #1 Make Scott the infant son of gypsy street entertainers, who at age eleven months already becomes the centerpiece of his parents' grandest scheme. In a grim Romanian ghetto alley little Scotty sits in a lap while the mother or father tries to balance a chicken egg on the palm of his tiny hand. They have an animal patience with him, careful to avoid sudden motions, other than when an expensive egg smashes and his mother tries to scoop up enough in the shell for dinner. One day he can hold up a chicken egg—large end down—on each flat palm, and his parents beam, put wet kisses on his cheeks, sing his favorite lullabies. The hours of sitting together on the steps in the alley continue. They buy (or steal) a crate of laying hens. Eventually, before he had even learned to run very well, the tyke could balance eggs with the small end down while rotating his palms, the eggs turning like sluggish tops. On Sundays, over at the weedy neighborhood park, gathered for a picnic near the statue of some victorious general who was later assassinated, his uncles and aunts and cousins watched the spinning eggs and cheered. Success being addictive, in due time the boy has eggs twirling on his upright fingertips: three on the right hand, three on the left, a total of six in simultaneous action. A friend of his mother paints the eggs with scaldingly bright fingernail polish, a different color for each egg. His child's imagination outleaps the programmatics of his parents, and soon they find him with eggs dancing on his toes, his chin, his forehead, his nose. Extraordinary. The hour has arrived for his debut at the busiest street corner in the tourist center of Bucharest, and ultimately—who can say?—on from there to all the capitals of Europe. The climax of his act, however, will always be the same. To add a dramatic finish, demonstrating furthermore that these whirling objects are, remember, fragile *eggs*, with his foot Scott sends one in an arc high, high into the air, landing the egg with a clownish *splat* right atop his head, letting it run down over his face.

Looney Tunes #2 Move Scott to China, to be the first-born son of a talented acrobat and a skilled contortionist. They massage, stretch, and manipulate the boy's limbs from birth onward, beginning there in the parental bed where the morning sun and their gentle hands form a unified warmth. He loves being touched. To him, having his legs rubbed and placed behind his neck is a caress. Outside live a billion countrymen, but inside the apartment live only three, with their own two rooms and their one secret. Together they build a minor miracle of human flexibility. Strange, how with tireless practice and a series of infinitesimal yet ascending steps, improbable goals can be reached, seeming to defy the rules of anatomy itself. The boy bends as if he has no bones. He can easily stand on his head and curve his legs backward—in a direction contrary to the joints—until his toes reach around and hold a toy tin flute against his lips, upon which he then blows a familiar folk melody. *Toot-toot-toodle*. Son, father, mother, are pleased to the core, and when Scott is on stage with spectators oohing and aahing, the family, their modesty overcome, feels pride. The boy chooses not to notice that other expression on the audience's gawking faces: a look of revulsion.

* * * *

If a person with sound reflexes sensed himself about to "fall in love," should he avoid it, like stepping around any other object about to trip him? Or could a clever mind find something positive about falling, such as the liberating sensation of soaring just before the inevitable smash.

Scott took the Ford on a southward loop near the Pajaro River, going up his town's main street, where California's Highway 1 once locked itself briefly between these eight blocks of buildings. Here the street's eastern tip was a straggle of store and cafe and bar fronts with signs that read *Tienda de Comestibles, Un Poco Mexico, La Frontera*. He turned off—right—in the center of town at the plaza, driving to a pinched side street that barely separated the white greco-hacienda post office from its white satellite, the public library. Parking, he rolled down the car window and looked back at the tidy landscaped plaza, obedient to his recent interest in the elderly inhabitants found there. In the rain those benches stood empty. There were bobbing umbrellas, black and sharp as silhouettes, and a few hurrying, vital, half-launched figures, but no old men. The hunched, talking, spitting, smoking sons of Portugal, Slovenia, the Philippines, Cathay, Mexico, Missouri, had escaped somewhere away from this weather.

While his Ford waits and while the girl waits, *S. Bakkan* sits, thinking of his sick grandfather. These recollections, in their sequence, draw together the actual Frankenstein story of how Scott became a homemade professor-boy, sewn together from dead academic parts.

Scott Lemay Bakkan is the child of Furman Bakkan and Elaine Lemay, and the lonely remnant of their once-upon-a-time calculations and dreams, now mislaid. These two had met in 1931 and married in 1932, when both attended the state college close by in San Jose, completing degrees in English and being certified to teach secondary school. No Bakkan or Lemay before them had scaled such educational summits, and to climb there during the economic disaster of the 1930s proved they had the grit besides the brains. Hence America gained two fresh instructors of language and literature. And they had an evangelical intent, the pair of them, as a team, of going out and giving America's classrooms their nervous new wisdom and their own living demonstration of literature's transcendence.

As ready as his mother and father were to serve their students, none would ever come to listen and learn. The crushing wheel of historical events rolled over them in the end. "Brother, can you spare a dime?" Or in this case father not brother, because it appeared that the only dime-paying job around was with Leland Bakkan, father of Furman. Leland Bakkan, widower, owned a sick back-of-the-house lumberyard at the edge of Ceres, a sandy San Joaquin Valley village audacious in mythological name but nothing else. They slid into a semi-desperate formulation called the Bakkan "business." The new Mrs. Bakkan, Elaine, cooked, cared for the home, and managed the paltry bookkeeping. Leland went scouring the big lumber distributors in Modesto and Stockton, occasionally up in Sacramento or down in Fresno, where he culled together off-sizes and sapwood, whatever they would practically give away. Furman sold or traded this junk, for a couple of dollars here, a couple of turkeys or lugs of peaches there. To go beyond these broke farmers he began loading up the '27 Chevy flatbed and grinding over the steep Pacheco Pass, making the half-day haul to the coast and Santa Cruz. Once arrived he would peddle the lumber, sleep overnight in the truck, return the following afternoon. Finally he rented a three-room shed (a pit toilet outside) near the city of Santa Cruz for seven bucks a month. Furman and Elaine Bakkan, teachers of English, moved in. Scott was born there. Now a pile of boards sat behind an old house in Ceres and another hopeful pile sat on an old Chevy truck in Santa Cruz.

With the 1941 Japanese attack on Pearl Harbor, Scott's father entered the Army and was away for huge chunks of four years, Elaine raising her son alone—a common family condition throughout America. By 1946 grandfather Leland Bakkan had money to invest, made during the war, as did Furman, who came back a discharged major. Scott's parents took a pause—on the way to line up their decade-delayed teaching careers—and they put part of their cash, and his grandfather's, into lumber. Then they put some into property. Then they put some into construction. Selling those houses, and borrowing more money, they bought and built again. Through bank dealings they came to know the Staliches, Marlee's parents. Although Elaine had another child, a girl, she continued doing the financial paperwork, hours of it a day. With the thriving boom times now arrived, buyers never paid with peaches anymore, and behold, one fine day the Bakkans possessed more money than the Staliches, although neither family would imagine that fact.

When Scott's father and mother got around to constructing

their own considerable home, off in a picturesque rural setting, they made a fuss that its hub be an immense library, almost institutional in size, with floor-to-ceiling shelves. A noble monument to visions past, this library bespoke much poignancy: the more the business flourished, and the fewer the hours for reading, the faster they ordered new books. Filling these shelves became the last available proof of their abiding faith. Soberly, they would crack open the latest shipping carton, turn each book with a welcoming touch, read the jacket notes to each other, skim a chapter, and find the newcomer a slot on the crowded wall. Many a good dollar went into furnishing this temple of regrets.

During those years of poverty, of war, finally of unrelenting business success, Scott was well-loved, and loved twice over, being doubly precious, both as a first child and the first and only student at hand. That combination had been irresistible, with Scott getting kissed, lectured, hugged, drilled, cuddled, cajoled, in general consumed without mercy. Few idle hours found a place inside his childhood life. Every literary treasure his parents carried in their recollections, or in their yellowing college notebooks, ended up funneled into Scott's head, passed on for safekeeping. He listened and memorized, happy about the family game, even if anything that earnest could never truly be play. He heard Homer's fables along with those from Mother Goose and the brothers Grimm. The blood of Beowulf and Grendel fit in there somehow. With *Winnie-the-Pooh* came the *Aeneid*. With *The Jungle Book* came *A Midsummer Night's Dream*. The anthology favorites from the Boston Brahmins (Longfellow, Holmes, Lowell, Whittier) Scott chanted from his mother's lap, while his father fought in the far Pacific and his uncle, Elaine's beloved brother Spencer, went missing in Germany. These evenings alone together, during the war, were intense, with their "goodnight" bedtime reading frequently lasting beyond midnight. The urgency in his mother's wide-awake eyes—which the young Scott took to be her fear that he might not understand their latest book—no doubt also had to do with her putting off sleep and its battlefield nightmares.

Poe he liked, and the whole crowd of Elizabethans. Chaucer and his fabliaux with their sexcapades were blushing held back until spring of eighth grade. ("Nothing in these old stories that you don't *already* know about," said his father, home from the war. Not so, not so.) Old English turned into a mutual flop but Middle English went better, credit given to those naughty fabliaux. His mother, never heard to swear, once and only once shocked the room with an irritated "Shit!" that permanently underscored Scott's duty to master poetry scansion. When she finished with her son he was a genuine technician, who with an eruption of pencil markings could scan any variant meter and rhyme of a Petrarchan sonnet quicker than the Olympic 200 meters was run at Helsinki in 1952. As a particular family obligation, on Scott's sixteenth birthday his mother insisted that he inherit the private documents of his vanished uncle, Scott accepting an informal oath that he would "learn it all by heart or at least definitely *in* my heart." This inheritance was a large cardboard box crammed to the top with Spencer Lemay's life story, from official university transcripts to Army records to correspondence to diary musings to twenty-seven pieces of handwritten poetry—what Scott classified as Spencer's "literary remains," a depressing phrase Scott knew never ever to repeat to his mother.

On and on the preparation went for Scott—different body parts dug up from different centuries and different cultures—until there he stood, more or less a complete creation, smelling around the edges of formaldehyde or at least of exhumed textbooks. Scott's academic storehouse was now an embarrassment of riches, his memory for quotation freakish. Like freaks everywhere he had to be on guard not to frighten strangers or his teachers at school. As of late the superseded parents had reduced their proselytizing to spare minutes, gestures almost, and the daughter Joyce, age eight, heard only echoes of the former thunder. Scott himself was reading the moderns and in independent orbit, put there under the power of his own escape velocity. Nowadays, when other local young men drove to San Francisco to sample the sins of North Beach, he instead explored, in that same merry cauldron of sleaze, the alcoves at City Lights Books, where were found the most extreme, avant-garde Beat poets—each one excitedly imitating Walter Whitman, Jr.

<u>Four</u>

Outside the library Scott let rain strike his upturned face. That failed as therapy to keep him from this mood of being loaded down in every pocket. He blamed his stagnation on the gray weather, its pressing sky, and because the mud had kept him from running his usual afternoon eight miles.

The aging library was branded with CARNEGIE at its entrance, in recognition of that philanthropist's generosity, imprinting into this western outpost a hint of legendary Atlantic capitalism. Scott knew the quaint place from top to bottom and it knew him, the librarian at the checkout counter now smiling hello. Mrs. Ade: her helpful name was a pun poised to happen. Scouting down an aisle of books he tipped out several and carried them to a table by the main banks of windows.

In October his grandfather had left the original Bakkan home over in the Central Valley and come to live with his son Furman. The old man hated going, but he had "highly advanced prostatic carcinoma," or in plainer talk, "cancer." Both proved hard for the family to pronounce. Medical experts defined the illness as "progressive," an otherwise positive term which here signified that his grandfather would soon, 1-2-3, worsen and die. Scott watched his father watching his father.

How it works, it appeared to Scott, himself perched on the third rung of the generational ladder, is that tucked away inside every living body is a biological voice, and after an imprecise period, after a devious self-serving delay, the voice calls "Time's up" and the body begins to wilt. Then you, along with other interested members of the audience, get to observe the results. First you note your tired skin, easing down to take a rest, and next, your squint, and next, your stiff knees, your list of six different aches, and next your shoulders' stoop, and next your nodding afternoons. Finally, look out, there goes a necessary part heading straight toward sleep.

The library books are full of these vital organs, these potential sleepers. Just pick out any page to frighten yourself with, including the one showing the prostate gland, "a muscular-glandular structure found at the base of the mammalian urethra."

But the disease. Back to the book ranges, in search of pathology texts.

Scott Bakkan resembled his grandfather Leland's Norwegian facial contours—strong cheekbones, stubborn chin—and a head squared at the corners and edges rather than rounded. Both had eye color of a raw blueness. In his mirror at home Scott could manipulate his features into an even closer imitation of his grandfather, by sucking a hollow in each cheek, crinkling furrows at the eyes, with one hand pinching a dewlap under his chin, with the other reaching up to blot out the hairline. Artfully, Scott could build a preview of himself.

Among the 616.000 block of Dewey classification numbers, Scott poked at book spines, checking titles, finding mostly veteran volumes that had been re-lettered in webby lines of white ink. Sickness was a popular subject. He extracted *You and Disease* and *Pathologia II,* the latter a donated work lost from its mate, and he went to the nearest window, leaning there, scanning pages. *You and Disease* explicated itself in battle analogues: the gallant human fortress under siege by microscopic invaders. The skin puts up the shield or outer wall of the fortress, which, if breached, is backed by your army's hemostatic corps, those engineers who cement the blood and patch the wall. Should any invaders slip inside they face your shock troops, the furious Prussians, or white corpuscles. Behind them brigades of seasoned antibodies stand on guard. If need be, your fortress could stoke its boiler room, raise its temperature, weaken and fry the enemy. *Semper Vigilans.*

The battle goes well, nevertheless the war badly, said the accruing evidence, if not the esprit, in *You and Disease.* Hordes— clouds—of parasites continue charging in through the vulnerable entryways of your fortress. They hurl themselves across mucous moats, dodge barbwire hair, advance beyond all fortifications. The enemy's ranks are legion, the defenders valiant but outmanned. *Dulce et decorum est pro patria mori.* The fortress shivers, moans under the assault. Viruses infest storerooms of protoplasm, bacteria infiltrate lung sacs, tapeworms feast in intestines, a platoon of cells, obeying a muddled battlefield command, constructs a tumorous, self-destructive bomb.

Above his head, rain gathered into shifting designs on the library windows. New droplets added themselves as others slid in trails, down, off the panes, presumably like tears off a glassy cheek, given the subject matter of these books. Beyond the windows the December sky was concluding its somber day. Scott's little sister, Joyce, had already twice asked him, in private: "Will we, maybe, have to look at it, when he dies?"

Pathologia II ("pathology," from the Greek for "suffering") was an avalanche of erudition as cold and direct as alpine snow. Scott focused attention on the book's gallery of illustrative plates—not the circus sideshow shots of, for instance, deformed stillbirths, or "Symmetrical gangrene of toes," presenting a forlorn set of amputated feet—but instead the distracted art of photography through a microscope. "Tubercle bacilli in lung tissue" might be mistaken for distant seagulls wheeling against a background mass of summery clouds. "Acute abscess in kidney" was a July 4th star burst. "Muscle fibers from atrophied heart" were long narrow banners aflutter in the wind,

"Fatty degeneration of kidney" a bouquet of flush pansies seen from overhead, "Polylobular cirrhosis" stones under creek water, "Calcified pudic artery" a setting sun. With their blithe and insidious scenery, conceivably finger-painted by happy schoolchildren, these pictures were more eerie than that pair of feet hacksawed through at their arches.

When Scott found what he wanted—the cancers—the deceit was greater yet. Their magnified secrets revealed nothing but dreamy abstractions, innocuous points and splatters and swirls, glossy, rather lovely. "Myoma uteri," "colloid stomach malignancy," fibroma, sarcoma, melanoma, myxoma, "Note malignant cells invading and destroying fibers of the heart"—any of them could be inflated, suitably framed in modern metal, and hung unsuspected in an art show.

At the end of *Pathologia II*, among the appendices, lurked the mortality tables. All art vanished here with these columns of simple numbers. What the charts could not explain about his grandfather was the how of it. "Tell me, what's gonna happen?" Joyce had asked big brother, while stretched on his bed, his pillow under her stomach. "No, don't tell me, I guess. No, tell me, I guess."

Back, back to the shelves again for information. Weary, he rested a minute or two there, as outside the daylight quit altogether. He began advancing along the lines of vertical titles. One can stray off course inside Dewey's roomy palace of decimals, and when Scott came across *The Human Body* he reached out. He flipped pages, finding a series of photographs: embryos, fetuses, infants, babies, children, all in their natural state. The book's topic is developmental morphology. He flipped onward, idly, ascending the chain of enlarging bodies, until he met page 104. Page 104, margin-to-margin, fills up with a black-and-white photograph (figure 84). Page 104, fig. 84 has the official designation: "Fully Pubescent Female, Age 18."

He carries *The Human Body* to the closest ceiling light. This nude girl, age 18, here in his hands, stands facing front, feet together and flat, arms at sides, fingers extended, not unlike an obedient soldier ready for inspection. Available free for public view she is female pubescence, a piece of evidence on display, and from face to foot her body permits no interference with the sight, not even suntan boundaries. Her head is level, her eyes on Scott, the way eyes in photographs do.

He brings her closer, within the brightest center circle from the hanging lamp. He concentrates. Somehow she emanates her own brightness, illuminating her own page 104. Against her white he sees her dark, the dark of that flaring fountain of tendrils ornamenting her middle, the two dusky rosettes (roses on a larger pale rose), the hair curving in dark borders about her face, a shadow between the parted lips. Those eyes are also dark, and darkest with intentions that are impossible to come from a photograph. Even a foolish Scott is no complete fool. He understands that the paper stranger on this paper page cannot be recognizing him.

But *S. Bakkan* is sweating without his eight-mile workout run. He could be stumbling, could be feeling that dangerous substance, which people name "hope."

<u>Five</u>

She made him late for dinner, this p. 104 paper maiden. He apologized to his family seated at the table. "At the Staliches?" they assumed.

"I was," he answered, calculating, as he sat, whether in a larger spirit that might be another lie for today.

"And Dorothy?" asked Elaine, in reference to Marlee's own mother. "She show you the new car? Hm? Their Cadillac was delivered today."

"Let me think. No, she didn't show it to me."

In the Bakkan household the kitchen had triumphed over the library, and Elaine used recipes the way some preachers come to cite biblical verse—from excessive use, if not always from devotion. The Bakkans feasted more than they ate. At each end of the table a lazy Susan offered nibbles, contents varying with the seasons. In the glass compartments of one would perhaps be olives, sliced tomatoes, cauliflower segments ("accent with bell pepper rings for color"), carrot sticks, celery stalks with troughs smoother than a glacial Sierra valley ("fill these with cream cheese, peanut butter, or other spreads"). Silver relish forks held out their handles. The opposite tray might contain at its center—as it did tonight—a dome of cottage cheese ("top with bright quarter moons made from peach slices"), encircled by asparagus tips, artichoke hearts, and two dips—one tangy horseradish, the other cool sour cream.

Scott's father, Furman, announced: "Those twin Santa Cruz houses, the two off Portola Drive, sold today."

"Both?" asked at once grandfather Leland and granddaughter Joyce. The grandfather had on a red cardigan sweater, a Christmas gift. She wore, mostly as a scarf, his matching molten red tie.

"Yes," laughed Furman, "both to both of you."

"We shouldn't talk business during dinner," suggested Elaine, arranging Scott's salad. "But what did they sell for?"

"Full price."

"Well, well, well," said Leland, "well, well, well . . ."

Scott said, "For my 21st birthday I'll take a '55 Merc." At that his father laughed again, clapping his hands four times, which, unintentionally, equaled the number of Bakkan homes sold since the last family holiday of Thanksgiving.

A "Merc" was a car, wasn't it, Joyce wanted to confirm. Okay then, she said, she needed a "big 1955 something" for her birthday, like Scotty.

"I was only joking. Got it?"

She rolled an olive between her fingers. "Me too. I was joking."

Leland, inevitably, said, "Now put our dollars right back to work. For every fancy $16,000 house you can sell, you got ten buyers for an ordinary place. Why not build two $8,000 houses and quick put the money back into four more?"

For years the family had heard this catechism. The lesson was to build cheap, keep it modest, draw up a simple box floor plan under 1100 square feet with two bedrooms, one bath; downsize where possible the headers, joists and rafters; use laminate doors and standard dimension windows; put on composition roofing instead of shakes; lay more linoleum than carpet; plant a flowing plum by the entry but no lawn. To Leland Bakkan these criteria were less marketing theory and more world experience. During his life—Leland would explain, with appropriate gestures—the fat times he could count on one hand minus its thumb (showing a few fingers), while for the hard times he had to take off his shoes and socks to add 'em up (pointing with emphasis at his feet).

Furman had been ever ready to advocate the New Era, where "People want quality in their houses nowadays, three bedrooms, two bathrooms, a patio, some tile in the kitchen or bath, add a fireplace." Since the cancer news, noticeably, the old debate had lost steam, and any discussion went tiptoeing around a fight.

Scott could not forget another night, an August night two years ago, with the family on one of its summer trips to Leland's house in Ceres. Although past bedtime his grandfather must have been waiting awake because he called out Scott's name, and as Scott entered the east bedroom Leland said, oddly, "Shut the door." With a short, sharp breath, he had gone on with "*I found out something tonight*" in such a shaken voice that Scott at first thought this had to be about death, and Scott had cringed, wanting himself out of this hot antique room and over in the Santa Cruz Mountains, running on trails under the trees.

Leland bent forward in his bed, as if painfully scrunched, a revelation to Scott of his grandfather's advancing age and frailty. "I just heard it, here, tonight."

"What?"

"About your father."

Now Scott was the one being bent.

"Damn your father, damn his hide!"

Scott's great relief was part anger and part snigger. For he knew instantly that a *damn* could only mean money. Fine, he had countered, gleefully, silently, damn my father and damn my grandfather.

But Leland Bakkan on this sticky August night had been shivering. "Your father, he tells me tonight, has bought thousands of dollars of stocks. Thousands of dollars of STOCKS. The New York Stock Exchange, you know?" The cooler fan in the window rattled and whirred while Scott sat by his only living grandparent. The blood scent from the Wall Street massacre of 1929 smelled in the bedroom. Leland could have afforded any new house anywhere he wished, yet preferred living in his old place, and his dead wife's. Accordingly this spot had become a second home to the grandchildren. From over the coastal mountains they would come, down into the vast Central Valley, where the summer heat settled in for the entire burdensome night and the pendulum clock in the parlor went more like an audible skin tic than the customary tick-tock. "Sell the whole pile of turds, is the only thing to do." Scott had squinted at the faded lavender-and-lime pinstripes on the wallpaper, a favorite pattern from a buried decade. This bedroom setting, reflective of his grandfather's past, signified toil and the ghost of a reduced life. "We're no Rockefellers. The big guys lick their chops and swallow up little folks like us. Stocks? Us? You ask Furman if he remembers hiring out at the lumberyard in Modesto for twenty cents an hour. Oh, we got money today, and we can lose it all the quicker, too, and *Jesus*, we want to keep ahold of our money for once. Talk to him, Scotty, 'cause he thinks a lot of your opinion. I'm old-fashioned, see. I'm not up-to-date enough to speculate in paper certificates, see. I'm not ambitious enough. Well, listen, sir, I remember what happened when my own father got ambition and tried his Bakkan Canyon sawmill over in the redwoods, losing every penny we scraped together for a lifetime, long and hard, $25,000, and that was a heap of dollars in 1904." After that famous page from the Family Chronicles, both Leland and Scott Bakkan on that night had nothing more to do other than examine the wallpaper further.

Furman, for his half of the debate, would buttress his position with data gleaned from Maynard Stalich, Marlee's banker father, or the *Wall Street Journal* and *Time* magazine. At the dinner table he might have a drumroll of statistics ready, rim shots included. Were the Bakkans aware, for example, that this year "Americans saved more money than any year since the war? That six out of ten families own their own homes, more than ever before? That 11,000 babies get themselves born each day, enough for a new Akron, Ohio, every month? That the population of the USA was now 164 million?" This year, the Bakkans learned, Americans enthusiastically bought "5,300,000 cars, 3,400,00 refrigerators, 7,000,000 television sets, 1,200,000 houses. Some of those houses were ours."

"How come," Joyce had wondered, "it wasn't seven million and *one* television sets. Or *two*?"

In Furman's pocket was often a slip of paper filled with these scribblings. The grandfather stood an inch shorter than his son, and the son an inch shorter than the grandson—"the reverse in brains," Furman liked to tease. Unfolding his creased square of memo pad he would read: "Stocks are yielding 4.35% dividends compared to bonds at 2.89 %. During the year General Motors went from $60 to $98 a share, Jersey Standard Oil $72 to $111, DuPont $107 to $167, Boeing $49 to $148—that was, I repeat, Boeing from $49 a share to $148. Airlines went up an average of 95%, oils 45%."

"You don't own any of that Boeing, do you?" Leland had

said, amazed. "You got better sense. God spare us. Those air companies flip-flop from boom to bust before you can get up off the can."

"The can? What can?" Joyce had asked. She asked again.

On that occasion Furman had been caught in a slight embarrassment, since he had no Boeing shares. Despite his bravura, when he bought stock he chose the bluest of the blue chips, mostly royal purple.

* * * *

Furman, who was fond of hot dinner rolls and chilled butter ("My appetite is more for bread than stone," he would almost accurately cull from *Measure for Measure*), tonight ate his rolls and asked if the family had heard the day's other exciting news. Scott was in the *San Francisco Examiner*. It quoted there a slogan heard making the local rounds: "Bannister in '54, Bakkan in '55."

"Bannister?" asked Leland.

"It's track," explained granddaughter Joyce. "It's some running stuff."

"Not *stuff*, please, Joyce," corrected her mother. "Use a specific word instead."

"Roger Bannister," said Furman, "was the Englishman who broke the four-minute mile this year, the first runner ever. How did your slogan make the newspaper, Scotty?"

"Mine? Not mine." He, too, tore apart a soft dinner roll with its three automatic mouthfuls. Ice glittered in the butter dish. "I don't make up that stuff."

"Scotty was the newspaper!" shouted his sister. "Whoopee!"

Furman jabbed deftly at his lettuce, spearing clots of blue cheese dressing. "I suppose it was too catchy to let pass: 'Bannister in '54, Bakkan in '55.' Rhetorical balance and alliteration. Every writer loves alliteration."

"What's 'literation?" asked Joyce. She took three rolls. Her mother put one back. Joyce compensated by crunching a piece of cracked ice.

"Alliteration is repeating a certain sound or sounds, especially consonants," Elaine answered in a teacher's voice, uncovering a vaporous bowl of succotash. "Take *Love's Labour's Lost* by Shakespeare. And take some of these vegetables, without complaining about the corn, if possible."

"Love's *what*?"

From her father: "Now pay attention, sweetie. Listen for f's and b's. 'The fair breeze blew, the white foam flew . . .' Hear it? Coleridge."

From her brother: "Listen. 'Sick Sally still sells splendid succotash beside the sunny seashore.' That's 'literation."

From her grandfather: chuckles.

From her mother: "Don't encourage her to mispronounce the word, Scott, please."

"Could I eat just the limas?" asked Joyce.

"Certainly not," replied someone.

Joyce forked in an indiscriminate mound of the succotash,

chewed thoughtfully, let her rainy-day twitches escape by tapping her loafers on the floor and bobbing her towheaded hair. She was, as a rule, an object in motion, limber, rhythmic, confident to the point of carelessness and prone to small playground accidents. In better weather, she could be seen whizzing up and down their country road on her candy-cane bike, painted in pink and white. The family struggled not to pamper her. America might be in the middle of its baby boom, but for the Bakkans little Joyce represented a depleted resource.

Grandfather Leland turned to Scott. "You hope then to run the four minutes this year?"

"No. That was a world record."

"Sick Sally still sells—" began Joyce, halting in a spray of alliterative succotash.

Elaine went for soup. "Scott probably does have *visions* about going that fast."

"Four minutes plus four seconds is my vision."

"Only four more seconds over a whole mile?" asked Leland, poking an olive without eating it. "Not so much difference there, would you say?"

"It's different," said Scott.

Joyce, having picked up her succotash litter, tried to impress her grandfather by impaling two olives in a single thrust. She impressed him. "Gosh, Scotty, four seconds. You can do that. 1-2-3-4—"

"Honey," interrupted Furman, "those seconds mean running

yards and yards."

"Scotty? Couldn't you run kinda harder, part of the way?"

Cream-of-potato soup arrived ("sprinkle with parsley, float several pats of butter") and made the rounds. Nearby was a wicker basket full of bread sticks and assorted crisp crackers. Elaine rotated the pepper grinder over her soup bowl, raised her shaped '40s-fashionable eyebrows in invitation: Pepper, anyone? "No American has ever broken the four-minute barrier, Joyce. Not even the older runners."

"Scotty can be the first American."

"Forget four minutes," said Scott. "The main goal is not losing."

Elaine attentively lifted cocoa-colored eyes, a Lemay contrast to the Bakkan blue. "Do you worry about that? Being beaten?"

"Not much. But I might be lying to myself. Every pound of confidence is gained by swallowing at least one fat lie. And lately it seems I figured out how to lie."

"Why would you lose?"

"Why not?"

"Or how, then."

"I train three hours a day, some other guy does three hours and twenty minutes. We race together in a mile. The king is dead: long live the king."

"Whatcha mean?" asked Joyce.

"New runners pop up anywhere. That's the beauty of the sport. Maybe a skinny sophomore from Nowhere, Idaho, shows up, all hyped with adrenaline, not knowing himself how good he is, not knowing he was born with a greyhound's lungs."

Joyce's hand sprung open, dropping a saltine, which luckily landed in her cream-of-potato soup. She fished it out with two damp fingertips.

With measured reflection, Furman crunched a bread stick. "Anxiety's a healthy sign, keeping us competitive. But I have to say, for my wager, you're the fellow who'll do the whupping, when any whupping gets done."

Leland agreed, repeating a bit stiff-tongued, "Bannister in '54, Bakkan in '55," this loyalty prompting Scott to respond, "I'm off to Melbourne and the Olympics in 1956. Does that satisfy everybody?"

"What if precisely that came to pass?" said Elaine, leaving the table again for more food, stiffening her son's backbone by trailing behind a quote from *Paradise Lost* on the ecstasy of ambition.

Scott reminded her, "Too bad that 'Better to reign in hell than serve in heaven' also comes from there. And, I believe, Milton never had to run any miles, just compose an epic now and then."

Joyce said, "No person can ever be born with dog lungs inside him. Period."

* * * *

The entree: tender veal casserole made with noodles, button mushrooms, a cup of sour cream ("add half-tsp. paprika and a hint of garlic, lightly brown and top with buttered crumbs").

The side dishes: sweet potato/sausage puffs and Boston baked beans ("dry mustard, molasses, one onion, five cloves, pineapple chunks"). Furman and Leland drank coffee, Elaine had tea, Scott milk, Joyce chocolate milk. Joyce wanted to pour hers into a coffee mug, one like her grandfather's. "Consent given," said her mother, "if you fetch the mug."

Their food had an amplitude in common with the surrounding rooms—food bountiful, rooms outsized. The furniture, also paralleling the meal, was an expensive, flavorful, uncoordinated hash. In the sunken living room alone could be seen a black leather couch (before the flagstone fireplace), a second sofa covered with nubby silver linen, an antique rocker with caned bottom, a rattan settee group, various chairs and tables made from walnut or cherry or oak. Clearly the Bakkans sought their satisfaction object by separate object, going to the furniture marts to shop chair by chair, table by table, unguided by any scheme of decor. In the same manner the family enjoyed their meals, dish by random dish, eating along a series of culinary non sequiturs, savoring the plenitude as much as the flavor.

These days, Leland's stomach had difficulty keeping up with the competition. What food he ate might not stay down.

"Don't hurt the cook's ego," said Elaine, adding casserole to Leland's plate.

"Mother," objected Joyce, "no."

"He needs nourishment to stay strong, dear. Same as you do."

Joyce raised her voice. "No more for Leland, Mother." It made her sick, herself, to hear her grandfather vomiting behind the neighboring bathroom door.

They called him "Leland," including his son Furman, who had since childhood. This formality followed Leland's own intent, from the conviction that too much sentimentality is risky in this life of disappointments. A favorite wisdom was "Never spoil a dog by either petting or feeding it every day of the week." What, after all, had the Bakkan forebears amounted to, after 150 years in America: a 20-acre farmer, a crippled arthritic stone mason, a pair of swindled shopkeepers, a bankrupt logger.

As talk of business dwindled, the dinner conversation slid its customary, if choppy, path into politics. Leland asked, out of nowhere, "How did a mortician ever become vice president of the USA?"

"Nixon was a lawyer, Leland," corrected Elaine.

"He knows," said Furman.

Elaine thereupon clarified to Joyce, "Leland hasn't cared much for anyone in government since FDR."

"Me either," said Joyce.

"FDR," began her father, "stands for—"

"Franklin Delano Roosevelt. I can name all the presidents since back to Tuft."

"Taft, you mean, sweetie?"

"Daft, maybe?" suggested Scott.

Elaine said to Scott, "Describe their new Cadillac for me. Supposedly it's Aztec Yellow, whatever color that might be. Is that as awful as it sounds? Sounds garish."

"It definitely sounds garish."

Joyce said, "I have a question for *every*body. Who has the biggest potty in the world?"

"Pardon?" asked her mother.

"It's a riddle. Hippo-potty-mus. Betsy told me that."

"Oh, mercy," said Elaine.

"I like it," said Scott. "Congratulations to Betsy."

Elaine cut through a flaky crust, exposing the mixture of sweet potato ("beat into a golden smoothness") and ground sausage. "Scott, your mind must be a billion miles away this evening. Think I haven't noticed?"

"Don't exaggerate. A million miles."

"Or ten miles. You could be thinking about some*one*." With a small prodding grin she paused, much like Marlee left strategic vocal spaces to let in his Final Word.

"Yes, about someone."

"A young lady, possibly?"

"A young lady, exactly." Was his poor heart racing, or, more an aching? "Is there pie? I smell it."

She carried in dessert on silver trays. One tray held wedges of apple pie, radiating heat, oozing thick juice ("top with sweet whipped cream, highlight with shredded cheddar"). The other tray, for palates tickled by a different fancy, carried fruit cocktail cups ("chill thoroughly, garnish with crushed candy mints").

Furman and Joyce had both. Scott and his mother, the pie.

Leland took a fruit cup and explored it with a spoon. Coffee, tea, milk, chocolate milk again.

Sipping her herbal tea, satisfied with her evening's labor, Elaine asked Scott, "Dorothy was there, wasn't she?"

"She lives there, after all."

Leland was mistakenly calling the "United Nations" the "League of Nations." Furman described the new nuclear submarine, christened the Nautilus. He went on, using saucers, to show Joyce the position of the islands Quemoy and Matsu relative to the "red monolith" of mainland China.

Elaine said, "What on earth did Dorothy say about the new Cadillac? Wake up now."

"Let me think. Truthfully, I didn't hear her say anything about the car. Mother, once again a masterful pie. Or rather, please change the *p* in pie to the, ah, twelfth letter of the alphabet."

"The twelfth letter of the alphabet? You silly ninny."

<u>Six</u>

Describe it as the dawn before the dawn. Scott is awake and already dressed in the battle gear of his workout suit. He will run through the mountains, loop back, shower, eat, read, rest, eat, read again, run again. These vacation days are an opportunity for hard punishment. Bannister in '54, Bakkan in '55. Even daring to repeat that jingle demanded 80-mile-week payments. The dark mass of his house slumbered, between two redwood groves, while in front waited the road. "Here we are again," he ordered his laggard body. "Crank yourself up. Roll."

The body whined and objected, being groggy, cold, stiff from yesterday. Only after ten minutes of prodding it through the motions did the body settle into efficient rhythms, the ragged breathing now leveled out, the muscles and joints limber. Once in this lubricated condition the body agreed to float along indefinitely, without any further supervision, regardless of the terrain, steep or not, transforming into a dutiful mechanical gizmo. It just *went*. Scott's mind, freed from caretaker chores, found its own rhythms and cast off into its own kind of float. Years ago as a boy loping over these same lanes and trails for fun, he had, by accident, discovered this hypnotism. Scott could look at his track records spotlighted up on their wall and wonder how incidental they might be, and whether the trigger behind his success was nothing more than chasing after reverie.

Mind and mechanism always found their separate stations by farmer Overton's apple orchard, thirty acres of Gravensteins, Bellflowers, Newtown Pippins, that filled a strip of benchland between Fern Creek and Fern Road, where Scott ran. His legs—mesmerizing automata—went into their power glide, making Scott a serene picture, deceptive in speed, the bounce of his hair (a moribund blonde) the sole vertical aberration to his forward flow. Through the dissolving night the apple trees cut a leafless network of branches, their stubby leaders pruned close to the limbs, bark black from the dew, tree after tree, row after row, sharp and exact. Scott passed them, absorbing these meticulous etchings, appreciative, aloft inside the fixation of this Open Road. Hello, hello, the clue to join poet Walter, Jr., again. Afoot and lighthearted . . . the world before me. Away we go, Walter.

Fern Road climbed a grade, fell back into a slender vale bent beside its ferny namesake creek, became covered by the abrupt neo-night of a redwood forest—*Sequoia sempervirens* at their mature regal height, their drooping arms holding a hush underneath, water over stones the only sound. Out of the creek bottom went road and Bakkan, up another ridge, along its spine so that wakening vistas opened to show pastures and orchards below interrupted by woodland tangles—conifers, oaks, chaparral—and above, stacked in loftier ridges, mountains deep green with more redwood cover. He flew. Daylight grew. A couplet, they were. Half the sky was clouds, benign cumulus, stained a crushed seeping pink on their eastern edges. Between the clouds a violet haze brightened toward blue, as he took a turn at a private graveled road and headed the long way back home. His spectral shape was recognized in these hills. (The Bakkan boy who runs at an insane early hour. Come springtime, read about him in the newspapers.)

Scott astonishes himself once more. He feels giddy with strength, feels so alert he captures the multitude of sensations around him, large and small. Fern Fork: a bouncy gurgle, sluicing through a corrugated culvert, off to augment Fern Creek. Official state bird: four startled quail, topknots erect, join the runner and leg it alongside. Gravel to pavement and back to Fern Road: where under Overton's apple trees crowds a field of wild mustard, yellow flowers brilliant enough to be fresh from a paint jar. Other plants flourish by the road and on the hillside, paradisal trappings of the Pacific slope, where greenery confounds the winter season, including California poppies waiting to unfurl under sunshine. Watch out, Walter. This Bakkan is, really, going to *fly*.

✳ ✳ ✳ ✳

Three o'clock in the afternoon and here is Scott running a second session, on his former high school track, where it classified as technical training. Keeping company—in stride—is his friend Lyle, also back home on vacation, an athlete himself, a football player who would be the starting quarterback in the fall at Furman and Elaine's alma mater. Lyle grumbled intermittently about sopped shoes, about being hungry, about panting already. But Lyle did have the breath left to be Lyle, and he was reconstituting his very own Krafft-Ebing case study of a "Bernice . . . a tall one in a white sweater in my botany class" and the actress Grace Kelly, seen in "Dial M for Murder." Both had appeared to him in the same lucky dream, both forgetting their clothes, both wanton, contrary to their public sham as aloof beauties. "I asked her out for New Year's Eve. Bernice. She accepted." Girls seemed drawn, resistless, to him, which amused and irritated Scott, in tandem. "Animal magnetism" was Lyle's lighthearted explanation when he let his brindled hair curl uncombed after a shower, or wore a tight T-shirt, lounging in a chair with those muscles of his innocently flexed, like the proverbial trap ready to spring if you touch any part. "Know what? Maybe I'll blurt out . . . 'Bernice, I dreamed of you . . . last night.' She'll be surprised . . . to hear that. And curious. Slow down, Bakkan . . . I'm getting winded. I'll tell her . . . 'No, no, you *don't* want me . . . to repeat this dream . . . to you.' But she will."

"She'll say . . . she's already heard about boys . . . and their creepy wet dreams."

"Not with her in one. Hey, isn't it a . . . compliment? Being dreamt about? She'll ask. She'll promise she won't get mad. She'll promise to understand me . . . and my dream."

"You wish."

"She will."

"In another dream."

"There you go, laughing at me again."

"*Qué?*"

"You always laugh about me and my luscious women."

"*Qué?*"

"Sure you do. Hey, slow down, man."

"Well . . . I do think you're funny."

"Funny? If you saw Bernice . . . you wouldn't say funny."

"White sweater. Botany. Tall. White sweater. Long hair. White sweater. Long legs. White sweater. White shoes. White underwear probably."

"Damn what an . . . imagination. And you're even *right*. You should be the guy to tell Bernice . . . my dream."

"I have my own dream."

"You bastard . . . are you . . . speed . . . ing . . . up?"

He was. "I need my pace work now."

"Then 'bye. Go beat . . . Gunnar Nielson . . . and Wes Santee. Go on, champ. Bernice and me . . . will find you . . . later." Lyle dropped back into a warm-down shuffle, hollering in Scott's direction: "Would any other football player run with you in the winter? You're welcome!"

Their friendship had—always—been judged unlikely by everyone else, but never by them, and over the years they stayed tight. Lyle ricocheted through his days with the total freedom of an instinctively clever thinker turned loose inside an anarchic family life. His house was a stucco box near the slough, occupied, marginally, by a troublesome younger brother and an over-challenged mother. It took a shovel to make one's way through the rooms. Lyle's father worked "in the merchant marines," said his mother, to explain the absence. "Correct, and his home port, somehow, is anywhere but Oakland or San Francisco," pointed out Lyle, blithely, who lived in this disorder without any detectable early sorrow—as Scott once in admiration said to him, citing that Thomas Mann allusion free of charge.

Scott ran on alone, ahead into the proper crucible for building a runner's body, not to mention a runner's mind. Unlike the mornings, now he received no aid or comfort along his pathway. Instead of a sunrise there were blank stadium lights. Instead of trees, power poles. Instead of quiet, traffic on the side streets. Not hills and canyons, instead he had a formal oval with the rulebook geometrics of chalk lines dividing the dirt, a tedious tabletop where—to look at it bluntly—Scott went around in circles, arriving nowhere.

* * * *

He made certain to ask Mrs. Stalich about her new 1955 Cadillac Coupe DeVille, who insisted he and Marlee take it for a test drive. At the wheel he felt lordly. (Scatter to the curb, peasants!) The seats were leather, the chrome flawless and thick as tank armor, the Aztec Yellow as rich as real Aztec treasure: the car a suitable Tenochtitlan altar on which to sacrifice a vestal virgin. He repeated the notion to the closest virgin. She agreed, saying, "Let's ask Mom if she knows of any."

Back in the Stalich living room they sat with Marlee's mother and drank apple juice with ice, chatting. The word virgin never came up. The three made a regular family circle, with no one playing the host and no one the guest, since the proprietary connections between the Bakkans and Staliches, business and private alike, were too interwoven for anything less.

Mrs. Stalich was speaking of her "husband's bank," which she did as commonly as a physician's wife mentions her "husband's hospital." "Maynard wonders if you might, possibly, like to work at his bank this summer, Scott."

"How's that?"

No faded flower, this Dorothy Stalich. She turned heads on the street. Junior-sized like her own daughter, as immaculate and groomed, she dressed ten years younger than Elaine Bakken and looked those ten years younger, although their ages were identical. Sometimes Scott viewed Mrs. Stalich (in an investment appraisal that any banker's clan could respect) as an encouraging prospectus of Marlee's own eventual appearance at middle-age, off in the distance, when the century waned. Today mother and daughter wore a shade of creamy lipstick identified as Silent Desires, an intense hue akin to pomegranate juice. Mrs. Stalich could sip her drink and keep the glass rim unmarked. Punctilio came easily to her. "Maynard thought," she said, "and I thought, that you might be scouting around for something different to do before graduate school starts in the fall. Want to hear our idea?"

Scott, needless to say, smiled his polite willingness and Marlee smiled hers.

"Maynard can open a summer position down at his bank, a flexible arrangement, where you move from department to department and learn what goes on in a bank's operations. There'd be a regular salary, but mainly, it's an opportunity to explore a new field, like a trainee. Could be fun?"

"Could be fun," he said.

"Think about it?"

"I will. Count on that."

He made the lengthy passage out through the Stalich house, down a hallway with echoing hardwood floors. Marlee, the only child, joked that her parents had twice lost their baby when they forgot which of the four bedrooms held the crib. The house was decorated with an expensive spareness that preferred to seduce rather than assault the viewer, much as a single $5,000 note, in a plain frame hung off-center on a wall, compares to that same wall plastered over, seasick green, with a tidal wave of dollar bills. The Staliches, Scott noticed, were smoother, calmer, more rehearsed with money than the Bakkans.

At the end of the corridor, in a cozy niche with a west window, Scott and his Marlee, leaning together, said goodbye. "What's this banker business?" he asked.

A sexy enough sprite, she burrowed into him with a laugh. "Every daddy wants a boy, people claim. See, you're a boy. I'm a girl."

"Silent Desires, that lipstick's called?"

"Shhh. Silent."

"Speechify for me. Come on, yell 'em out."

Her lips did part, not for talk but to share her flavor with him. Marlee was quite the edible girl: sugary, bite-sized, fine of texture, tasty as a Bakkan dessert. She told him, "You make me dizzy when you kiss me. Every day, every time." Face turned up, blushed by pleasure and the sunset's light, she seemed irresistible, and feeling himself a fortunate fellow, he held Marlee with his arms and with his Daily Word.

"You're so affectionate today," she whispered.

"Your fault." He placed a hand under her upraised chin, sliding it down, and up again, along the taut throat. "Your fault. 'There's a certain slant of light, on winter afternoons' . . . and it charms you and you charm it." The partial Emily Dickinson reference did not register with Scott himself. This weave of stolen words with his own happened too often to always recognize.

"Tomorrow," said Marlee, "stay just this way for me, this tender, okay?"

He nods, earnestly.

* * * *

Halfway home, he swung the Ford into a perilous U-turn, tires squalling, back toward town.

"Are you serious? Are you totally nuts?" He warned his face in the rearview mirror, "You'll miss dinner again. You'll . . . miss . . . everything."

From atop a rise he could see the city lights blinking on. Coming from the north into Watsonville he first passed, at the head of Main Street, the Saint Patrick's Church (wood, 1864; brick, 1903), the town's most imposing structure with nearly sufficient steeple to qualify as cathedral instead of church. At the town's center he drove by the five-storied Hotel Resetar (1927, the most ambitious secular building), Ford's Department Store (founded 1852 and the "oldest operating department store in California"), turned left at the plaza (donated in 1860 by the Don Sebastian Rodriguez family from the Bolsa del Pajaro land grant). And there on its corner stood his Carnegie library, built for ten grand in 1905 from plans drawn by busy architect William Henry Weeks.

Mrs. Ade, the librarian on evening rotation, sat at the circulation counter. "On a night schedule now?" she commented, a woman trained by profession and by a meager book budget to scrutinize who funneled past her desk, and with what.

For Scott, the more nervous, the more frequent his quotation snippets. It made for problems. He said, "Hi. 'I must become a borrower of the night, for a dark hour or two.' From *Macbeth*."

Mrs. Ade's eyelids fluttered, or graphically sputtered.

He faked browsing, before getting his hands on *The Human*

Body. At an isolated reading carrel he built a sight barrier on its tabletop with five volumes from an encyclopedia set. Only then did he open the blue-backed book with the gold lettering, and followed upward the numbers on the page corners: 58, 68, 77, 90, 101, 102, 103, 104. Figure 84.

Those eyes said—said what? Was it "I missed you, too"?

Checking behind him to see if anyone else had heard, Scott elbowed over two of the encyclopedias. *Bump, whump*. But the sleepy place was paying him and his secret no heed.

So, Bakkan. Then what do we have here, after all these dramatics? *Who* do we have here? We have no rare beauty—not that—not that quick Hollywood fix. Marlee suited better for any Miss America 1955.

Helpfully, fig. 84 offered to reveal her many details. She shows Scott her fingernails and toenails, all short and unpainted, her arches, veined, her shins, unshaven with their downy blur. She unclenches her thighs apart the space of an edgewise hand. On her soft blank stomach crosses the faint impression left from an elastic waistband. The bony ladder of her ribs vanishes, paradoxically, under mature breasts and she has too-thin shoulders, a lengthy neck, a narrow face, emphatic eyebrows. From a perfectly parted centerline her hair falls in increasing disarray, either rumpled by her undressing, or head-tossed, or waiting for this photograph she had anxiously twisted fingers through the ends.

Such minutiae, those bits and pieces of her, proved nothing

to him by themselves. The sight that jolted him, that captured him, was larger. And it was that this young woman had made . . . a mistake. Yes, a huge mistake. She had forgotten to neutralize her face, forgotten to vacate her body and leave behind the safe photographed husk of universal form, an anonymous "Fully Pubescent Female, Age 18." Instead page 104, recklessly, stood there more exposed than all those other unclothed specimens in *The Human Body*.

A somebody, an actual living person—name unknown—looked back at him. Because of this, every facet, each curve, angle, texture, pronounced its honest correctness for him. He traced the ankles, the long thighs, the symmetrical flanks, the scoop of her abdomen, the arcs of her eyebrows, the stray shadows creasing her at the elbows and between the lips. She wore no other lipstick. Extending the tip of a finger he put it, with accuracy, on the solemn mouth. He asked, out loud, in the library, "Have no Silent Desires?"

At that he shut p. 104 away, with a loud ugly slap together of the bookends.

In the Ford, on the way home, late again, he ignored a regal show of the constellations, being preoccupied with regal self-ridicule. Tell me the difference, Bakkan, between you, and Lyle and his girl-in-a-white-sweater Bernice, except that you, you book parasite, whip it up into Dante and his glorious Beatrice.

Or, my dear Uncle Spencer, should I blame you for this tomfoolery. Possibly. Probably.

<u>Seven</u>

He never ran without her anymore. No other way to explain it. On this day, this dawn, off they go together, *S. Bakkan* and page 104. No use denying the embarrassing fact.

They pass by Overton's apple orchard. Today there was Overton himself, his rubber boots glistening from dew where he walked to probe the ground for soft spots, before hauling in 500 gallons of lime sulfur and spraying during the windless morning. "Hello-o-o-o!" Overton hollered to them, with a flapping wave. He fit well the formula of the simple farmer: religiously in denim, slow of speech, stoic when Newtown Pippin and Bellflower prices slumped under fifty dollars per ton. A bachelor, in place of a wife he had his trees and his tractor, a graceful new orchard model Caterpillar D2 crawler, series 5U, which Overton was known to wash on weekends and rub with automobile wax.

Once beyond Overton's benchland, an alternate route led

eastward from Fern Creek up into the escarpments above the plunging depths of Eureka Canyon. It was an abandoned dirt logging road, much steeper than along the creek, with sections where running felt more like digging out a flight of earthen stairs with the balls of the feet. But she stuck beside him, escorting him to unknown levels of focus, hence powers.

"I'm happy you found me," she says.

He answers her, actually does. "What's your name?"

"Come to the library and be with me again today?"

His muscles cycled, in rhythm. On the downgrades he set sail, an illusion that he carried five yards, ten yards, twenty yards between steps, until he launched himself, airborne, across swales, gullies, entire ravines.

"Or am I not real enough for you yet?" she asks.

Upward again Scott ran, the logging road narrowed by slides of decomposed granite and Purisima chunks, fans of eroded sandstone. He reached the first outlook—the Monterey Bay visible, eight miles distant—and on he went. Overhead, the sky clarified into a dome of clean blue, its sole accent a tawny band of ocher along the eastern horizon. At last he topped out on a commanding ridge, stripped once into a pasture. The sun was on the rise, the bay agleam, a California thrasher in a toyon shrub preening with its scimitar bill.

Scott braked to a stop: a cardinal sin against his supercharged cardiac motor. He was remembering Marlee Stalich, waiting at her house, for him, for a New Year's Day breakfast.

From his vantage point he could view the summit forming the county boundary, beyond which the Santa Cruz Mountains slipped down into *terra cognita* or the urbanized world of the Santa Clara Valley and the San Francisco Peninsula. On this side of the mountains, his side, formed the headwaters of Corralitos Creek, flowing hidden below inside Eureka Canyon, beneath square miles of redwood forest. "No, no," he sent out into this void, "borrow your mother's Cadillac. Come and get me. I'm late!" He shouted louder: "I'm l-a-t-e!" The dun thrasher flew off, ungainly. Only its bill and its song had elegance.

Without fail Marlee would be ready to welcome him at the door, wearing her happy greeting like a nimbus. Marlee and her mother will fulfill their parts, holding vigil out their front windows, and as the assigned hour passed, Marlee would no doubt telephone the Bakkans ("Has Scotty left yet, Mrs. Bakkan?"), amplifying her unease, further spoiling the special plans. Now he had to come toting excuses, packets of costly apologies to hand around, first to his own mother, next for Marlee, finally for Mrs. Stalich. And what would he confide into Marlee's ear? "Missed you," should he say. "Missed you this morning more than any morning you ever missed me more than, if you ever miss me mornings." Alliteration again, my terrific little sister.

Scotty B. might stand for Bastard, but he dare not tell the truth, if he had truth. How could he? "My book maiden is the one I miss. That's right, a photograph, in a book. No name. Just make it p. 104. Just paper and my desire. What, Lyle? You bet I desire her. What else is this about, when you dig down, right buddy?"

In the spring of Lyle's fifteenth year he had gone camping with a youth group to Yosemite National Park. There he met a girl standing along the Merced River, skipping pebbles off the water, wearing cut-off jeans outgrown from the year before. Her hair was a rat's nest from a night in a sleeping bag, the jeans stiff with camp grime, yet no matter, Lyle tagged after the girl and before the trip ended he got friendly enough with her to discover "not much of a chest, but otherwise a body ready for a harem or a whorehouse." What did Lyle, upon his return, report to Scott about the translucent charms of Yosemite's ponds, or of snowmelt plunging over thousand-foot waterfalls, or about the granite colossus of El Capitan, or stupendous Half Dome? Nothing was said, because Lyle wanted instead to celebrate thirty-five inches of pelvic bone.

* * * *

Under his jacket in a plain 9"x12" manila envelope Scott carried three glossy, scandalous B&W stills, the elite from Lyle's pornography collection. One picture was a flight stewardess prostrate on a mattress saying "Welcome aboard" with her legs; one was beyond civil description, but involved a woman and two empty wine bottles; one was a young woman in the approximate posture of p.104, fig. 84.

These photos, courtesy of his friend, he had reviewed before, out of brotherhood obligations. Borrowing them, however, required running the gauntlet of Lyle's curiosity. "It's for an unusual experiment," he volunteered to admit.

For some reason, when winking, Lyle always rapidly alternated his eyes, like a six-year-old proud of this new skill. "I know what they're for."

"You don't. It's an experiment."

"Then I'm a regular scientist. Shucks, never mind, your business is your business."

"Why are your eyes twitching? Is that a nerve problem?"

They had been at Lyle's house, in a scruffy neighborhood lodged between the municipal airport and Harkins Slough, had been in his bedroom, surrounded by an acrid gym suit, two footballs, two basketballs, three baseballs, a Louisville bat, a Wilson first baseman's glove, football shoes with grass clumps still between the cleats, an intestinal pile of unraveled Ace bandage rolls, a weightlifting bar with 220 pounds of disks, unhung posters of Johnny Unitas (the Baltimore Colts), Frankie Albert and Hugh McElhenney (the San Francisco '49s), Marilyn Monroe (breasts), Otto Graham (the Cleveland Browns), Jayne Mansfield (bigger breasts), Bob Waterfield (the Los Angeles Rams), and Bobby Lane (the Detroit Lions). There also lay, about, copies of the new magazine *Sports Illustrated*, sports sections from newspapers, and, seven feet up in Lyle's closet, guarded under lock and key—actually a combination bicycle lock—his

Photographic Nude Annual (genitalia prohibited) and *European Sunbather-Nudist* (soporific) publications, several issues of the new magazine *Playboy*, and his "good stuff."

"I am, no bull, doing an experiment," Scott had insisted, a trifle lamely, tapping the manila envelope, "comparing these with the picture of a girl I know. She's, um, in the raw."

"Whaa? Jesus, somebody from Stanford?"

"No. A girl from far away."

"You and your San Joaquin girls. Damn 'em, bless 'em. Wait, who took the shot?"

"Who do you think?"

"Not you. You? In her house or something?" Lyle sat on the floor, fingers pushing at his forehead, his imagination under total assault.

"Maybe her family has a camera hobby and she developed the film herself. Maybe."

"Holy smokes. She poses, you take it, she develops it. Me, I drive way up to Oakland, sneak around a liquor store where everybody wants to put a switchblade into my guts, and it costs five bucks for a dirty picture. Bakkan, listen, I'll pay five dollars for a quick peek at this girl. How about it? Fifty dollars. Tell me her name anyway. I can imagine from a name."

"I don't know her name."

"What's the harm. I'll never meet her. Give me a name, a bone, to chew on, at least. A favor for a favor?"

"Call her Sara. Spelled without an H."

"I like it. Sara what?"

"Sara Serendipity."

"I'm on fire. Is that Italian? She must be a farmer's daughter. Clothes are just a city nuisance to those farm gals. She probably gave you a basket of grapes to bring home, to slobber with while you look at her. Describe her a little?"

"A head, two arms, two legs, two this, one that, the usual."

"Ah, I know, I know, ain't it wunnerful?"

As Scott was leaving, the manila envelope tightly tucked under an armpit, Lyle had asked him, "What's to compare then, anyway, if they all have the same parts?" and Scott had replied, "That's my experiment."

* * * *

His arrival on an early Saturday impressed Mrs. Ade. "It's our best customer," she enthused. "Good morning to you!"

With the 9"x12" manila envelope under his jacket he swept past with the audacity of a hardened shoplifter. He gathered *The Human Body* and four or five other books—camouflage books—going to a spot forechosen, a corner where the sole approach to his table was a long aisle formed by book ranges. Once inside this defensive cul-de-sac, Scott spread out the books and the manila envelope, ready for business.

Overhead the window let in a clean blast of sunlight, washing his corner with its sterilizing clarity. Scott had come to the library at this hour not only to beat the crowd, but precisely for this, the morning's fresh light and mentality, both uncongenial to sentiment. It shall be proven: he would reduce this tyrannical whole number (p. 104) down to its accurate sum, namely a sexual sublimation, a fraction, a bare Bernice-on-a-page.

Folding up the clasp of the manila envelope—those tiny metal butterfly wings—he slid out the three bright photos, of studio quality. Lyle had gotten his money's worth on that score. And, giving professionalism its due, they also delivered a fair market value—three works of invisible desserts made visible. *The Human Body*, when Scott picked up the book, opened itself automatically, through habit, to p. 104, fig. 84.

On Scott's left, there on her mattress, was the peroxide blonde, wearing a stewardess-style pillbox hat with the rest of the uniform stacked neatly on a pillow. On Scott's right was p. 104. On the left was the second woman, darker-haired, with fishnet stockings and a garter belt of rococo lace, the censored wine bottles in both hands, her face replicating a passion. On the right was p. 104. On the left was the stewardess again, her rude, mocking eyes unrepentant about her public performance. On the right was p. 104.

To be systematic he chose the girl who stood in a posture similar to p. 104, for better comparing them side-by-side, strictly left-right, in a delimiting 1:1 ratio. Scott arranged body against body. On the left, one female body, and on the right, another female body. The young woman in Lyle's photograph, on the left, was pretty, twenty or thereabouts, maturely developed. Page 104 was eighteen and "fully pubescent."

His comparison started with their faces and never reached lower. On the left, Lyle's girl holds her mouth in an oval, ablaze with Unsecret Desires: "O, are you staring at me?" Page 104 has only that shadow between her lips. On the left, the girl's come-hither eyes are taunting: "Naughty boy, do me some naughty." On the right, p. 104's eyes watch him.

Scott Bakkan stuffed the glossies back into the manila envelope. "Excuse these pictures," he apologized to p. 104. "Seems I'm anxious about something." He untied and retied his shoes. "You win," he told her, "but what do you win exactly? A dunce. You win somebody making a total ass of himself." He fingered the edges of page 104, before crossing into its middle. "Yet total is what I want in my life."

At the library exit counter, a solicitous Mrs. Ade wondered if he had "found what he needed." The unintended perfection of her query appealed to Scott. "Absolutely," he said.

"I don't notice anything. Did you put it in that envelope?"

Scott looked at the suspicious manila envelope in his careless hand. He looked at the librarian, who up close had lively Gaelic-green irises. "No," he said, "I put it in my head."

"Pardon?"

"I was after two lines of poetry."

"And you memorized them. Now, doesn't that make me curious." She wore purple again today. Mrs. Ade had but three workday outfits, each dress a color without much subtlety: crayon yellow, grass green, and plum purple. These did, to their credit, complement the copper shades of her hair, which above one ear showed some dozen strands of recent gray interlopers. "Would you . . ."

". . . repeat them?" Scott's thrill was the prickle of playing with dangerous objects. He leaned near, an elbow on the counter with a conspiratorial smile, voice lowered, his breathing audible to his listener. "For you, yes. Privately between the two of us. I hope you appreciate sight rhymes. 'If these delights thy mind may move,/ Then live with me and be my Love.' Follow that?"

Mrs. Ade smiled herself—with nice teeth. "How romantic."

"How sixteenth century."

"Whose is it?"

"Christopher Marlowe's," he said, adding, since p. 104 had just given him the gift of boldness, "and mine."

In that case, warned Mrs. Ade, Scott should hurry on home before she stopped biting her tongue, and had to ask him, "Who else will be hearing your poem?"

* * * *

In Overton's orchard the leaf buds eventually were "in the silver tip" and about to split. Here and there a few had. The fruit buds, swollen too, would shortly follow. "This '55 year is gonna be a crop we'll be proud about," predicted Overton, who treated his apple trees like they were mothers-to-be.

In a novelty of schedule, unexpected by his pleased family, Scott came home from campus on every weekend and holiday "to run his favorite trails." Throughout January, and February, he established his secret life and his love affair. Day or night the faithful Ford came slipping back through town in a reversal of outward routes. He would pass the cathedral (designed by Wm. H. Weeks), the big hotel (Wm. H. Weeks, architect), the historic department store, and turn at the central plaza with its circular bandstand (Weeks, architect). Or he might approach from another compass point, passing by the Victorian splendor of the Tuttle mansion (built 1899, Wm. H. Weeks, architect), the Bockius home (state legislator, built 1870), Bockius' neighbor the Porter home (Lt. Governor of California, built 1900, Weeks, architect), by the Swiss cider plant (1868), turning left, past the former home of an Irish whiskey broker (1900, Weeks), turning right, and along a row of other formerly prosperous Victorians—two-storied, with turrets, verandas, scrolled woodwork, wraparound leaded windows, and carpentry that Scott the builder's son could appreciate. Today they were rentals and apartments for Mexican workers, but had once been homes for various entrepreneurs, including an English surveyor/lawyer (1892), an Italian grocer (1898, Weeks, architect), a Slavic fruit dealer (1898, Weeks). Leaving these houses he drove through a tip of Old Chinatown, or its location before being relocated over the Pajaro River in 1888 (no Wm. H. Weeks, architect).

Whatever historical circuit he traveled, Scott ended up at the same spot. Whether he came from the north, from the direction of Mt. Madonna (where Robert Louis Stevenson spent a few weeks writing) and past the county fairgrounds, or from the east through strawberry fields and past a Buddhist temple, or from the south, from the windy sand dunes and the Pacific (failed Port Watsonville), past canneries and alluvium-rich lettuce fields, or whether from the west and Santa Cruz (the cathedral route), all his roads into his polyglot village led to the cramped nexus of Trafton Lane and Union Street.

The library, yes, stood there. PUBLIC LIBRARY said its stones (Wm. H. Weeks, architect). As well as Scott had known this place, he learned it better.

He would park the Ford and walk a block or two since Trafton Lane never did accommodate the automobile. Approaching, he saw first the library's portico with its flag pole and its twin squared colonnades, filigree at their tops, and a band of bas-relief decorating the building's upper margin, above the windows on the second level. The entrance faced the street corner where the curb had been rounded to match the sweeping fan-shaped steps. There were seven tiled steps up to the entry doors and, inside, a flight of creaky wooden stairs leading on, past a bulletin board of book jackets, to the main floor. Here the circulation counter—curved like the outside street corner—controlled a figurative gate into the treasury of print. And here Mrs. Ade or an alternate librarian greeted him.

"Finish these so soon?" they marveled, because on a crude

pretext he signed out and returned a steady loop-the-loop of unopened books.

For convenience, if not for peace and intimacy, Scott wished he could take *The Human Body* home with his other books, easy as that. But library rules limited renewals, and furthermore, doing so would reveal the object of his fascination. Mrs. Ade already took a natural interest in him (her "most frequent and favorite client"), this middle-aged woman with the coppery hair who now often asked him "book questions," indeed anticipated his fancy quotations, in her own version of Marlee's Daily Word. And there was the issue of those cryptic symbols hand-lettered on the blue spine of *The Human Body*: **<XX>**. Scott suspected this odd double-X might even restrict use inside the library. Page 104, given this hazardous scheme, could be put away for keeps. Being a Bakkan, he never gave legitimate thought—never gave any thought—about a razor blade, and mutilating the book, robbing it of p. 104, fig. 84.

Instead, he did a lot in minimal space, considering the size of the old library and its 1938 annex. Together he and p. 104 sought the protection of every obscure niche, rotating the best ones, varying the sectors within the library—behaving like cautious hunted animals switching lairs. One afternoon found them behind the Seth Thomas grandfather clock, which had measured the shush of this room since October 1905. One day they carried off a Reference chair and isolated it far in the backwaters of Philosophy/Religion. One night they leaned beneath a faulty lamp too dim to attract anyone reading text. One day this, another evening that, around and about in this devious dance they maneuvered, from alcove to aisle to cubbyhole and back.

Wherever they did settle, Scott would patiently confess, in essence, "Here's your maniac lover again."

Incredible she was, vivid and spontaneous, no cheap curio tarnishing with use, regardless of how many days he met her. She never permitted any timidity between them and he had to tell her directly, "You exist for me, you know. How many different faces have I seen in my lifetime? Thousands. Only yours convinces me that for some reason we make two matching pieces, the two with the shapes cut to fit and lock together, without forcing." He told her, "I have these new pleasures with a new restlessness, too. I might be a big dreamer. Well, look at me—I *am* a big dreamer. But you should understand how every Bakkan has a poor man's practical streak. Both my grandfather and my father, in the end, want to bank their money and keep it safe. That's how I feel about you. I need you in the bank."

Part II

"I think I'm not lying."

<u>Eight</u>

"1948," said grandfather to granddaughter, tilting a copper coin toward the ceiling light. "1948. Phooey on Dewey. That's what happened in '48. How many pennies you saved in that tin box of yours?"

"Way over a hundred. Listen."

"Don't shake the box, sweetie," Furman said, eating a (no surprise) dinner roll.

Joyce reviewed her facts. "Truman got elected President first in 1945."

"Not elected," Elaine corrected her. "Roosevelt died. And when a President dies in office . . ." She was serving a cottage cheese salad in a gelatin mold. ("Peppy lemon gelatin is a delight in any season. Cottage cheese provides texture and mild taste, sour cream its zest, crushed pineapple and maraschino cherries their fruity goodness and cheerful color.")

"Quite a collection," Leland congratulated his granddaughter. "Here's 1927. Now we're getting somewheres. Lindbergh, wasn't it, Furman? Because that same year Wanda—your grandma—and me paid off the house loan and we drove to San Francisco to celebrate. We went in the '22 Star."

Scott asked, "Was that much of a car?"

"No. Wrong gearing made it weak in the rear end. You could always figure on rear end troubles."

That sounded "pretty funny" to Joyce.

"1948 again."

"A bad year for Dewey," said Furman, "but a swell one for us. We sold those two-bedroom stucco units on Branciforte, which started our business ball to bounce."

"I think 'swell' is finally passé," Scott advised.

"Is it. Good riddance. It's been hanging around for more years than there are commas in a Henry James sentence."

Elaine said, "I pass those same buildings occasionally. Now the stucco is a tannish color, thank god. We painted half the units a Bluebird Blue and the other half a dirty Flamingo Pink."

"Very ornithological, my dear," smiled Furman. "But those colors were all the vogue then. Hollywood Pink and . . . Sea Azure . . . no, Sky Azure, were the actual labels on the cans. Notice, Scotty, you're not the only one with a good memory. Besides, how could I ever forget? Leland bought the paint from an overstocked distributor in Merced, at thirty-five cents per gallon, and when I arrived to haul it—in a *car*—I found an entire driveway blocked with a mountain—or should I say flock—of bluebirds and flamingos. To this day we have a few gallons of that paint around."

Leland explained the principle behind "volume discount": You buy more of something than a person could ever use, and as a bonus you get charged less for the total, than if you had bought just what you needed in the first place. Everybody chuckled. Steamy pea soup made the rounds ("add in potatoes and onions, first simmered in butter").

Joyce asked, "Why do we make houses in Santa Cruz but not in Watsonville?"

"We have," answered Furman, "although not usually."

"Why not?"

"Why not. Because the same house will be worth more in Santa Cruz."

"Why?"

"She wants to know why," Furman passed on to his wife.

"Because," Elaine said, "the main street in Watsonville is named Main Street and in Santa Cruz it's named Pacific Avenue. Catch the difference?"

"I like this soup," said Joyce. ("Stir in celery salt, ground pepper, and the subtle seasoning of marjoram, a natural partner for peas.")

Furman requested his son's attention. "On the subject of houses, there's that rental in La Selva we want to remodel and put on the market. It might be a good summer project for you,

Scotty. We'll let you supervise the work, handle the whole shot."

"He done that before?" Leland wanted to know.

"No, but he's ready."

Scott asked, "Is it the crummy red shack with roll roofing and batten siding?"

"That's the one. We took it as a down payment on that new house we sold near the cement boat in Seacliff, the two-story, garage-under house with the ocean view. I suppose this place was a vacation cabin once." A resumé followed of the renovation program: add a bedroom, shingle the roof, combine the kitchen and the dining room with a breakfast bar in lieu of the present wall, strip the interior to the studs, adding some braces and fire blocks, framing in two new doors and a picture window, rewire, cover with sheetrock, and paint.

"With bluebirds," said Joyce.

Elaine brought in a choice of main dishes, the first being Broiled Fish with Deviled Cheese Sauce ("broil fresh fillets, brush with butter and spices, top with cheddar or other favorites like smoky provolone or frothy mozzarella"), the second being Crispy Chicken Olé ("melt butter into one deep bowl, combine yellow cornmeal, salt and chili powder in another deep bowl"). Furman took both, Leland neither.

Joyce asked, "Why is the cheese called deviled?"

"Because the sauce is saucy, the way you are sometimes, my love," answered her mother. ("Get the zip from mustard, horseradish, chili.")

Furman took pause to say, "I relish chicken with a noisy crust." ("Dip drumstick into the butter, then roll it in the crunchy cornmeal mix.")

After the partial eclipse of chicken and fish, Scott said, "About this summer. I received an invitation from the Staliches, offering me a summer position at the bank—a trainee deal."

His parents stopped eating in order to properly ingest this news. "Apprentice for what eventuality, I wonder," asked Furman, with Elaine responding instantly, "The obvious."

"Don't you think," said Scott, "this is a case of going to summer camp to learn the worthless art of canoe designs?"

"Your mother imagines the designs are the ones they have on you."

"Leland, did you hear that?" asked Elaine. "Scott might be working at a bank."

"At a bank?"

"Yes."

"You mean Scotty being a *banker*?"

"I guess he'd be a banker."

"What sky did that fall out of? I thought Bakkan and lumber belong together."

Furman reminded him, "Finance and construction go hand-in-hand you know."

"His fingernails would stay cleaner, anyhow," said Elaine, her fancy veering off into an altered Bakkan/Stalich potential.

"How about being in the Olympics?" worried Joyce.

A Cherry Ice Cream Pie was carried to the table, already cut into wedges, ready for the eating. Even Leland accepted a piece, although he picked up a penny instead of a dessert fork. "1919. Looks clean for 1919."

"That rhymes. I washed the whole bunch in Momma's dishwasher."

"My brother Woodrow caught the influenza in 1918, the plague that killed folks left and right, more dead than the war in Europe had. The World War, the first one. Woodrow fought that influenza till 1919 but he got weaker and weaker, and his lungs filled up. That was the winter of 1918-19."

("Put together two favorites for one grand occasion and you have Cherry Ice Cream Pie. Crumble vanilla cookie wafers into a melt of butter and sugar to form the crust, which requires only five minutes to bake. Cool and chill before swirling in softened ice cream alternately with cherry pie filling for a layered luscious effect.")

"He's buried in Santa Cruz, in that cemetery up on the bluff. I last saw his grave long, long, long ago. Our father had talked him into coming over here. Nelson, our father Nelson, had the notion that when the war ended lumber would boom, and he never did give up on the Bakkans owning a mill again. Woodrow went to check our old sawmill in Bakkan Canyon behind Soquel. About then he got sick and never left Santa Cruz County."

("10 minutes before serving remove pie from freezer. Whip 1 cup whipping cream until stiff, adding in confectionery sugar and vanilla. Gently fold in remaining cherry pie filling. Spread top of pie with whipped cream topping. Sprinkle with slices of toasted almonds. Crown with pitted whole cherries.")

"Woodrow cut off most of a thumb at our mill, about '03, thereabouts, not much before the business went under. Anything a mean man can wish to go bad did go bad for us, with so much rain we couldn't get into the woods to log. Floods and a landslide wrecked the stables. Our horses, heaven knows where they washed to, probably straight downstream to Capitola and into the ocean. The only luck we had was we missed the big shake in '06, 'cause by then we had gone to Fresno and hired out for wages. Later, when Woodrow died, me and Wanda had our house in Ceres and my father lived with us. He was too feeble after his stroke to come to Woodrow's burial, but direct afterwards he tells me, 'It's your turn to find out what we can do there.' Talking about our old sawmill, understand. I advised him, 'Nelson, business is still spinning its wheels. We got lumber right in our backyard we can't sell.' Nelson was a stubborn S.O.B. to put it plain. And before long sure enough I'm heading back over the mountains to Santa Cruz, with my Model T tourer, and that trip wasn't a picnic, though you took food along. Naturally, nothing happened about any sawmill. We couldn't come near to raising the money. Nelson died before things picked up later in the twenties."

Joyce, fiddling with a package of leftover vanilla wafers, said she knew, she thought, "what S.O.B. stood for."

"I hope not," said her mother, "because it's a bad word."

"Golly, I know some bad words."

"I hope not," repeated her mother.

"Well, I do. 'I see you in the ocean/ I see you in the sea/ I see you in the bathtub/ Oh, pardon me!' Betsy sings that."

"Betsy's a true friend," said Scott, "to pass along dirty Third Grade limericks to you."

"*Dirty?* In a bathtub?"

"Furman," said Leland, returning a latecomer 1954 penny to the tin box, "you can recollect when your grandfather lived with us in Ceres."

Furman could. Joyce wiggled a vanilla wafer out of its package, to finger, not eat. Her eyes held to her father's, who said: "The old boy talked about when he came to California—here to Santa Cruz—and worked in the redwoods. Seems I heard him tell of living in a burnt-out redwood stump and spearing salmon in the San Lorenzo with a pitchfork. In my mind as a youngster I saw him in buckskin, a Dan'l Boone swinging an axe. Buckskin. Now I see him in his bedroom at Ceres, sitting in the rocker with his feet up, chewing snuff, watching out the window at Leland in the lumberyard. I realize today that Nelson wasn't an aged man. A sick man, yes he was, but not ancient, not how he struck me then. And one day in his room . . ." Furman, uncharacteristically, floundered. "How to explain it. You know I witnessed some rough scenes in the Pacific. What I mean is, whatever I saw during the war, none of it penetrated, through-and-through me, like on that day I went into Nelson's bedroom. My mother had sent me to bring him for dinner. Every evening she sent me, when dinner was ready.”

“She did . . .” said Leland.

“I wasn’t much older than Joyce. In the bedroom the shadows made a patchwork of dark with a few sun streaks left outside in the sky. My grandfather sat in front of the window, napping in his rocker. He napped a lot. I shook his shoulder, which was normal for me to do. I said, ‘Nelson, Nelson, wake up.’ I gave him a good poke in the chest, just before I noticed that one of his nostrils was plugged tight with red, as red as this cherry pie tonight on our table right here.”

Pop, went Joyce’s vanilla wafer, and shattered, no less loud than breaking a stick of dry kindling wood.

“I kept shaking his shoulder. On and on. It got darker and darker in the room. My mother shouted up. I shouted back, ‘We’re coming, wait a minute.’ I knew I didn’t want to stop trying to wake him up.”

* * * *

Elaine vanished, returning with an additional dessert, one less red than the cherry pie. On the plate were displayed Date Star Cookies. (“Fold cream into your butter-and-brown-sugar dough. Mix, chill, add chopped dates, grated lemon peel.”)

My dear Book Maiden:

Today I thought of you. Yesterday the same.

Tomorrow the same, I know. It's getting to be
something. It's getting to be Something.
      Shall we agree with Cap'n Ahab
(or with mastermind Herman Melville himself)
that "all mortal greatness is but disease"?
Or, in terms closer to our case, what else is
"lovesick," but a splendid disease caused by
gulping down so much ambition.
      Wanna get sick together?

Drinks were refilled: black coffee, coffee with cream, herbal tea, milk, ice water.

"About summer, and the bank, or the remodel job," said Scott, "some vacation time would be appreciated, to sightsee America before graduate school gets me."

Furman, sampling a Date Star, chewed, nodded, indicating either approval of the cookie or his son.

"There's a girl I met," said Scott. "I want to visit her."

"A girl from school?" asked his father.

"Not from school. That's why I need to visit her."

"You met a new girl?" asked Elaine.

"A new girl, a new girl, exactly correct. A wonderful girl."

"A*wonderful*girl?" With a piece of cookie held between her teeth, the slur of his mother's speech provided comedic echo to her double take. "What's this. Do you mean you like her?"

"I mean I love her."

"Scotty's teasing," predicted his sister.

"Does Marlee know about this?" asked Furman.

"Not yet."

"I'm stunned."

"Mother's stunned."

"I am. I can't swallow." She reached in and removed the wet bite of cookie from her mouth, laying it, a sorry rejected lump, on her saucer. "Okay now. You're playing a little game with us."

"No, I think I'm not lying."

"Let me count. Is that two-and-a-half negatives? Does it add up to maybe you are?"

"Ask me where she's from."

"Where?"

"I don't know yet. But I intend to find out soon. Ask me her name."

"Which is?"

"As of now, unknown. But I love her."

"You're smirking," decided his mother, "smirking like an idiot."

"I told you," said Joyce. "Can I have two more cookies?"

"Ask me how I met her."

"All right," scolded Elaine, "no more Jabberwocky. Now I see where your sister gets her devilment."

Joyce said, "I'm taking two more cookies."

"When I learn her name, does anybody want to hear it?"

"Lordy, aren't you quirky tonight," said Elaine.

"I are. Hand me two of those stars, too, please." ("Re-roll dough and cut into star shapes.") "By the way, are we rich? Could we be considered rich yet?"

Furman: "The Du Ponts are rich."

Leland: "If this was 1933 we'd be big rich."

Elaine: "To others we seem rich, and we'll get richer, knowing us. 'No one lives content with his condition.' Horace."

Joyce: "I'd go for banking. Banks are always the nicest-looking stores in town. They smell important inside even. Mmm, the cookies mmmelt in my mmmouth." ("Lightly brown in 350-degree oven. These stars taste like they fell from heaven!")

<u>Nine</u>

Dear Sirs:
  As part of my Master of Science thesis, I
am conducting a survey of publishers/authors
of Developmental Anatomy textbooks. My
intent is to investigate whether such texts
unsuspectingly distort standard body types
by photographing models from insufficiently
diverse ethnic and geographic backgrounds.

  Accordingly, my study requires a thorough
statistical tabulation of the full names and
<u>complete</u> addresses from a scientific sampling
of such models. From your textbook <u>The</u> <u>Human</u>
<u>Body</u> the following models have been randomly
selected: p. 17 (fig. 23), p. 62 (fig. 59), p.
104 (fig. 84), p. 205 (fig. 111). Please send
the requested information pertaining to these
individuals.

  Of course all data incorporated into my
formal monograph will be summarized and
anonymous. Thank you for contributing to this
important academic project.

  Self-addressed stamped envelope enclosed.

* * * *

Dear Publisher Company:
  Will you help me to my lost sweethart?
  The Army tole everbody I got killt on training oversea in Korea (it was a mix-up-ed mistake). I just thot maybe my sweethart stop writting when she was mad or something.
  When I come home (USA) she and family had moved and nobody hear wear. But I see her picture in your book The Human Body page 104 and tole myself will the book company help me?

* * * *

Dear Sirs:
  I write representing the Futura Model Agency of California. A young woman in a book of yours—THE HUMAN BODY (p. 104, fig. 84)—has been called to our attention by several publication scanners, or "talent scouts." In their opinion, and ours, this amateur model shows potential and could be a candidate for fashion magazines, even possibly films.

  Therefore would you or the book's author please furnish our agency with the information needed (name, address) to contact the young woman? This might be the start of her new career!

  Should you feel it prudent, you may send only the address of her parents or guardian.

These asinine letters never had to be sent. One March morning Scott read the Forward to *The Human Body*, written by Martin T. Frazer, M.D. In the middle of this plodding apologia for Anatomy and Greater Knowledge lay a nugget of purest gold. This Dr. Frazer believed "professionally, and, indeed, personally, in the fundamental values of open exchange of information about the human body, its conception and development, its natural cycle, which should be a study not of mystery, but of science." As evidence of his belief he would mention, "in the briefest of asides," that his own daughter, "eighteen years of age," serves as one of the "subject photographs in the present book."

Miss Frazer. That information, an uncalculated injury to his family's privacy by dedicated Dr. Frazer, was for Scott an omen that destiny was firmly freighted on its track. On this March morning Scott sat in the library savoring his good luck like a birthday boy slowly, slowly, unwrapping the largest package. For at the end of the Forward, signed from his desk at home, the doctor had closed the commentary in a traditional manner and given his place of residence: New Hope, Illinois.

Now Scott had to write another letter—one more important than before, more precarious.

* * * *

Dear Miss Frazer:

No, this isn't some early April Fool's Day joke. But I do feel like a fool. I don't know all your name, actually. However, I have met you, and my simple wish now is your permission to strike up a proper introduction between us. Awkward, isn't it?

No doubt you wonder where I did "meet" you, as I claim. Probably you suspect. Probably you have a scrapbook labeled Crank Letters or Mash Notes. Please understand me when I say

When I say

When I say

* * * *

Dear Miss Frazer:

This isn't easy. This

* * * *

Hello!

Well, if I can't meet you, then I'm just talking to myself.

Don't you agree?

* * * *

Dear Miss Frazer:

You live in a town named New Hope. I assume the first settlers gave it that name, following their 19th-century agrarian visions for a prosperous life in virgin midwestern lands. Here in California the pioneers did the same. I like the thought myself, the idea of starting off without encumbrances to cripple your best instincts. In fact, New Hope does have everything to do with why I'm writing you today.

Slick segue.

* * * *

Dear Miss Frazer:

Allow me to be blunt and quick, in hopes that candor will pull off what could never be diplomatic anyway.

I'm about your age. Not long ago I happened to see your photograph in a book called <u>The Human Body</u>. You remember the picture. Being normal, I found your body attractive, but my motive here isn't sexual. Believe that or not, as you choose. The truth is, the lust you put in me was the desire to know you better. I want to learn your full name. I want to know what songs you sing.

> Bakkan
>
> you sleepy
>
> sloppy
>
> bone brain
>
> go to bed.

* * * *

Dear Friend:

Let me tell about myself, before explaining this letter. That way, I won't be such a stranger, and it's only fair to answer a few questions about me before asking a few about you. Inside this envelope you'll find my photo.

To begin, I'm writing you at dawn, because shortly I have to do my usual early training run. According to <u>Track</u> <u>&</u> <u>Field</u> <u>News</u>, S. Bakkan is one of the top young milers in the world. But the earth's a fairly big planet and I think I just heard it snicker.

What else. My parents got college degrees to be English teachers but with the war, etc., ended up owning a successful construction company. We build houses, mainly. Want to know how to frame a door? Just ask. My parents also taught me more about literary history than you'd ever believe. I have a younger sister, and my grandfather (seriously ill) now lives with us.

What else. I do the normal things. I have a "girlfriend," whose name is Marlee.

* * * *

Dear Friend:

I've just come, tonight, from my girlfriend's house. May I tell you about Marlee before explaining why an unknown person writes you this letter? By introducing the young lady already in my life, it should make clear my intentions don't threaten you in any way.

Marlee's a delight and fulfills every reasonable expectation for a sweetheart. Marlee, besides being considered the prettiest girl around, is probably the friendliest, and the least deceptive. She can be a friend and not only a girlfriend.

Darn, I'm the deceptive one here. The truth? You're my real girlfriend. I wouldn't be writing this letter otherwise. You should feel threatened, after all. I should.

* * * *

Dear P. 104:

My greeting above tells you something about me, but not the critical part. Yes, I saw that picture. No, I'm not after a naked girl.

Dear p. 104, with your eyes you've spoken to me (excuse this mysticism). Dear book maiden, a fear comes upon me, in the day and in the night, that we shouldn't miss meeting face to face, not miss talking together, and at any cost not miss finding out what might happen between us.

Your state is far away from mine, yet I'll gladly drive there this summer and visit with you under any conditions that put you at ease—either at your home with your parents, or with friends, or in a public place such as a school.

Do I still sound like a shrewd rapist?

Or how about in an Illinois National Guard armory surrounded by troops with full battle weaponry?

* * * *

Dear Friend, dear Girl, dear Woman:

An emerald fog of jealousy settled over me the other night, after figuring out that while I was caressing Marlee here, some lout might likewise be caressing you there. I imagined his hands fondling your face and breasts—a drooling oaf with satyr's hair sprouting out his nose who for impossible reasons you like. Very painful for me.

Possession is nine-tenths of the law and I possess you (or the reverse, anyhow). After discovering you, I want to hoard my treasure, because romantic love is ultimate greed. So don't share yourself with any other lover, please. I suffer enough already, knowing p. 104/ fig. 84 is scattered across the nation, beguiling the eyes of strangers, inciting my competition.

Be patient. I'll send a letter soon, come to your door soon, and provide, soon, any attention and fondling you may ever require.

* * * *

Dear Friend:

On this day I carted you directly beneath the librarian Cecilia Ade's nose. (It looks halfway like yours, her nose.) She wore the Irish green. I wore grays and tans. You wore . . .

She knew nothing. We knew all.

* * * *

Dear Angela:
Today I'll name you Angela. You can be my good angel.
Dear. Angela. Angela, dear. I'm dopey but I mean it, my
lovely angel. I may tear this paper up immediately
but I mean it, Angela.
Angela Bakkan. A.B. We could start an alphabet together.
Get ready for a Watsonville postmark.

* * * *

Dear Book Maiden:

Dear, dear, book maiden. I hardly care who finds out about us. Let me seem absurd. Let me seem unhinged. Let me kiss your paper eyes in place of your real ones. I haven't done that yet, but I might. Why not. Why be shy in front of you, who stands so openly, for me, on p. 104?

How does the poet Whitman put it. Something like "amorous madness" or "madness amorous." I'll look in my book here and check. Yes, madness amorous. "Hark close and still what I now whisper to you,/ I love you, O you entirely possess me,/ O that you and I escape from the rest and go utterly off, free and lawless."

Good old Walter, Jr. Or good old Spence, because this reminds me of my uncle Spencer, who also could foam at the mouth on this topic. I guess it runs in the family genes.

<u>Ten</u>

Saturday morning, the opening of track season, 1955: Scott lingers in bed, while already in focus. He had allowed himself his trip home to p. 104 because this first invitational meet is at Stanford, only an hour's drive from here. Today is an *S. Bakkan* day when he will be his own question mark and his own reply.

"I can't find my left leg," he told sleepy-headed Joyce, entering his room. "I think it ran away during the night."

She yawned, her mouth a full circle, climbing up on the bed. "What's this then?"

"You found it, bless you. What'd I do without my sister?"

Joyce held one of his hands with both of hers. They were child's hands, Joyce's, exquisitely proportioned, with a hint of the woman's hands to be. "Well," she said, "what would you?" A tousled flounce of hair kept falling into her eyes, despite sputtery upward puffs of air blown off her lower lip. With the fingers of his free hand Scott combed the hair back out of her face. "Thanks," she said, her drowsy gaze examining him with the same blue softness as her blue flannel nightgown.

"Want to hear a secret?" he asked her. "I do have a love who lives far away."

"Honest?"

"Honest."

Joyce sat beside him, patting his outsized hand, until she was fully awake. "Now I'll get you up," she threatened. "I'll tickle you. You'll laugh till your guts come right out."

"No, no. I need my guts today."

Shortly he was off to Marlee's house, herself back for the important event. In effect, he went from his bed to another one, since she made him lay down in her bedroom. On these race days Marlee hovered around him with a smothering protectiveness, urging virtual immobility on her bed in order to "save every speck of strength" and to keep from "twisting an ankle while walking outside for no good purpose." She would stretch out alongside him, on her back, maintaining a slight, guarded distance. "Will this disturb you?" She held his hand—not too differently from how Joyce had—and chattered, avoiding certain sensitive words, the same way that small talk with a patient before surgery avoids the words "scalpel," "pain," "accident."

Before his departure, Mrs. Stalich fed him what she held to be energy fuel: unsalted nuts, juice, a weighty chunk of Swiss chocolate. She then gave Scott a quick, self-explanatory encouragement squeeze as he left and so did her daughter. Both of them were sweeter and more aromatic than their imported *Schokolade*.

* * * *

Scott entered the other, more exotic corner of his life. At his gym locker he dressed with the ritual and the colors of a costumed matador. The racing shorts, ironed to a mother's standards, shimmer along with the shoulderless singlet, and when he ran the race, on his feet would be gold-on-white Adidas track shoes, made from featherweight perforated kangaroo skin. These German imports, in motion, suggested Pegasus' winged swirl.

The afternoon, one of sun and warmth, as a California spring equinox should be, had its brightness scumbled by a mild filter of upper haze. In the stadium a crowd has gathered. Why the unusual excitement for a preseason track meet is not hard to imagine. Into the seats file the Bakkan family, Joyce and Leland included, and with them the Staliches and Marlee.

When the loudspeaker grandly intoned *"First call, Mile Run,"* Scott did several fifty-yard bursts: sprint, jog, sprint, jog. This procedure was intended to duplicate, for his body, the section of road before arriving at Overton's orchard, and he pulls himself, mentally, into a concentrated center, a point of compact purpose.

"Second call, Mile Run."

Up above, in the beckoning emptiness of the sympathetic sky, a coward could find an escape, momentarily. But in his warrior attack mode Scott refused any and all weaknesses, turning up instead the fires of determination. Under his warm-up suit he had heated to the proper degree for action, his skin damp, muscles loose, lungs and heart on the alert. A loping pace, with a periodic pump of the knees to chest height, held this readiness until, "*Last call, Mile Run. Runners report.*"

A swell of applause—an upswell of expectation—greets the announcement. On the track the milers, shuffling, advance to the start line, while an official goes through the entry checklist. A scattering of athletes from Bay Area schools are present—persons and uniforms familiar to Scott—and four unfamiliar faces, three down from Oregon, one from Seattle. For Scott the individual, the loudspeaker at this opportunity broadcasts a hometown spiel: a resumé of last year's deeds (records! records!) and this year's prophecy (ranked #1!). His fellow milers view him from the corners of uneasy eyes. This prelude itself could cripple Scott's opponents, or it could until the major national meets, when aspiring gunslingers from afar would be anxious to confront him and put a bullet through his ballyhooed reputation.

"Don't shove into the lanes at the turn," the starter is instructing them, stealing his own glance at *S. Bakkan*. ("I started a mile of his once, back in '55, and I could purely tell that we'd watch him in the Olympics someday.")

The runners toe the line in every sense, leaning ahead toward four repeated ovals, 5,280 feet exactly—toeing, leaning, waiting for a pistol to fire. Scott in his white-and-gold shoes crouches with the rest.

"*Gun up*," goes the loudspeaker, for it was.

Shoes tied. Knees bent. Lungs full. ***POW!***

Like a miniature mob they bolt to the first turn, cut in there from the outside lanes, jostling, finding positions. Avoiding this danger of sharp spikes, Scott dashes ahead before settling back along the curb into his miler's stride. Behind him he can hear chasing feet and, already, the grunt/gasp of breathing. At the head of the backstretch *S. Bakkan* is the leader, and rearward trails a string of assorted followers that would grow longer and thinner as the yards passed. Bannister in '54, Bakkan in '55.

Near the end of the backstretch Scott hears footsteps closing. Some fantasy-bedazzled kid must have lost his head. A runner scoots by, capturing the front, the runner from Seattle . . . someone very brave or very scared or very good. So okay. Scott lets him hold the lead position, through the turn, down the home straightaway where timers are shouting lap times, and on into another turn and the backstretch again. Up in the stadium seats the crowd is quiet, raptly intent, either from surprise, or from discovering that a potential entertainment more riveting than Bakkan winning was Bakkan the record holder getting squashed by an unknown.

Tight behind the Seattle runner, tucked inside his slipstream, Scott evaluates the body ahead of him, mere inches away. The shoulders are steady, the arms smooth, hips rolling, thighs driving onward in muscular ridges—the genuine deal, these features advise. Have we a new king, already, in this first throwaway track meet?

On the next turn the Seattle runner's neck begins to flush, but he holds the stiff pace, indicating he was after the big prize, nothing less. Coming down the grandstand stretch his head bends over on a slight starboard tilt, like an object gathering weight. Scott recognizes these signals. At the start line again, a half mile completed, the timers shout out their splits, the crowd, coming awake, yells advice, and the runners enter the third lap. The Seattle runner, rounding the next turn, runs upright instead of powering through on an inward angle, his track shoes hitting flat-footed. Too bad. Scott knows these indicators well, these machine gauges sending needles into the red zone. At least a dozen expressions exist for this ignominy. The Seattle runner had "hit the wall," "stepped into a hole," "stripped his gears," "shot his wad," select whatever worn words you choose to humiliate him with, not excluding the classic "run out of gas." Physiologically defined he was lapsing into oxygen debt after squandering too much on premature pleasures. Bodies—like budgets—need to keep within their means. With a kind of regret, Scott sees the swinging, struggling elbows ascend from waist level to halfway up the rib cage, and he hears the torn breathing, can practically feel bits of it flapping back into his own face. The legs shorten stride, chopping instead of gliding, their elastic muscle fibers reluctant to expand anymore, about to snarl into twisted rubber bands. Scott eases over and closes up to the runner's outside shoulder, getting struck there by flying droplets of sweat, looking across at the disappointment, the desperation, in the eyes. "You did fine," he tells the Seattle runner, sincerely, while realizing— the inevitable predator in him—that his steady voice brought blood, sharp as a knife blade.

The third lap is the reality lap, where surplus energy vanishes, each yard eating away the meager strength left at the core, until the runner prays a mistake has been made. *What*, this quarter mile here, and still another quarter mile to go? Mind and spine start bending, and shift from hot ambitions of glory to the chilly condition of survival. Perversely, the third lap, for Scott, was a strategy and an indulgence. He would run this cruel lap cruelly, having learned that if he took a risk and went quicker here, it broke the spirits of the others, and the race was won. Therefore Scott presses his acceleration button and explodes past the Seattle runner. From the stadium a hungry howl rises.

Remarkable, how quickly he surges 100 yards ahead, 200 yards, running free, giving himself over to the intoxication of power, letting his body exploit its gullible self. From the airflow forced across his chest he judges his speed, maintains forward drive. He can hear his spikes biting into the track, hear the punctures, feel them break away, kick up, and he can feel his momentum build, feel the tug of centrifugal force as he runs a curve, his elbows pumping. He pushes, but relaxes, having found the efficiency groove. Those mountain roads and trails yield at last their spendable dollars-and-cents dividend.

A rhythmic clapping originates in the crowd, joined by athletes on the field: Go-go-go. Insignificant meet or not, too early in the competitive season or not, Scott blasts into full flight, ratcheting up his pace faster and faster. He can hardly resist his own talents. About when predicted, in the final lap, a bile taste bubbles up in his throat and a matchstick catches fire behind his sternum. This is how his body knocks on the door for Scott's attention. "Stay calm, stay loose," Scott reassures his physical partner. "We have this bad part in every race. Trust me and I'll get us through this again, the same as before. Afterward we can worry about what hurts and how much."

He had seen, earlier, Mrs. Ade coming into the stadium, wearing in the sunshine her indoor purple. The librarian could never suspect that he was about to use this public commotion to join with her most private book page, the scandalous p. 104. And Scott did now visit with Miss Frazer, where they mimic a Rumpelstiltskin dialogue.

Would your name begin with a C, say Carmen?

Too dramatic, I'm afraid.

An A. Amanda. I like the sounds of Amanda.

Too beautiful for me.

But it means "worthy to be loved." Abigail, Adelaide, Amber, Anita, Arlene, maybe Astrid?

None of those.

Something from the other end of the alphabet? Vivian. Violet.

Yvette. Yvonne.

Not those either.

What about Daisy, Rose, Lily, and I already tried Violet.

No flowers.

No flowers, no animals, no months of the year, no rare metals?

And no jewels or gems.

If I guess your first name, I get to keep you, isn't that the agreement?

"Whooeee!" celebrates Lyle, appearing out of nowhere at the finish line, draping his personal jacket over his friend's wet skin. Scott trembles under the reverberations from his thudding, stressed heart and that wind sound must be his own breathing. In front of his eyes, in a snowstorm of white spots, Lyle's face pokes through, like a St. Bernard to the rescue. Normally a manly guy whether enduring a broken nose in football or his mother's gin-and-tonic snoozes at home, Lyle almost plants a kiss. "Wow, hero," he tells Scott, "wowee, can you ever knock down a mile." Not an overstatement. *S. Bakkan*—it will soon be announced on the loudspeaker—has just run the USA's fastest mile for the new season.

<u>Eleven</u>

Scott had gone to a United States atlas, turned to Illinois and scanned down the index, down its N's, confirming that the town New Hope did exist. The map showed a dot on a rail line in the center of the state's western bulge, where farmland bellied out to fill a 200-mile curve of the Mississippi River. His packet to her was addressed:

> Miss Frazer
> c/o Dr. Martin T. Frazer
> New Hope, Illinois

On the late March morning that he let his envelope drop into the mail chute, the weather promised clear skies, low-70s temperature, a friendly breeze to stir the air. The year, 1955, marked the hundredth anniversary of Whitman's *Leaves of Grass*. Therefore all omens were favorable. After leaving the main post office he went across the narrow street to the public library, to Miss Frazer, trying his best to connect her body with that obscure speck on the Illinois map. Soon now, he told her, these eyes of yours will read . . .

Inside the oversized mailer he had packed a newspaper sports clipping, his picture, and the four most reserved of his many trial letters to her, but included the latest, his most daring, a confession guided by Spencer Lemay's incorrigible hand from the grave.

> Dear Miss Frazer:
> I found you one gray day
> in a gray library corner.
>
> In that December dark
> I grew bright,
> grew a crimson need for you
> and came back again.
> And again, Miss Frazer.
>
> There was miracle to your bare body,
> its relentless innocence, caught there
> behind the opened paper door.
> Naked girl,
> cynosure of pubescence,
> you stood straight, looked straight, and
> trusting me, when cradled in my hands
> you always rushed to appear
> as p. 104, fig. 84.

I wanted your name,
your how and your why.

In a studio, against a cold wall,
did Miss Frazer undress alone
or in loneliness?
In the darkroom who first watched you
bloom onto paper,
and what happy printer
saw you pass, hundredfold,
and how many greedy viewers
have devoured hours of my own p. 104?
Miss Frazer, I yearned here
in this library for more of you
than other eyes could ever see.

I believed you gave me that
or would.
I sent a letter
from the heart
to Miss Frazer
to find you.

Please, Miss Frazer, be free to answer with only a polite goodbye, or not to answer at all. Please be free to laugh and laugh and toss this whole package away.

Please be free to feel disgust.

<u>Twelve</u>

Ten days pass, during which Scott reads a pair of books daily and forgets them daily. The eleventh day is April 8, 1955, a Friday. He arrives home for the weekend and parks his Ford in the garage with the gas gauge on the ½ mark. Joyce's bicycle lies flat on the asphalt, wheels splayed in opposite directions, regardless of her having been scolded about this before. He rolls the bike into the garage. The sun sits a fist's width above their redwood grove and he dallies in its light.

Inside his mother greets him from the kitchen. Scott can hear the voice without seeing her. "You have," the voice adds, "more fan mail. This one from Illinois. Female."

At the immediate stroke of great events people are known to check a clock, making it possible, generations later, to inform children exactly where and when history fell on Grandpa or Grandma. Today the time is 5:41.

* * * *

At 5:49 the letter, unopened, still waits alongside Scott on his bed. It was from her, no need to emphasize that sentence further with rhetorical sledgehammers. The return address shows clearly **V. Frazer** and **New Hope**, formed by female, unpostured pen strokes. He can only think to say to the letter, "Don't hurt me." At 6:02 he slit the envelope's back, while ordering himself, "Take it out by 6:05." At 6:15 he removed the folded letter.

> Dear Scott,
>
> Your package came and for a few days I sat down a lot, too amazed to stand. I wondered what I should *do*. Then I decided just to let myself be overwhelmed by you. Of course, I already was.
>
> Now I want to pass on something from a diary, written in the past. No one else has ever seen this Book of Ultimate Secrets before. Here it is: "Today I'm 18 years old. I don't feel unhappy and not happy either. To find out what I really am, I'll wait. I intend to hear from a friend."
>
> Could that have been more right? Mr. Bakkan, sir, you're talking, and I'm sure listening.

The letter went on—more conversational, less stupendous— which as she had planned he could now read in comfort, being snug in the harbor of their twoness. Her home was located on Lincoln Street, "one of nine runty streets in New Hope."

According to an informal survey she herself had conducted (she said, smiling on paper) "38% of all people in Illinois live on a street, road or lane called Lincoln." Her personal language was a pleasure in written harmonies, in accord with Scott's own. "Write me," she ended, "whenever you desire. My desires you seem to know already."

Scott ate no dinner that night, never went to the table. He stayed on his bed next to the letter, not reading it again, not daring to, because another dose of this ecstasy might crack him apart. "Imagine, after all," he said to himself, "happiness happens." His father tapped on the closed bedroom door, asking if Scott would be healthy enough to race Saturday. Scott responded that he plans on breaking his half-mile record tomorrow. "Really?" said his father, before hurrying to agree, "Why, sure. Swell."

Her name was Victoria. The family had shortened it to "Ria" at early childhood, when she had trouble with four syllables.

* * * *

He wrote: "I bought twenty-five stamps today."

She wrote: "I bought twenty-five stamps yesterday."

Like a heart getting excited, their exchange of letters increased its beat, from one letter the first week to two the next and suddenly enough mail to take even a runner's breath away. Before the letters switched to his campus address, Scott's mother, naturally, asked questions. He admitted, "We're both spending a fortune on postage. I guess love's expensive." "Oh my god, oh my god," Elaine said.

He wrote: "Can you send me some photos? Would begging help? In the meantime I hurry to the library to see you whenever I come back to my town, which isn't often enough. By turning this 1905 cracker box into a labyrinth I escape the possessive curiosity of librarian Mrs. Ade. Once, after I skipped a weekend, she claimed that she 'felt abandoned' by me. She assumes I must be reading her priceless books A through Z. If she ever discovers I have you held in my hands, right inside her (figurative) house, her cheeks will match her purple dress."

She wrote: "Tonight a thunderstorm parked itself over our house and let us have both barrels. Simply ferocious. Lightning snapped and cracked and lit up the sky without any pause between flash and sound, striking so close the windows rattled and we could smell the electric scorch in the air. Despite my being born here, our local plot of prairie was giving me a bad case of the jitters, until I imagined you imagining me, out there in California, and then I felt myself protected. I even relaxed enough to appreciate the stormy display outside. In sort of the same fashion, I feel safer when you keep me the same in your mind instead of having any disruptive new pictures."

He wrote: "According to my calculations, you deserve 60% credit for my racing triumphs every week. In order to go on beating the rest of the world I need help and you provide it. How? What a question. What a question! You know perfectly well that

I'm courting you, and when I walk up and ask for your hand (and the rest of you) I intend to have with me the tallest trophies possible—and you, pretty book maiden, will swoon helplessly into your hero's 1951 Ford. Until then, mail me at least a single photo, maybe, huh?"

She wrote: "I wonder if you have a clue about your own powers. Over vast distances you sweep me off my feet, spin my head, turn me into a girl who actually *giggles*. You're positively a risky man, Scott Bakkan."

He wrote: "Never believe you only exist for me from afar. Let me explain how I exploit you right out here. After the quarter mark in a race, when the traffic's clear and I'm running alone, I call up the image of your face and speed toward it. I chase after you through those long straightaways. I lean into the curves on the fourth lap like a sprinter, sling myself around: 'The last lap already? They call this scrimpy thing a mile?' I dig down deeper, and I stay limber, concentrating on your approaching face. At the finish line there you are, the clever reward I arrange for myself."

She wrote: "You flatter me and you downright spoil me. Truthfully, now and then I'm ashamed of myself for not objecting more. But most of the time, oh, I slurp it up like a greedy little pig. Oink, oink, snuffle. Obviously, I've been starving for ages. Excuse my messy table manners, dear Scott?"

He wrote: "Handing out cheap flattery doesn't interest me, too much work involved. And Ria, with eyes like yours, flattery is always an understatement. Now. About a picture of you. Are you tormenting me on purpose?"

She wrote: "Have you noticed? My language keeps escalating. I've been calling you 'dear Scott' lately. What's next, 'dearest,' then?"

He wrote: "Notice, I did. And was that a 'dearest' you already managed to slip in there?"

She wrote: "We sound more and more like what some folks might call love letters. But I wonder, am I living only inside your dream . . . or you only inside mine?"

He wrote: "Tell me that a new photograph will be in your next letter. Tell me. You can't expect me to live with just p. 104 forever."

She answered: "We both know that this girl from page 104 is with you forever, unchanged."

<u>Thirteen</u>

"Not unexpected." A surgeon and a urologist both made this useless comment. Grandfather Leland had been hurried to the hospital, where he spent most of a week, the doctors performing the medical equivalent of shrugging their shoulders. When he returned home again Leland had the look of an animal backed into its final corner. Elaine, unconsciously, borrowed her impression from the poet Yeats: "His clothes don't fit. He's a tattered coat on a stick."

Joyce woke up Scott at an hour when waking up comes hard, and he said, "Where's the clock? Holy Toledo."

"I wanted to tell you something."

"Wait, let me clear my head. Wait."

"Leland left blood in the toilet and I had to flush it down."

"Wait. Sit here. Sit. So you went into the bathroom."

"And Leland left blood in the toilet. Real blood. The water was all bloody red."

"I know. He forgets to flush sometimes."

"I don't get where the blood's coming from."

"I explained his problem to you before."

"You didn't say anything about blood coming out. You didn't. Anyways, if he has blood coming out like that, why don't the doctors fix it?"

"Because these guys, these doctors, finally run out of medicine that works on very sick people. That's the deal with Leland. I tell you this about every week."

Joyce shook her head, doggedly. "It's not right. You know it's not. Somebody else should invent the medicine, if the doctors won't. We gotta check around."

"Crawl in under the covers."

"Thanks."

"No tossing and turning?"

"I promise."

A promise broken.

For Scott, despite being pinned solidly in place by the heavy demands of academics and his running, daily life swung violently between his happiness with Ria and the distress with his grandfather or with Marlee. The equation proved mathematical. One hour of joy presupposed an hour of guilt. An afternoon of warmth meant an evening of chill. This predicament brought Scott to the edge of resenting the two troublemakers—Leland and Marlee—his unjust accusation, in turn, making him cringe.

Scott swore an immediate double oath: to lay the truth in front of Marlee, and to drive his grandfather in search of the lost Bakkan sawmill.

Elaine continued the substantial dinners, an effort to nourish her family in the broadest sense, keeping one apprehensive eye on her father-in-law, when not on her son. (Salad bowl, cheese crackers, salted nuts, raisins. Roast duckling and gravy, apple sauce, mashed potatoes, cauliflower with browned and buttered crumbs. Baked Indian pudding and vanilla ice cream, gingerbread, coffee, tea, milk.) "Wonderful eats," Leland would vouch, although, given the cellular facts, his body was starving away. "My share goes to the growing girl here."

In agreement, Elaine urged her daughter to load up: "Have some sweet corn." (Or sweet potatoes, sweet pickles, sweet peas, sweet onions, sweet relish.)

"Okie Dokie," Joyce would politely say. Onto her plate went the corn, etc. There it got poked around.

"This is wasteful," her mother was required to observe afterward, scraping the dishes.

"Okie Dokie," said Joyce.

(Clear broth, escalloped salmon, warm French bread, artichoke hearts, fruit tapioca, graham cracker cream cake.) Furman slogged forward through the courses, like the sturdy soldier he had been, 1943-45, in the Pacific. He sat poised over his plate, mouth set to its chewing business. In appearance Furman resembled more his husky grandfather than his father, as Scott also leapfrogged one generational way station to his own leaner grandfather.

(A tray and pitcher of chilled Cranberry & Ginger Ale Cocktail. "Cranberry syrup one-third to ginger ale two-thirds. Stir. In each individual glass drop a whole candied cranberry.") "Say," Leland told Scott, "I saw your picture on the front page. You must be doing big things to end up there instead of the sports section."

For everyone's plate, a lamb croquette, wanted or not. ("Into the meat/rice mix goes 1 tsp. grated nutmeg, 1 tbsp. chopped parsley, 1 tsp. salt, 1 tsp. rosemary sauce, a dash of pepper and 1 cup cream sauce. Coat top of mix with beaten egg and crispy bread crumbs. Bake for 30 minutes. It's juicy, it's crunchy, it's creamy, it's dreamy!") The spring season of anniversaries had arrived, starting with Franklin Delano Roosevelt. "President Roosevelt died ten years ago," Elaine told her daughter.

"I know. Somewhere in Georgia."

"He had a job to do in '33," said Leland. "The riverbank by Modesto was thick with hobos camping out. Families, too. Recall that, Furman?"

Furman had committed himself to the demolition of his Kidney Bean Salad. ("Combine chopped eggs, beans, celery, onion, relish and salt, tossing together lightly. Gently stir in sour cream. Chill an hour to blend flavors. Garnish with ovals of sliced hard-boiled egg. Place a plump black olive inside each tasty white oval.")

Leland went on, "They came knocking on our door, hoping for

work. Work? I was stealing vegetables and fruit out of the fields myself. Scotty, Joyce, you kids don't forget that your grandpa went stealing in the night to save a few cents on food."

"I won't forget," vowed Joyce. She requested permission to "put two orange cubes in my milk." Permission given. ("Blend ½-can orange juice concentrate, 2 tbsp. sugar, ½-cup milk, 2 scoops vanilla ice cream. Freeze in cube tray. When ready, drop cubes into glass of cold milk. *Good*, and good for you!")

Elaine had memories of their tabletop Crosley radio she said, could feel still, at her fingertips, turning the knobs, could hear again the uneasy prologue of its hum and crackle. "Those years, when Scott and I lived alone in Santa Cruz during the war, I spent a goodly chunk of every day warming up the radio and listening for the latest news. There was early morning news, mid-morning news, noon, mid-afternoon, dinner-hour news, and news when we went to bed at ten, not to mention all those special reports. 'Radio-holic' people called me. But I had you, Furman, in the Pacific and Spence in Europe. My brother Spencer." That addendum was superfluous, "my brother Spencer." She drank a swallow of tea, with the quick toss of taking medicine. "Where is the old Crosley? Scott, did you tinker it to pieces? Ah well, we got that radio ages ago, secondhand at that, and the war is ten years gone."

"Ten years ago tomorrow, May 8," Furman reminded his father. "Ten years since V-E Day."

"That stands for Victory in Europe," Elaine said to Joyce.

"My, you should have heard the radio on V-E Day, Furman, how it went on for hours without any commercial ads, just singing, music, speeches. Outside, in the streets, everywhere over town, we could hear drivers honking their horns, or faraway shouts, and church bells peeling."

"A happy day."

"No. Not with you in the thick of it in the Pacific and with Spence lost, lost or whatever, wherever, or however. Not a happy day for us. We kept in the house. Frankly, I preferred the early days, when I had a better idea where you and Spence were, and when I watched the dial on the Crosley, its glow, and I listened to the newscasters get excited. I suspect those men were grateful to have a world war to report. The excitement of the great storm, or some such. Poor Mr. Roosevelt, he died before having the chance to enjoy V-E Day either. So many anniversaries, Furman."

"I know, I know."

Elaine had prepared a "marginally experimental" recipe, identified as "Baked Slice of Ham with Grape Juice Sauce." ("Place ham slices in baking dish, rub with mustard and crunchy brown sugar. Coat with milk. Bake 1 hour. Guaranteed to make mouths water.")

With a knee on her chair, Joyce leaned over. "What's that stuff in the gravy boat?"

"Use a proper word, please. It's the grape sauce for your ham. Take some."

Joyce checked with her brother, her only trustworthy adviser on food taste.

"It's good," he reassured her, smacking. ("Use 1 cup grape juice. Mix cornstarch and cold water. Add scalding water until mixture thickens. Pour in fruit juice. Serve tangy hot and sticky sweet.")

"About a week before FDR died," said Elaine, launching helplessly into her inevitable, fatal subject, "we received Spence's last letter—'Dear Sister' on that tissue paper the military called V-mail. The letter's stored in his box of papers." She referred to an old cardboard box that held the family's most poignant archives, the box that had in its entirety been gifted to Scott on his sixteenth birthday. "Only later, with the missing-in-action notification, did we realize it might be his last letter. That began the mystery."

Even when Scott was younger, too young, his mother had made him read, as proof of his uncle's curious disappearance—not his death—a copy of the 1945 military field reports, made up of the company commander's logbook notations. Elaine devoted over two years wrangling this unusual document from the U.S. Army. Considering her lengthy effort, the summary sheet of paper was mockingly slight, although Scott had recognized, among its typed abbreviations, censored blanks, and terseness, the eloquence of omission found in good poems.

```
Overview: typ Swabian forest & terrain.
         Enemy contact spotty.
```

<u>4 April</u>, 0800: Weather clear.
    Recon Probe,N-NE,Sgt Lemay
    leads Cpls ***, ***, & ***.
    1200, Cpls ***, ***, & ***
    start return, per orders from
    Sgt Lemay. No enemy contact.
    1600, Sgt Lemay absent.
    2000, Sgt Lemay absent.

<u>5 April</u>, 0800-1600: Full search.
    No evidence Sgt Lemay.

<u>6 April</u>, 1600: Comp adv twenty (20) km.
    No evidence Sgt Lemay.

<u>7 April</u>, 1600: five (5) voltr teams
    X-ed rear area.
    No evidence Sgt Lemay. MIA filed.

<u>8 April</u>, 1600: Major engagement w/enemy.
    Enemy position destroyed.
    37 POWs taken.
    Unconf civilian claim, rifle fire,
    <u>6 Apr</u> 1400.

"Was he tall," asked Joyce, "like Scotty?"

"He'd picked up a giant 1930 V-16 Cadillac phaeton," said Leland, "the kind of car that folks dumped in the late thirties. It would carry the same load as our truck and drank gas like it owned shares in Standard Oil. One summer he was delivering to me cartons of nails from a hardware store in Santa Cruz that went bust. Furman, you paid eight bucks for the nails and we promised eight to Spencer for hauling over the boxes, plus gas. But in Gustine the Cadillac runs dry already. What did Spencer do about it? He sold enough nails at the service station to fill up the Cadillac, then sold the rest to this dairy co-op and handed me in Ceres twice the money I could have got myself, and he wouldn't take more than the eight dollars, for his part."

"I can't begin to visualize sixteen cylinders slamming up and down in one engine," said Scott.

"He could talk," confirmed Furman, "could be persuasive, and be hilarious in a sideways fashion. *Tristram Shandy* was a favorite book of his. That says a bunch."

"God, how I still miss him," Elaine urgently informed Joyce, the only one at the table mistakenly looking at her mother's face. The others brace themselves. The others know what comes next. "God, I do. Being the big sister, I practically raised him myself. And yes, he was tall like your brother, and the older Scott becomes, the more alike they are, in ways small and large. Indeed, the similarities have been troubling me lately." Once Elaine's seasonal high water of emotions crested the dam, hang on for the flood. In any April or May this solid, savvy businesswoman, Mrs. Bakkan, could transform, in a snap, into a wobbly handful for the family.

"Whatcha mean?" asked Joyce.

"Your uncle was brilliant, is what I mean. I mean he loved the wrong woman. And I mean he was a decorated war hero who one day drops into oblivion and I mean it was completely, completely, completely, completely strange."

"Golly," Joyce said.

Furman elaborated, in his most subdued tone, to counterbalance his wife's rising pitch, "Spence had a nickname in the Army back then. They called him 'GMC' for General Medals Corporation. He was awarded a chestful of medals, which does make him an official hero, believe me."

"My golly."

Elaine raced onward, partly incomprehensible, but most the family knows the sentences beforehand: "Months and months and months of surviving these horrible extreme unbelievable dangers and he vanishes *poof* vanishes on a peaceful day ordinary day *poof* at the end the very very end of the war. Guess what? Guess *guess*. The Army offers up 'missing in action, presumed dead.' If that were *correct* I could rest easier. Well, I couldn't manage this frustration by myself, that's why Scott has Spencer's box now. That's my salvation. You'll understand him better than anyone, Scotty. Who else could? You and Spence, Spence and you."

Scott said to his grandfather, "Had you heard that Spencer wrote poetry? A family affliction kept in the closet. Do you like his poems, Mother?" No response. "Mother?"

"I think not. Too much there about that woman."

* * * *

The evening that Leland unintentionally destroyed their dinner, what was the *hors d'oeuvres* dip? Ground black walnuts blended with mayonnaise? ("Garnish with olive slices, parsley sprigs, pimiento bits.")

Said Leland, "While we're together here tonight, I want to settle a thing or two."

(Or had the dip been "peanut butter and bacon crumbs, topped with dill pickle." Or was it "boiled egg yolk mixed with melted butter and mustard, topped by a strip of sardine or anchovy paste.")

"What's inside me feels like a man dying. Fact is, I'm hanging on by my fingernails."

Furman informed his father he was "a tough old bird," and "didn't he remember" his gallstone troubles, how he got through that. Acting irritated, Furman spooned himself a messy portion of the Golden Yam Casserole, ruining the arrangement of ringed marshmallows, toasted and crusty, a lump of melting butter highlighting their center.

"You mean good," said Leland. "You, too, Elaine. But this time, it's over for me."

Furman returned to the casserole and scooped up the entire butter glob. ("To each 4 cups of yams add 1/3 cup cream, 1/4 cup honey, 1/4 tsp. nutmeg, salt to taste. Sprinkle top with cinnamon.") Elaine gave Joyce an extra napkin and added to her plate a mucky pile of yams. Unless it was instead, that night, Peas in Turnip Cups. ("Brush turnip cups with butter. Use peas, a grating of onion, a sprinkle of salt, and 1/2 tsp. of sugar. Simmer, add 2 tbsp. rich cream, then fill turnip cups.")

"Sit up, sweetie," Furman told his daughter.

"I figure I'll be gone before the year's over," said Leland. "So I'll check my testament documents this week to be sure each point is written down right. There won't be any loose ends for you to bother with."

"Leland, Leland, Leland," complained Furman.

"My whole estate goes to you and the kids. No surprises anywheres."

Elaine reminded Joyce about her napkin.

"I'm not crying."

"Everybody just takes whatever's around and loose. My odds 'n' ends. Joyce gets the wicker baby rocker she likes. The antique one. Of course Scotty gets my tools 'cause Furman you have plenty. Elaine—"

"Elaine is going to pour you more coffee." No easy trick for her to do, with the cup already at the brim.

"I'm *not*," insisted Joyce.

"And we'll sell my place in Ceres."

Furman took the coffee himself, dug out a scoop of Vienna Noodles with Poppy Seed. "No rush to sell the old house," he said tightly.

"I'm thinking about your mother, and those boxes of hers up in the attic, fifteen or so, altogether. Wanda's boxes need to come down where I can sort through them, before some lawyer does it for me."

Banana Pudding. ("Give pizzazz with a topping of sliced bananas, sliced cherries, almond sprinkles. *Smooooth*.")

"Why are you talking like that?" said Furman. "It upsets me. No outsiders will rummage through our family items."

Leland said, "Excuse me. When your mother was dying I

thought she behaved peculiar, too, but now I understand her. She had to have every piece of hers packed up inside a box—her clothes, her hats and shoes, her combs and brushes, her sewing goods, her pens and paper, her purse, her medicine bottles even. Why, she made me help her walk around the house to show her the empty closets and drawers."

Butterscotch Pie. ("For a finish, spin a meringue so frothy it dances, so airy it melts in your mouth.") Apple Custard. ("Isn't it great?")

"But cleaning up isn't what worries me the worst."

Hot Milk Sponge Cake with Apricot Icing. ("You can't eat enough.")

"No, not the most." Neapolitan Loaf Candy. ("Three colors, three flavors, three million delights.") "I worry most about dragging all of you along through a bad time. That's not fair."

Honey Cupcakes. Jam Squares. Lemon Tarts. Furman and Elaine wanted to know "what on earth" Leland means, "not fair."

"Look over there," said Leland, indicating Joyce. True, Joyce could not spell her name with j-o-y tonight.

"What?" she asked their investigating glances. "I'm *not*."

Leland sighed. "It's not any sight for children to watch, day after day. It doesn't make for a good home. There are special places for cases like me, professional places."

"No, no," objected Elaine and Furman.

Grape Chiffon Pie.

"Sorry for this," Leland said. "I apologize."

Does Joyce want to wash her face?

She shook her head. "I might be sick, though."

Did she wish to be excused?

"Should I go, Scotty?"

Bavarian Cookies with Ivory Frosting.

Leland said again, he regrets this had to happen to them.

They replied, he has it backward.

Six-Spice Cake with Sea Foam Raisin Frosting.

* * * *

Under a sky filling up southward with stacked clouds, the 1951 Ford carried grandfather and grandson to the village of Soquel, whose name and locale—the story goes—had been clumsily detached from the Costanoan Indians. It lay in a niche between bay and hills.

Leland rested against the seat's back, occupying scarcely more space than 101-pound Marlee would have, his bony hands cupped on his bony knees. He was telling Scott, "Here you're giving me a ride, and I remember when I took you, only the two of us, from Ceres to Santa Cruz, in my 1936 Studebaker. You stayed there in Ceres with me a week and I brought you back over. I sold that '36 Studebaker eventually for $340 and a set of snow chains."

At Soquel they turned on Old San Jose Road, snaking out into the mountains. Their destination: Bakkan Canyon and the old sawmill, and Leland Bakkan, fifty years absent from the legendary spot, chewed his lip. New roadways, new houses, disguised the land. "I'm lost straight off the bat," he murmured.

"We'll stick with it, agreed ?" said Scott.

At least the timbered ridges, up above, and Soquel Creek, down below, had held their fundamental geography in Leland's mind. He judged, "We got to top that grade ahead." There they pulled to the roadside.

"On farther?"

Leland had the instinct that, no, they had gone far enough toward the summit, because Bakkan Canyon went "down through the low ground" parallel to those upper mountains. However, he was still "flipped upside down." He felt "foolish" not knowing how to get to his "own" place. Slowly, they drove again, back and forth a mile or two in each direction. They asked a knapsacked hiker the whereabouts of Bakkan Canyon. At three houses Scott knocked and asked, "Bakkan Canyon?" At a sand quarry they asked an entire crew, with several oldtimers, "Bakkan Canyon?" Never heard of it.

Letting in heretical doubts, Scott considered whether this Bakkan Canyon could be a phantasm, a vanity nourished over sufficient years, first by Nelson Bakkan and later by his son Leland, and to have grown a mock substance. Yet Leland had more than cobwebs and self-deception in his head. Concentrating, he insisted, "There'll be one big-sized feeder creek in this stretch here. That stream ran by our mill. Find the creek and there'll be a road going off west. Take that road and you find our canyon."

They located a bridge and under it the tributary. By an

overgrown, tree-choked ravine a gravel road invited them in, past its No Trespassing sign.

"Maybe we shouldn't," Leland hesitated.

"The Ford can't read."

The gravel dissipated into dirt more than rock, as they wound along the creek, blinkered on the sides by forest, Leland with his forehead flush against his window, saying, "It should, it *should*, widen out and the canyon *should* open up." And it did. "Yep, yep, here we are," exclaimed Leland, under an open sky. "Scotty, we owned this—2,000 acres!" Steep pasture land and meadows alternated with redwoods and arroyos, the road ending at a corral, set in front of a weathered hay barn, the barn in turn in front of a few charred beams—black and mossy, easily mistaken for stones—that had been the Bakkan mill.

For more time than it required for his grandson to run a mile, Leland sat in the car, speechless, surveying near and far, up to the reaches of the canyon where horizon and memory converged at terrestrial infinity. What could he see there across a half-century of distance? What was left? Scott tried to ask him that. Only afterward, when outside poking in the ruins, explaining eight-foot saw wheels and steam engines and drying yards and bank mortgages, did Leland answer: "Everything's left, and nothing, too."

Back at home that night Scott stood outdoors as those southern clouds—the wayward fringe of an equatorial air mass—darkened and roiled the moonlit spring sky. Black traveling clouds tore open into even blacker windows, where stars would gleam and the moon sail into view, until the shutters closed again. At intervals tiny rain droplets came trailing around Scott in a lacy water wand. It happened that a drop of rain, floating down from its long descent, landed on his cheek when the sky directly overhead was stars, not clouds. An incantation, Ria.

Fourteen

Marlee, talking to him, had her face near, available to sight and touch. They drove along Mission Street in Santa Cruz after a late afternoon of clothes shopping. The Spanish padres in 1774 had chosen a panorama for their construction site, and this Mission Street ran atop a headland with the city center down below, built out and up from its own river, the San Lorenzo. While Watsonville was mostly flat, rectangular, presumed to be overrun with farm yokels and *braceros*, Santa Cruz draped itself over bluffs, plateaus, small hills, where retirees dozed in sunshine to be rudely interrupted, in season, by beach-and-boardwalk tourists.

The street joined West Cliff Drive—aptly named—and the Ford followed the cliffs, westwardly, the world's largest ocean at their side. As the city fell behind, the landscape widened into scattered houses, upland pastures, borders of redwood forest. A promontory, beaten by automobile tires into a parking vista, was the destination. When they arrived, sunlight lay low across the water—glitz on the swells, shadow in the troughs. "Good," said Marlee, "we're in time." She hoped for a wide, showy sunset, the more chromatic the better, no mere fizzle and fade, please. "It'll hit the horizon in five minutes," predicted Marlee.

Snappy onshore gusts buffeted the Ford, rattling its outside radio antenna. To gain height for her view, plus a psychological advantage over the evening wind, Marlee sat on his lap. The sun began slipping under. "There it goes," she said. Against a last radiant fusion of diamond flash and cooler golds, snowy gulls hovered before sliding into lateral drifts, taking their free rides on the air currents.

"Look," Marlee said, "oh, look . . ."

A distant cloud bank became reverse-lit with a classic rose color (American Beauty) that oozed upward and merged seamlessly into swatches of amber and chalky violet, the canopy of daylight blue in retreat, pastels painting the global curve. His arm was held, crossing, beneath Marlee's breasts. The crown of her head rested against his lips. They kept inside this snuggled ball of contact until the sun was gone, the afterflush was gone, and only ambient grays remained.

Marlee expected to be kissed. Within the Ford settled a secure gray. Outside, the sky was dove gray, the sweeping Pacific a naval gray—its polymorphic skin an undulation of gray, breaking here and there into pearl. Instead of kissing her, Scott asked, "Want to walk on the beach?"

"Mm, it's too breezy for my dress. Let me put on the pullover and pants we bought today." She changed in the front seat. "Your hands are cold."

"You're warm everywhere."

On the path down the cliff she stopped twice to hug him, with strength in those slim arms. At the bottom they shuffled through dry sand, picking their way over a fringe of kelp—deposited by an earlier high tide—and went on to the damp and firm sand where the Pacific Ocean, at the moment, began. Seawater vocalized, everywhere in a slosh against the land and itself.

"How do you like my name," asked Marlee, "as names go?" They leaned together, so that both, as one, could lean against the wind. "Would you change it?"

From Stalich to Bakkan was she suggesting?

She said, however, "I never felt like a Marlee. My parents might have pulled a name tag out of a hat and stuck it on me. 'That'll be you.' But who wants to gripe about such a thing?"

Scott faced out toward the ocean, this water which always rolled at you, in your direction, regardless of where you stood, on any shore of any continent. He rummaged among flotsam until he found two staffs of driftwood. With these, they poked at sea froth. Marlee—with her almost black hair, almost black oval eyes—could have been a gypsy lass on a Dalmatian strand, a love amulet hidden in her shawl. "Let's call you Camille Stalich," he said. "You can be a Slavic gypsy girl, a wild gypsy with beach grit between your toes."

"Ugh. The wild part, possibly."

She began kissing him. They kissed until the tide scooted up to their feet. Back in the car she encouraged him with her smile, as inviting as a cabin's glowing window to a traveler in the night. At this opening Scott should please her with her Daily Word. He should. In panicked recompense he kissed her on the forehead, the cheeks, the hair, but not on her lips again. Being a generous girl, Marlee made no mention of his creative impotence.

* * * *

In a crinoline skirt Marlee created an impression that she, and her petticoats, might levitate off the Ford's front seat. She and Scott were parked in the Stalich driveway on another Sunday afternoon, preparing for separate returns to their universities.

"My trouble is," said Scott, "that after so much lying before, now when I need to tell you the truth, it'll sound like a lie."

"What are we talking about?" After a long day, her head is tilted back against the seat, relaxing.

"I'm not the person you want me to be. And not the person you deserve. But you don't believe me."

So correct is Scott about her convictions, Marlee never troubles to turn in his direction. "Are you teasing? Because you do that sometimes."

"For you to believe me, I have to hurt you. I've spent weeks trying to think up ways around it and can't. I just wish you'd despise me when I hurt you, except I won't be that lucky."

Now she does turn.

Scott said, "I care about you very much. I almost love you."

"Almost?"

"Almost. Lately I learned the difference, because I did fall in love, with another girl."

"Another girl?"

"No matter how much I want to protect you—and protect me from myself—I'm exhausted from pretending."

The first tears showed in her dark chasm-brown eyes. "You wouldn't tease me about this. Not you."

"Cry all you can. Punish me. I need to be hated."

She sat there defenseless, recoiled against the car window, against its square of sky, resembling a delightful doll that thoughtless hands had ruffled. How often, too often, Scott and others had stooped to this convenient image with Marlee. Once in his sister's room he read a costume catalog for Joyce's doll—a Madame Alexander doll named "Wendy"—but instead of little Joyce he had seen reflections of Marlee on each page, in each of the thirty separate and exquisitely detailed outfits. ("WENDY calls on Grandma, wearing Grandma's favorite ensemble, a mauve taffeta dress, prim nylon pinafore and a cute straw hat. Next WENDY wears this smart jacket outfit for a train journey, a white wool felt jacket with matching pixie cap worn over a chic pleated plaid dress with white top. Next WENDY goes to a matinee attired in . . . WENDY helps Mummy serve luncheon, looking charming in . . . WENDY wearing an outfit she likes for a plane trip . . . WENDY makes a lovely bride in a gown of heavy white satin, Juliet cap of lace and nylon tulle bridal veil.")

Mrs. Stalich appeared at the house entryway, pantomiming a fork or spoon serving her mouth. "Bring Scotty," could be heard faintly inside the car.

They sat for a while longer. Marlee used tissues from the glove compartment. Her fingers and Scott's, obeying their own logic, met in the empty space between them on the seat. At last Marlee opened the car door, stepped out, and stood there, reluctant for this parting to formulate, definitively, a complete farewell. In the advantageous silence she said, "Don't be surprised to hear me say I'll want us back together. You realize, I won't be able to stop from thinking that."

Here Marlee provided him a gracious avenue for a gimcrack to carry into the house and into tomorrow, a final Final Word, or at the minimum a chance for simple courtesy. ("When you come to get me back, I may never have left.") He resisted, he fought, for once, further gentlemanly or cowardly lies. Marlee, kind Marlee, did not let him dangle long and she flashed a crippled smile and went away, up her concrete drive. As he watched, one of her shoes slipped off a distracted foot—size 5 shoe, sunflower yellow, I. Magnin. She refitted it without using hands. He cranked over the Ford and she looked rearward. Both waved.

On his trip home he took the old highway route, known nowadays as Freedom Boulevard. "You see, Ria, I do give myself to you at all costs."

Fifteen

Dear Ria,
My shrinking thoughts hold just one Big Idea.
But it's a very big Big Idea.

Following my math and my maps there are
2117 road miles to your house. If I travel them,
then waiting for your photographs is unnecessary.

Enclosed find a calendar page showing the June
date when I can leave here and how many days
I need to reach your front door.

You'll be there to open it for me?

"Is something momentous happening?" asked his mother.
"You should count," said Scott, "on my being gone during

June, to visit her."

"I know who he means," Joyce informed the shaken family, another dinner shot to smithereens.

For Lyle, his solution was a preemptive strike: "Look for me to marry the girl in due time." Soon thereafter, Scott found himself escorted into Lyle's bedroom by his friend's mother, who like a zealous tour guide pointed out what her son had done to his room, how it was stripped Spartan and spotless, the only noticeable dust being on the exterior of the windows. The Monroe and Mansfield posters had disappeared.

"No, I can't figure it out myself," said a sheepish Lyle. "You tell me about this new girl of yours and, ugh, I hate my damn bedroom. I hate my clothes. For some reason I'm nervous. Hardly any appetite, either."

"Don't be afraid. When you meet her, you'll see why."

In Ria's answer to his latest letter she playfully scolded Scott for tempting her with an image of their meeting in Illinois, when he knew that would not happen.

"It'll happen," he reassured her. "That's why I sent an 'actual' calendar, to pick an 'actual' day, for us to be actually together. I always promised we would."

She wrote, "We are together. Right at this *moment* we are and we'll stay together. You made that clear from your first letter."

He wrote, "You forgot to send me the date again. Is this a form of deliberate torture?"

She wrote, "Remember once when you asked me about my

parents, and I said that Scott Bakkan was my father and my mother, because he created who I am. Yes, that dramatized how important you are to me, but please say you also understood I was explaining about us and the book. Dear Scott, we can't jeopardize ourselves by forgetting about the book. I admit, I forget about the book, myself, more often than I should. It's terribly easy to do."

He wrote, "Ria, write me immediately and detail, in a simple sentence, how we can meet. The book's our past, isn't it? We need the future."

Dearest Scott, now I'm scared. Did I misjudge us?
It startles me, when I think back on the letters I sent you,
or what I let myself believe, in private.

From the start I assumed you had every fact
about me, you above all, who misses nothing in
a book, especially this one. Underneath you saw,
I thought, why I never sent the new pictures you
asked for, and the most wonderful part, I believed,
was that you knew the truth but pretended you didn't.
I adored you for that.

Don't you know the truth? I've lacked the plain
courage to ask you, and I still lack the courage,
because I dread ruining what we built together.
I can't express how well you comprehend the
Ria you found and love. You'll never in your
lifetime imagine how much you expanded my
small existence back here.

If forgiveness is needed, and possible, please
forgive me. Please.

The book, the book, the book. *The Human Body* was in his agitated hands at the first possible opportunity. Page 104 tried to open for him—that spinal signature forever creased by repetition at this spot—but Scott forced the book backward to its front, to the publisher's imprimatur, where his bitterly frigid suspicions told him to check.

HAMILTON PUBLISHING
COMPANY

╫ New York, N. Y.╫   ╫ Chicago, Ill.╫

Part III

"Even my truth is a lie."

<u>Sixteen</u>

The worse that bad news is, the more it resists belief. Scott needs to open *The Human Body* again.

The plaza had been designed (Wm. H. Weeks, architect) with intentions of fulfilling more than one concept: Alhambra courtyard, *fin de siècle* Sousa bandstand, convenient promenade, public greensward. Occupying a full downtown block the plaza was crossed by an X of walkways, the circular bandstand at the X's intersection, the walks lined with benches. These benches seldom stay empty on mornings with sun and when Scott arrived, to await the library's opening, he had to share seating with an unshaven old codger who somebody had thoughtlessly bundled in a mackinaw, and with a Chinese elder whose pallid skin seemed tearable as paper. Neither spoke to him, nor to each other. A likelihood was that between the three of them they possessed no native language in common. Yet they sat intimately, Scott restlessly banging his knees together with a surplus energy vulgar to display in front of his aged companions.

"I didn't sleep much last night. Practically didn't. How about you gentlemen?" No answer. "I kept trying, last night, to remember if I had read a page from a book, or read it correctly, or whether I was remembering a dream about reading a page. My dreams, lately, have been extensive. Gets confusing. Gets maddening. 'My life's a little dream rounded by a sleep,' to borrow from Shakespeare. Either of you gentlemen a dreamer?"

They appeared to be studying the tops of palm trees, whereby they hoped to avoid this loud youth. Scott clapped his hands, briskly, until the two, lurching, faced him. "My grandfather's dying, and I submit his condition as my ticket to sit with you on your bench."

The old fellow in the mackinaw, agitated, did something unsavory with his nose.

"Also my uncle's supposedly dead, disappearing in Germany during the war. That gives me more surrogate points. Dead did I say? In a contradiction, Spencer became alive to me over the years as I dissected his literary corpse. You heard right, literary corpse. Turns out, the joker wrote a stack of poems—more poems for me to read, for cripes' sake. Think it was *my* idea first to sit here? No, no, and to prove my point, would you gentlemen care to hear Spencer's poem 'Day Star'? Our sun is a star, you know. Yessiree, that sun right up there. Only twelve lines this poem is, in four three-line stanzas, so short, if not sweet. I have it memorized, of course. Of course.

Noon, with all the sky white and blue.
Bright delight it seems: true to those idylls
of old men dozing in the park safe from cold and dark.

Has your attention, gentlemen, does it not? Sit down, both of you. You have nowhere else to go. We know that, and don't pretend otherwise. Sit. Good, thank you. But gird yourselves because the poem turns kinda nasty. By the way, how's your Latin. Weak? Then I'll tip you off that the famous Latin means 'Let There Be Light.'

Fiat lux. What a mockery in that command!
For just as skulls grin and men do die at noon,
so blue sky hides a sight black as moonless midnight.

What the heck does it mean, eh? Blue is black as midnight. Keep with me—pay attention. I know I'm being rude. Sorry, sorry for that. But the next stanza:

Such is great love that our familial sun
wraps us around with its one own warm embrace,
and which stupefies, like a blanket drawn over the face.

No, it's not noon yet, sir. That's your mackinaw making you sweat. Shuck the dumb rag off.

Beyond the blue mask billions more stars shine.
They wink to catch our eye, while we only smile,
content each day with the brightness of being blind.

There you have it, twelve lines to think upon between now and sunset. Get it? Maybe we should be more honest and come back and sit here at midnight. Note the hide-and-seek rhyme scheme, the stanzaic balance, the entire contraption courtesy of my uncle Spencer, and who can guess why he put it on paper. Well, thanks for your patience, and speaking of great love, and great blindness, I'm off to the library."

* * * *

His book he carried to a library table, although he examined it standing. Why trouble to sit when a speedy glance would check the copyright date to confirm yesterday's nightmare. Sadly, it did. Further, Scott enumerated what should have alerted any awake book veteran back in December 1954: a sickly fade mark along the exposed spine, flakes from the gold-stamped cover, a printer's typeface now out of favor, the melancholy scent of confined paper. And as for the girl herself, her eyes clarify their old message, "I'll wait and wait and wait and wait for you."

He could not hold himself back from descending, skidding, into his own Depression, a spiritual 1929, brutal as the economic one his parents and grandfather had endured twenty-six years ago. *The Human Body*, acting its part in this conceit of history, crashed to the library table.

It was his misfortune, a week later, to be in front of 12,000 people. With the close of May, track superstar Scott Bakkan had reached the Western Regional Championship meet, the elite competition to qualify toward the national championships.

Proud Watsonville citizens had caravaned for the trip, among them the town's librarian, and the Staliches and Bakkans, who not discarding tradition had come together, without grandfather Leland today. Lyle sat with them in the stadium.

Scott ran in the middle of the pack until the half mile, when he lifted his tempo and began picking off the leaders. He carved in, about, past, a festive collection of different uniform colors, exotic blends and designs from distant schools. Four other uniforms still in front of him. Three. Two. One.

"B-A-K-K-A-N!"

The crowd began whooping it up, anxious for the usual explosion. Ahead, the remaining uniform shone, ruby and white, with copycat Adidas shoes. Scott pulled alongside that ruby-rimmed shoulder, noticing how nature had complemented the picture by putting ruby acne welts across those shoulder blades. Voices, multiplying, intensifying, fell like sharp projectiles onto the field: "Now, Bakkan. Now!"

What the spectators were viewing, without ever grasping it, was a harlequinade—a stage show featuring a buffoon. There Scott pranced, wearing the donkey's head, whispering endearments to a piece of paper. (The audience yowls with laughter.) He coos, pirouettes with bliss, nuzzles the page, steadies his palpitating chest. O, love! O, rapture! (The crowd points, hoots.)

Ever notice how many songs and stories depend on Boy & Girl? These hankerings have entertained the ages. The Greeks had their Aphrodite and Romans their Venus and Norse skalds sang of Freya. The Church had its Mary, the British their Guinevere and Moll Flanders, America its Hiawatha and Hester, Tarzan Africanus somehow his Jane, and Scott Bakkan made do with a textbook nude. (No kidding. A book page. Laugh everybody. Everybody applaud!)

"Go, go!" exhorted his coach at the bell lap, without panic, confident.

On the contrary, this premier miler prospect was already drained, vacant. Scott had never suffered this depth of exhaustion before and, savagely, it pleased him. What better penalty for prideful *S. Bakkan*. As prophesied, a world was ending in a sweaty whimper, not in flash and boom.

He toiled at the other runner's side, laboring down the track. Scott's feeble loss here would have its proper finality, and anyway, this Nobody with ruby scars on the shoulders surely had a justified surprise coming due, in the grand payoff of life, for a good deed somewhere. But when the finish line loomed ahead, beckoning with its ancient glory call, Scott's body stirred—the instincts of a dying warrior on the battlefield, raising his sword for a last kill—and in a surge it carried him across the winner.

"Saving yourself for nationals," surmised his coach. "Smart."

He said, "I'm sick. I think my season's over."

Seventeen

Returning home at the finish of school, in place of waving his new baccalaureate degree he should be holding a warning sign, lettered *noli me tangere*, the Latin equivalent of the rebel flag "Don't-tread-on-me," hand-embroidered, with coiled rattlesnake.

Scott confined himself in his bedroom for unreasonable hours. His parents wrung their hands. Was he sick? ("Sort of.") Would he come out and sit down at a regular dinner? ("Not much hungry.") Would he, please, explain what's going on, for his own parents? ("I prefer not to.") What should they tell those newspaper reporters calling about him? ("Too ill to run.") Both his coach and the athletic director, separately, arrived at the house, hat in hand as it were, hoping Scott might recover in time for the national meets. He preferred not to see them. Both Marlee and Lyle left repeated messages by phone. Shouldn't Scott return those calls from his best friends, suggested his mother. ("I prefer not to, actually.") Furman was overheard in the next room, asking, wasn't this "I prefer not to" from a Melville story, the one about the lawyer's pathetic clerk who goes screwy?

In short order his father sat in Scott's bedroom, for a talk. "The university informs us that at the graduation ceremony you'll receive three—that's three—achievement awards. They leaked the news, I surmise, to encourage you to attend. Any chance of that happening?"

"None."

Furman ducked as if delivered a glancing blow to the head, before righting himself again, his mind having let in a wounding possibility: *His own son might be a stranger to him*. Distracted, he rubbed a thumb across the crease in his chin, where a noisy clump of whiskers had survived his usually careful razor. He said at last, "Bad days come along. They do. Life in certain periods is a matter of being caught between Scylla and Charybdis. Be prepared to find yourself unprepared."

"Why is it," said Scott, "our family can't get through discussions without tossing down a five-dollar literary chip on the poker table? I'm the worst." With that he broke out into forms of ragged laughter.

"What's so funny?" asked Furman.

"I am. I'm a pretty comical guy."

Later it was his mother's turn in his room. She sat, stood, sat again, seeking the appropriate position, whether to be interrogator or mother. "I've given up cooking dinners," she complained.

"The family has lost its appetite apparently."

"Sorry, Mother. Maybe we ate too much anyway?"

"Too much? Too little, is what I see. Go on much longer and you'll look like your grandfather. Scotty, what's wrong? The girl, I guess. Did she break your heart?"

"Heart? Feels more like broken bones."

"That's it then. The girl. That girl. And so you're not sick, really, after all."

"I'm sick."

"You are?"

"Sick of myself is my sickness. I can't, in fact, at the moment, think of anything in the world I'm not tired of, including this whining of mine."

Elaine's mouth moved. She wanted to speak, but had problems. "Mother?"

She gestured, indicating with pushes of a flat hand that he should hold on, wait for her words.

"Mother, now don't start with the tears. Besides there aren't any tissues here."

Elaine blotted the inside corner of each eye with a knuckle. "Please tell me, Scotty, please, that I'm not hearing, not seeing, Spencer all over again."

"Mother, you made me into a Spencer already, years ago. The job got polished off when you gave me Spencer's cardboard box of poison, the one over on my desk." That box on the desk had **GOEBEL BEER**, Detroit 7, Mich. printed on it, and against a background of various stains, **BUY WAR BONDS FOR KEEPS**. Inside the box was that untidy cache of intimate papers: scribbled notes, rumpled letters, private poems.

"I only wanted the *good* Spencer for you, the magnificent one, not the dangerous Spencer, not the weak one." Within her restless hands could be detected the emotional essence of Miss Elaine Lemay, the not-quite-handsome, brainy girl who had worked for wages afternoons and summers since age twelve, had gone to college, who had tutored and inspired her young brother as she would her son. "Spence was dear to me but don't repeat his mistakes. I beg you, don't. You need to understand how we lost Spencer *before* he went to the war. Sometimes I hate that girl he writes about. Sometimes I nearly hate him, for not resisting her. See . . . see me shaking. Scotty, you must be stronger than I am, and stronger than Spencer."

"Mother, what's done is done, for me. But Joyce must never get a chance, even by accident, to look inside that box. I'll make certain of it. And in front of her please shut the hell up about Spencer being somebody special."

"Yes."

"Thank you."

"And can I get one little promise from you?"

"I would, for you," he said, "if my supply of lies wasn't used up. I wish I had just one left." When his mother hustled out of the room, she likely was off to a far corner and to more tears, Scott had to believe.

Only Joyce never hesitated to enter his bedroom. She stayed home her last two days of grammar school "because Scott was." Her parents decided not to interfere.

Scott said, "Your class party's tomorrow. I want you to go."

"I'm staying here."

"Why are you stubborn?"

"Why are you stubborn then?"

"Good point, sweet sis."

"Don't you love her anymore? That girl?"

"Hippo-*potty*-mus *no*. That plain enough?"

"Hippo-*potty*-mus *yes*."

* * * *

Full of his venom where did Scott return, but to the library and page 104. He wanted to inflict some violence, or return it in kind, since her picture injured him to the equal degree it once gave pleasure. He carried a sewing needle and intended to pierce her eyes. Why not? They were paper, simply, and he was entitled to vandalize a single book in his bookish life.

Opening *The Human Body* he avoided Ria's face, paper or not. Hurriedly he erased the evidence of his juvenile pencilings, where in block letters he had, one lonely night, doodled the word LOVE. Then he brought forth the needle, placing its tip against her kneecap, increasing pressure, harder, until there came a *pop*. The vicious sound caused the reverse of relief and Scott put the needle away.

Lady, ma'am, what were you up to, he asked her. Why did

you ever write those letters to me? Here is what I should change about page 104. I should scratch out the deceitful label and put in its place: "Onlookers beware. Fully pubescent witch. This 44-year-old girl may already be your mother."

The Human Body lay abandoned on the library table only briefly. Before Scott was out of the building, Cecilia Ade had the book in her hands, where on automatic hinges it swung apart, exactly to p. 104, fig. 84. There, in the top margin bordering the photograph, could still be read enough fragments of the hastily erased proclamation: LOVE. Mrs. Ade wore her green-as-a-shamrock dress.

Eighteen

Scott compared himself to a lizard trapped at the bottom of a pit, surviving because its excrement draws flies which can be eaten and pass into more dung. The lizard and Scott were marvels of minimalism, yet the pit did stink, and Scott had to crawl out and catch a breath of fresh air.

"I'm ready for that remodel project," he told his delighted father.

They poured cement under the sagging beach house, once a cute bungalow, circa 1922. Or 1929. Scott the carpenter ripped into the building with a power saw, inhaling sawdust. He cut in a new door, two new windows, removed a wall, rearranged and replumbed the kitchen, braced the ceiling joists. The old fabric-sheathed electrical wiring was yanked out, the studs doubled, rebored, and strung with modern insulated wire.

"This is like installing a new set of veins for yourself," concluded Baxter Neef, a Nebraskan with tangential thoughts who had worked eight industrious years for Bakkan Construction. He also was a veteran of the war in the Pacific and called Furman "the Major."

Scott said, tangential himself, "Who touched this old light switch I'm tossing into the trash? Where are they today? Where are the snows of yesteryear?"

This yesteryear fancy stuck with Baxter Neef, who embellished it throughout the workday, culminating at five o'clock with, "I tell my wife I like remodel jobs best. Now I know why. A fella keeps a house alive, don't he?"

The two of them sat together on the stripped subfloor, relaxing before heading home. Scott asked him, "Where'd you meet your wife?"

"Back in Nebraska."

"Childhood sweetheart?"

"Yessir."

"Baxter, could I ask a personal question?"

"Shoot away."

"You love your wife, I expect."

"I sure do."

"Speculate with me for a second. These are what-if games. What if you'd never known your wife—Maxine, isn't it? You call her Max. That always tickles me: Bax and Max. What if Maxine had lived in another state. Would you've fallen in love with a different girl in your town?"

"Phew. That's a question."

"And to turn it around, what if you'd been killed in the war. Would Maxine have found someone else and loved him?"

"Well, I don't like the idea of that."

"The nub of it is, how many loves are there for you in this world?"

"That's the nub. Phew. 'Course I can't see me and Max not being husband and wife. Still, we'd have ended up with some other somebodies, I reckon. Folks seem to go and get married, wherever."

"And this different woman, would you love her?"

Baxter, unconsciously, retrieved his hammer and began tapping on the heel of a boot. "I'd love her. Just not as much."

"Not as much. What's love, Baxter? Are there grades of love, like grades of lumber, #1 heartwood for the best construction, #3 common for the nonstructural parts, or maybe like pennyweight with nails—the higher the number, the bigger and stronger?"

Whacking at his heel, Baxter said, "Oh, wowzer. You're an educated fellow and what's your thinking about it?"

Over subsequent days they put on new shingles, replaced the exterior trim, and subcontracted the sheetrock work, the painting, the floor coverings. Before the project even got tidied up, Bakkan Construction sold the house for $6400. Baxter Neef bought it, $500 down, $75 per month.

The remainder of summer was said to be Scott's "vacation," his parents repeatedly letting drop the term, with its assumption that Scott would carry out his autumn graduate school enrollment at the university. He began meeting, mornings, with Lyle, to catch passes and help him prepare for an extra football season at San Jose State, having suspended a season's eligibility back in his first year of college.

In Lyle's bedroom the leading quarterback candidate lifted weights, lying on a bench covered with pillows, where he pressed 200 pounds in ten explosive reps, elevating his impressive pectorals. Lyle had meanwhile grown a mustache and somehow another half-inch.

"The pros may want you after San Jose," claimed Scott. No grin from Lyle. Uncharacteristically, a mood of diminution clung to him. Lyle said, "I should be out of college, same as you. But I'm throwing a football instead."

"You'll end up All-Conference this year. What happened to your enthusiasm?"

"Think I've lost something, do you?"

"I never see you smile anymore. I don't see any fire when you sling the football."

Lyle cocked his head, checking his friend for irony. Finding none he said, "I don't see you smile anymore either."

"Hey, you were always the one with the grins, not me."

"You piss me off."

"I know you're mad at me."

"Forget about football. I haven't seen you running this summer. Nowhere, not once."

"Well. That's over."

"No, it isn't."

"It is."

"Isn't."

"I'm afraid it really is."

"You do piss me off. How can it be *over*? Nobody who's on his way to the *Olympics* suddenly puts on the brakes and *stops*. Christ no. Why would he? Why, why? I'm a dummy jock scratching his head."

A pause gathered size in Lyle's bedroom, where over the years, between them, there had never been silences. Lyle dismantled his weights, sliding the disks under the bench in carefully matched stacks. Outside, in a neighbor's yard, a lawnmower in need of a clean spark plug struggled through its task. Folding up the end of his T-shirt Lyle dried his face. His mustache made him simultaneously older and dashing, youthful and absurd. A fleet of dust motes, wafting along a shaft of light, caught his attention, and irritated he sent them tumbling with a swipe of the hand.

"I just quit," said Scott. "You never saw me limp. I never went to a doctor."

Lyle went to his bed, fell across it, face up, feet still on the floor. "I phoned you."

"I know you did."

"It went like this. One day, no more Marlee, you tell me. Another day, no national championship, you tell me. Another day I phone, and no *Bakkan* anymore. I thought, shucks, my own house will disappear next."

"My apologies. I might have vomited if I had to talk to anybody."

"Right in your palm you had *everything*."

"No, but everything's what I wanted. I wanted to fall in love more than run. You might say that I wanted to win the Olympics of being in love."

"With your Miss Serendipity. She didn't love you back, your serendipitous fluke?"

"Where'd you pick up the vocabulary?"

"In that fat book with all those alphabetized words inside. Where the stupids go to figure out the smart people's talk."

"Don't act the dim blue-collar boy. You haven't pulled that in ages. Excuse please the deception. I thought you'd just make fun of me."

"I wouldn't have."

"You would have. And you'd have been right. And go on, keep me honest, keep me from turning against my own town, like one of those Big City snooty types, who think Watsonville is a place—when you drive through it—better head north to Santa Cruz or south to Monterey before stopping for lunch, or it's a town where two or three letters have rusted off its sign. **WAT--NVIL-E. WATSO-VIL-E.** What-so-vile. Is that a smile yet? Give an all-clear signal when you forgive me."

Nineteen

Marlee, driving the '55 Cadillac, came to the Bakkan house with a bag of knitting. "A sweater for you, Scott," she perkily explained to him, and the others.

"Let me try it on," he said, but found a single butterscotch arm in the bag.

"Why, you silly Billy, I just began." Marlee brought out a tape to measure around his chest. "I need to size you." She added, in a loud aside to Scott's mother, "Any trick to get my arms around a particular man."

"Love your color," Elaine said of the yarn.

Furman loved the color. Joyce loved it. That left Scott the potential ingrate, and he joined in. He *loved* this color, applying the one short word that could be reverentially scarce, and cheaply abundant.

Outside, Marlee included, as part of her goodbye, "Am I making a comeback yet?" In place of his straightforward answer they settled for a fumbling squeeze.

Back inside, food was served. The menu? Not much: yesterday's soup, yesterday's casserole—both dishes, however, noted for improving as leftovers. Furman got his fresh dinner rolls, which may have improved his frame of mind. "A nice girl, Marlee," he said.

"A very nice girl," Elaine agreed.

"And she can knit," said Scott.

Joyce said, "Somebody'll want to marry her."

"Indeed. Exclamation point." This was Elaine again.

"Somebody'll want to marry you, too, my pretty sister. Will you marry?"

"Sure, why not?"

"Sure, why?"

Joyce looked over at her mother. "To have babies."

"A practical reason," said Scott. "I appreciate that. Babies."

Joyce protested, "Not just babies. Other reasons. Right, Mom?"

"Certainly."

"Let me guess another reason." Scott concentrated. "From *Romeo and Juliet* ought to do it. 'My bounty is as boundless as the sea,/ My love as deep; the more I give to thee/ The more I have, for both are infinite.' Right, Mom?"

"Yes."

"Right, Sis?"

"Whatcha mean?"

"I mean love. You'll marry for love?"

In astonishment, Joyce slapped the top of her head. "I'm not even nine!"

"Where, in history, when," Scott asked his parents, "did love of love supplant religious love and love of knowledge?"

His mother and father, recognizing this tone, hitched themselves upright in their seats, defensively adjusted their thinking caps.

Scott said, "Once, people put their devotion into whatever was larger than their own lives. They adored gods and not each other. Later, they restricted their absolutes to the purity of ideas, whether religion or philosophy or science. But read our books today, see our movies, listen to our songs. It's all a love-me-true plea."

Scott's parents forked thoughtfully into their dessert, yesterday's Ginger Rum Cake, and figuratively, scraped up the crumbs they could reclaim from Cultural History courses. They remembered a morsel about "the Virgin Mary cult"—which within the strictures of Catholicism itself, directed passion on a personal level. They repeated several standard tidbits from medieval romances and the "chivalric tradition," with its "courtly love" and knights and princesses and other idealized damsels. They traced a few stations along the developmental road from late Middle Ages through the Renaissance, Enlightenment, Humanism, and Industrialization, following the steady elevation of earthly life over abstract ideals, i.e. (Furman literally said "i.e.") the secularization of love. Finally, the present "natural" culmination of this development is reached in "modern" Democracy, where the individual stands at the apex, where thereby romantic love is the ultimate inheritor of our best impulses. Summation: love—in our world today—is "the perfect egalitarian religion," non-authoritarian, self-reliant, classless, without external boundaries of any kind.

"Without limits," said Scott.

"Without any outside limits," Elaine said. "The inner ones, we make ourselves."

"Time and place, for instance. They can never be a boundary."

Elaine finished her piece of aromatic cake. "Do I detect a verbal chess move from you, Scotty? I'll risk it. If you refer to authentic love, then no, like authentic faith, time and place are not boundaries."

"Love is a timeless absolute."

"Yes, by definition."

"By definition. Mother, let's go back to 1929. Elaine Lemay is in love with someone, we'll say, in 1929."

"1929?"

"1929. You were about my age. Don't you remember 1929?"

"I didn't meet anyone in 1929. That is, I met your father later."

"This is hypothetical. You fall in love with young Mr. Right. Now, is your 1929 love the same love as you feel in 1955?"

"Can you ask your question another way?"

"Girls fell in love in 1929, correct?"

"Of course they did."

"Is it the same love that girls fall into in 1955?"

"Yes."

"Love itself does exist changeless in time, as promised."

"Yes."

"You loved Furman Bakkan in 1935."

"Yes."

"You love Furman Bakkan in 1955."

"Yes."

"Those loves are interchangeable."

"Essentially, yes."

"Is 'essentially, yes' different from 'yes'?"

"No, it means 'yes.' Don't be so edgy."

"Now we use our imagination," said Scott. "And now we shuttle, back and forth, between 1955 and 1935."

"We do? This is *odd*."

"Granted it's *odd*. Still, how hard can the concept be. We have different years yet the same people and the same love. Does it matter what year you find yourself in? Mother, if you two got separated, you here in 1955, and your husband back in 1935, would your absolute love suddenly diminish?"

His mother, running out of cognitive space, or patience, flummoxed through a sentence. "It wouldn't lessen, it couldn't, because by definition, no, delete that, because according to our logic, our syllogism rather, love is—"

"No syllogisms. Are you telling me, you'll love a man who's no older than I am?"

Furman rattled cup against saucer, attempting to brake the increasing volume. "Your mother is answering rhetorically. You presented her with speculations, and her answer was that love is immutable in theory. In theory. Whew, I'm glad Leland's in his room."

"Was I being rhetorical?" said Elaine.

"What the bullcrap does 'in theory' mean, when we're talking about love?" Scott asked all those present.

"Don't swear, please," said Elaine.

Scott stage-whispered across the table toward Joyce. "When you reach your birthday, you can blow out your nine theoretical candles."

"Are you mad at me, too?"

Furman reassured his daughter, "He's not mad at anybody."

"I'm just mad," said Scott. He inserted the end of a spoon handle into his nose and let it dangle. "Look Ma, no hands. I can serve myself with my nose."

Joyce snickered. "You *are* crazy."

Her mother told her to watch her language.

Furman's next strategical response was to request another slice of cake. With the rum cake gone, and no other dessert in reserve, Elaine took the situation as a major household lapse. She was "very disappointed to have let this come about." Furman said that, oh Holy Moses, he "hadn't in all honesty wanted any more dessert" and that he was very disappointed himself, if she felt it necessary to be upset over such a trifle. Elaine vowed to start a new dessert right this instant—something quite elaborate—and went into the kitchen, followed by Furman.

Joyce, clearing her plate from the dining table, and Scott's, marched into the kitchen and back. "Kissy-kissy," she reported, smugly.

* * * *

Marlee's 21st birthday arrived. Dorothy Stalich, herself, phoned Scott, inviting him to the "family" evening. The four of them managed an unawkward meal together, for their talk repeating conversational scripts from past months and years. A stack of presents—dazzlingly wrapped in mostly silvers—stood nearby. With the cake and candles, Mr. Stalich led the singing. Mrs. Stalich, according to a formula of ascending importance, handed over the presents one by one, while Marlee, opening each, related in detail her appreciation. Mother and daughter, aglow, put those satiny ribbons and that shiny paper to visual shame. Scott's present was saved until last.

Afterward the birthday couple visited at the Bakkans, being welcomed with a smidgen too much good cheer. Driving Marlee home she asked to see a former haunt of theirs, known as the Big Bend, a sweeping viewpoint high in the mountains. Parked there, in the night, engine off, it was—back to basics. The 1951 Ford again. The front seat again.

Below them, in the distance, an electrified diagram of the town flowed out from its center, suggestive of a dropped bowl of bright baubles, erratic shatterings of light spread over the carpet of dark.

To the west and south was the blackness of the Pacific, the curve of its Monterey Bay outlined by a faraway golden haze from peninsular cities. To their left a black strip (the Pajaro Valley) led into black hills. Behind them—black again—the Santa Cruz Mountains lay like the excessive crossing of a T, forming the county's territorial line, holding back strangers.

Many of the names that rose in the night, the names of these high tops and twisting canyons, the creeks and big flats, the beaches, the villages, sang an Iberian lullaby: Laguna de las Calabasas, Rio del Mar, Loma Prieta, Pasatiempo, Valencia, Los Corralitos, San Cayetano, Zayante. This Santa Cruz County had held its privacy, and was, topographically seen, an enclave at the edge of a continent, ringed by these young, unruly, namesake mountains, further compacted by transverse ridges and ravines, where roads had to be chiseled into hillsides and the motorists frequently miscalculated the sharp bends. Rain drenched the mountains in winter, suiting the thirsty redwoods and readjusting the hillsides back across the roads. The Spaniards had learned better, and directed their highway—their El Camino Real—up the eastern valleys beyond the mountains, from Mission San Juan Bautista to Mission Santa Clara, leaving Mission la Exaltacion de la Santa Cruz to wither inside its stronghold. Every Bakkan now alive had been born here.

"Are you happy?" wonders Marlee in the darkness. She sat with legs curled under, her shiftings accompanied by the nylon rasp of hosiery. Her tentative voice, her shadowed body, all blend into vanishment.

He said, "I'm supposed to ask you that. It's your Happy Birthday we're celebrating."

"I'm happy. I'm probably happier than you're happy."

"Haven't we had this debate before?"

"Are you a little happy, anyway, to be with me?"

Although Scott had brought Marlee that clucked-over, expensive gift earlier, he knew she was saving another present of his for last and best. Their kiss tasted like birthday cake.

* * * *

An end-of-summer picnic. Marlee had wished this, had assembled the prerequisites: a blanket and food hamper. In ten days she must leave for her own graduate school opening.

The afternoon was splendid picnicking weather. Close to where Scott had done his mountain runs they parked the Ford, located a deer trail and followed it, deeper into the brush, until reaching a pocket of openness as isolated and screened as a Druid Circle. Down went the blanket on the dry grass. Out came the containers of food and drink. An understory of manzanita bushes bordered the clearing, as overhead, oak and madrone branches permitted in a crosshatch of sunshine and shade. Mountain quiet settled in around them.

"That hiking made me hot," said Marlee, removing her full-sleeved blouse and folding it over the hamper handle.

"You coordinate. Green bra, green shorts. Green trees."

"I can add another," she laughed, lightly. She undid a raspy zipper, sitting, and with a subtle lift of her hips slid her shorts off—one gliding move to the knees, a second final push, feet held together and toes pointed, ballerina-style.

"Green again. How can anyone not look at you . . . just to enjoy your fashion skills."

"You can look at me anytime. I like it."

They ate their snacks, Scott appreciating the artful contrast between Marlee's skin and the nappy blanket, the crushed leaves, the tree bark. For dessert she unhooked her bra. Her pale breasts seemed highlighted by sunshine, when in actual fact Marlee was in sun only from the waist downward.

"How did such a half-pint," he said, "get to be so stacked."

"I want to take everything off."

"Do you have a plan here?"

She did, retrieving from her picnic basket a small foil packet, playing it out on the blanket like a trump card. "Don't be shocked."

"I never read about this in 'Teddy Bear's Picnic.' We're supposed to have sex?"

"Well, we've been close enough to it before."

"Close, yes. Close enough, no."

For an instant she shivered, from a chill of vulnerability, not her bare skin. "I thought maybe you wanted to."

"I do."

"But not really."

"Really I do."

"Not really. You're not over here holding me."

"Should I make it plainer? When I get home masturbation might need to be on the agenda."

Marlee blushed—face, neck, down farther, tinting her upper chest. "You only have to ask me. I'll say yes."

"I choose not to ask."

"In a second I'll do it."

"I know. I believe you."

"I'm telling you yes, right now," she said. "I want to feel us together. I want this more than anything."

"We have sex," he said, "and we live happily ever after. The happy-ever-after part is what you want more than anything."

"You sound angry."

"Not angry. No. But I would kill myself if I hurt you again. Literally. Use a goddamn bottle of poison."

"Let me explain."

"I can guess already. You want us to prove something big together. Except I can't prove anything big, because I don't love anybody."

"Oh."

"No one."

"No one. Not the other girl either?"

"Definitely not her."

Marlee's face found an expression resembling satisfaction, and said, "That's good news."

He shook a finger at her. "You're relentless."

"I sure am." She was in no rush to dress. Once again Marlee demonstrated her flawless background for the social graces. "If we're not using these rubbers," she said, "what should I do with them exactly?"

"Put them back where you found them. Nobody will notice."

"But I bought these in a store."

"You bought them?"

"In a drugstore when I was shopping in Carmel."

"Gutsy, aren't you. Did he check your age? Was it a man behind the counter?"

"He asked me what brand, and Scotty, I didn't know any brands. I almost panicked. So I just stared him in the eye and said, 'Whatever you recommend.' Afterward I realized how personal that sounded, and how it could be taken."

Here again are the unpredictable advantages of growing up a confident daughter in an expensive brick home. She can stand there and look a pharmacist full in the face.

<u>Twenty</u>

When on a September morning Marlee left for her university, she telephoned a last goodbye, her voice resolutely normal. That night Lyle came to Scott's house, announcing he had joined the Marines. Scott rejected the news. "You didn't. You wouldn't. I never heard a whisper about this."

"You'd have argued me out of it. You always could."

"The Marines. They send the Marines into every death pit everywhere. It's dangerous."

"Good. I want to shoot guns. I want people to shoot back at me."

"Is there a reason behind this nonsense?"

"Reason?" He was in his car, wearing his white T-shirt, a tanned muscular arm bent outside the window. Scott stood in the driveway. "Reason. Nothing. That's my reason."

"You were going to be a star quarterback."

"You were going to the Olympics."

"What about those co-eds waiting for you at college?"

"What about Marlee and you?"

"Leave me out of it. I have no connection here."

"Not so. I'm your shadow."

"Shut off the motor."

"I should go home. There're a couple of weeks before I report in. We'll talk."

"Wait. You've never been anybody's shadow."

"No?" Lyle combed his fingers through his hair, disheveling it, in reality. "All that time we spent hanging out together, since way back when, you probably thought we were, uh, like brothers. You never had a brother. I did already. It was a father I missed, a grown-up guy larger than life, who could pull off anything. Does that freak you out?"

Lyle's car was creeping forward, with Scott walking alongside, saying, "And I let you down. I disappointed everybody around me."

"Naw. Here I am still copying you. You turn goofy, I turn goofy. I must believe you know something and see something I don't."

"If you follow me, then we're both stepping off a high cliff in the dark."

"I'm counting on you to pick the right cliff."

"In the twilight you look like James Dean in the movies. Must be that T-shirt and those sheepdog eyes."

"In the twilight you look like . . . Scott Bakkan."

"Don't get yourself into a war. *Hear* me?"

"So long, Dad."

* * * *

On Monday he received in the mail an invitation from Mrs. Ade the librarian, ingeniously typed to mimic an index card from the card catalogue, with the pertinent information (name, house address, time, purpose) put in place of the author, title, classification number, description. "Librarian asks favorite patron to join her for social visit. Friday night. Seven o'clock. Casual attire. No R.S.V.P., simply please come."

On Wednesday he pulled into Overton's ranch, recognizing him to be a serious pack rat who filled quart jars with the bent nails from repaired apple boxes. "Got any old magazines around here?" asked Scott.

"Come on in."

Overton's house was murky and formidably still, not even a dog in evidence. "I had this pretty sister who married in '28, and moved to Ohio in '29 to farm there," he said, opening a family album on the oilcloth of his kitchen table. The gangly Overton bride mirrored far too much her brother to be pretty, although the brother said so again. "Charming," agreed Scott. Overton expanded: "She stayed with me for a year during the war, when her husband went to work in the Mobile shipyards. She drove herself back here in a heaped-up '34 Ford pickup, full of boxes and barrels, clothes washer, magazines, whatnot and whatever.

And three kids." Immediately he located the magazines, tied by string into a neat rectangle, inside a closet that yet held a woman's coat and a dusty nest of children's shoes. *The Farmer's Wife*. "Look," said Scott, "the top copy is October, 1929." Overton could not miss the eagerness. "Take it directly home with you."

You could buy *The Farmer's Wife* four years for one dollar, back then, in Ria's life then. The pages had women with bobbed hair wearing flapper hats, waistless dresses belted or sashed low on the hips, sharply pointed shoes. One full-page ad showed girls in a dorm room, smiling in their underwear.

> This month two million girls are taking our
> rayon lingerie away to school and college.
> When a woman boasts she bought her lingerie
> for only 98 cents you may know she is a customer
> of ours.

> A few months ago we invited you to stop in
> and see our new subdued lustre rayon underthings
> and 5,000,000 of you came. In 1,400 J.C. Penney
> stores you bought these dainty 79-cent vests and
> 98-cent bloomers.

Scott felt the living presence of these five million anonymous women, each, individually, somewhere close or far, in both time and space, in their shimmery underwear with its cool sizzle. Each one also had a name waiting to be spoken.

When Scott returned the magazine he said to Overton, "You never married."

An emphatic shake of the head.

"Marriage is what most people do, isn't it?"

"I never got that far down the road."

"With girls and women . . ."

"With girls and women . . ."

"You had a girlfriend once?"

"No, no."

"There was a girl, or a woman, who you couldn't ignore. She stuck in your mind?"

"I don't believe so."

They had a meal in Overton's kitchen, tuna and tomato sandwiches assembled in brisk farmer's style with slices of white bread slapped on two plates and the basics dumped on the bread—all with the rhythm of another routine task to settle. How old was Overton? Fifty? His large, labor-stained hands threatened to crush the soft sandwich, although he handled it, and ate it, with caution.

"I feel we're friends," said Scott.

"Me, too."

"I ask these personal things because I'm having problems about this subject of romance. You dated some women, or a woman, once. Went out man-and-woman together?"

Overton ate the complete dangling crust of his bread last, likely an unbroken childhood habit. "Nope, never did that."

"Had a kiss in the schoolyard?"

"No."

"Never a kiss."

"Never a kiss."

Overton washed the plates using a bar of hand soap. Elbowing away, he worked up a substantial lather. Overton said, as he scrubbed, that he had always believed he would marry one day, and end up with a family. He had expected it of himself because he liked women, liked children.

"It never quite happened," prompted Scott.

Walking outside into his yard, or into his orchard, since the farm house was crowded by apple trees, Overton tried articulating what had gone awry with his marriage chances. Articulation, admittedly, was not his forte. "I never had much time for social goings," said Overton. "I was a boy with a sickly father. As a youngster I took over all the work done with horses." They continued walking down the rows of apple trees, Overton ticking off the list of seasonal work demands that his orchard made on him.

As Overton talked, instead of a litany of toil and complaint he spoke with rising satisfaction. It reminded Scott of the sunny day, last April, when he had stopped by here after a light Sunday workout. Apple blossoms were mounded in their glory with enough dizzying cream-and-pink fragrance to enthrall man and bee alike. Overton had been in the middle of the first spring disking and Scott watched the rank young grass get turned under. The Cat D2—Overton's series 5U orchard model Caterpillar tractor, the one he regularly shined with automobile wax—flew along in third gear. It went zipping down the tree rows like a yellow Jaguar sports car with tank tracks: low-slung, long hood, wide stance, balanced and agile. By comparison the '51 Ford was a shoe box with wheels, and Scott had looked on, impressed. The tractor shot slithering beneath apple limbs, its diesel engine torqued tight into a potent pitch, its track pads clattering and shining, their Peoria steel polished by clawing through dirt. At the orchard's edge sloped an embankment, and at the end of each row Overton sent the D2 charging up the bank at a jaunty angle, without side-slipping, a handsome machine strutting its stuff. Apparently it was for his audience that Overton had put on this display, as finally he had pulled alongside Scott, idled down, rapped the hood, shouting, "Best equipment in the world! The world!" He had then whispered a private remark to the tractor, lips moving, a grease smudge on his face and a broad grin.

And now, in September, they walked together under limbs bending with their load of apples, the fruit of, and the proof of, Overton's efforts. "These trees is all I know about," said Overton. "Of everything else, which I know nothing about, I know women the least."

"You feel unsure around women."

"I figure best just to do without 'em. That what unsure means?"

* * * *

On Friday evening Scott drove to Cecilia Ade's address, a small house with shiplap siding and a steep roof, vintage but immaculate, in a neighborhood of other older respectable homes. When Mrs. Ade opened the door, he listened for a party babble behind her.

"*Entrée, s'il vous plaît,*" she said with a labored accent, stepping aside.

No one else was visible in the house. "Am I early?"

"Not at all. Here, sit on the sofa." Mrs. Ade wore an angora sweater he had never seen before. He had, upon reflection, never seen her before in any sweater. It was lush lime in color, and the ends of her reddish hair snagged the angora wool's own tendrils in a riotous blend. She appeared lit up, her social switch set on full wattage, her bold makeup the envy of any schoolgirl ready for a splashy Friday-night date. "What to drink," she said. "A Coke. Or wine. Let's make it wine." She brought two glasses of white wine and sat by him on the couch. "A French wine, of course. I'm quite an unabashed Francophile. I lived there for six months. Shortly after my divorce. In France children can drink wine at meals instead of water. You won't report me to the library board, will you, for serving liquor to a patron?" Mrs. Ade laughed, a trifle coppery, like her hair.

What would be the best word to describe her. Tipsy?

Twenty-one

"My husband, or, now, my ex-husband," said Mrs. Ade, "hardly read a book after college. Well, he didn't complete college, to be accurate. I found myself married to a nice man who essentially had no interest in books. Isn't that funny for a librarian? On the other hand, he liked camping and boating and I didn't. We never argued. But one day we asked ourselves: 'Why are we married to each other?' After the divorce I went to France for emotional compensation and probably to meet, finally, Mr. Wonderful. The most I ended up with was a wonderful vacation. Excuse my chattering like a ninny. Please, let me fill up your practically empty glass."

Scott counted it as fill-up #3 for him.

"I'm happy we can speak personally. We can, can't we? We are, aren't we?"

"I think so. Am I the only one here, by the way, for the party?"

"Just us two. I arranged a chance for us to talk outside the library and become true friends. It'd be nice if you use my name Cecilia and not Mrs. Ade."

"Will do."

"We could practice a little. Try my first name."

"Will do. Cecilia."

She flashed her strong teeth. "I enjoy that. Again, please."

"Again?"

"Again."

"Cecilia."

Mrs. Ade drained her goblet. "Promise me you'll use my name a lot. With that same in-the-chest tone."

He emptied his own glass. "Cecilia, Cecilia, Cecilia."

They laughed and she said, "Look what we've done. We need a second bottle."

Mrs. Ade went off into what must be her kitchen, moving with good control on heeled pumps, the inverted-heart shape beneath her skirt on an even keel. Returning, she put a carafe ("more Chablis") on the coffee table in front of them. "Despite my stay in France, I'm no expert on wines." She filled their goblets. "Here's what has me madly curious. How did you ever learn so much and so soon? How does anyone memorize all those writers?"

"Simple really. For the same reason a wolf eats red meat. My parents fed it to me in the den. Once you have the blood lust, nothing else satisfies."

"You just eat and eat."

"That's not to mention the suspense of the hunt and the thrill of the kill." Scott made a wolf's yowl. "Watch me show off. What distant century do you want to hear?"

"Make it a love poem."

"You betcha, my specialty. First a swallow of wine. Okay, here's a guy who had his heart smashed to pieces by a girl around the year 1600. 'My rags of heart can like, wish, and adore,/ But after one such love, can love no more.' Something genuinely foreign? 'Einmal, wenn ich dich verlier,/ wirst du schlafen können, ohne/ dass ich wie eine Lindenkrone/ mich verflüstre über dir?' That's Rainer Maria Rilke in original German. I'd translate, but it's not 100% cheery news either."

Mrs. Ade toasted him with the Chablis. "My jaw has dropped. You're such a prodigy, or I should say such a master already, and will you continue your university career?"

"I studied my uncle instead. From him I picked up the Rilke. Right, yes, my own uncle. He was a secret poet himself, a diary poet, who are the best kind, because they forget to conceal much. I call the genre peek-through-the-keyhole *vérité*. My uncle left behind a box of assorted papers, the equivalent of a University of Bakkan, and it finished off my education."

"Is he dead then?"

"My uncle Spencer was missing in action in '45, in Germany. There are conflicting Army and family theories about what happened over there."

"Forgive me if that sounds intriguing."

"In particular when it has to do with a girl. His poems are full of her."

"More love poems."

"Mmm. They must be. Not everybody would claim so, but I do. Why write them otherwise?"

"I'm very moved," said Mrs. Ade. "Should I be sad? Were the two of them happy?"

"I expect they went beyond happy and sad."

"And now your uncle is your favorite poet."

"He was, possibly, along with another bare-assed idealist, my old favorite, Walt Whitman. But nowadays I despise them both, especially my uncle. Unfortunately, his story and mine had a bonded destiny."

"What destiny?"

"We were each two idiots dedicated to dedicated love."

Mrs. Ade drained her glass, leaning back in resignation. "That does it. I'm going ahead with this. Forging ahead. I brought you a gift tonight."

"That's backward," Scott protested. "The guest is supposed to bring the gift."

"Not in this case. I didn't buy anything. It's not new. Wait here, I'll hurry before I lose my nerve." She returned with a package wrapped casually in tissue, obviously a book, laying it in front of him on the coffee table. "So . . . for you."

Folding away the wrapping, Scott recognized the blue volume through the last sheet of gauzy tissue: *The Human Body*.

"This is an absolute first for me," swore Mrs. Ade, with emphasis, no doubt for her own benefit as much as his, "stealing from a library."

In a locked focus, Scott scowled at the book's cover.

"I'll say what I—" she began. "Drink your glass down. I'm going to drink mine." Mrs. Ade refilled them. "Okay. Big breath. The girl in the book. Let me be her tonight."

Her proposal he tried to assimilate, tried to simplify, tried to fit into his complicated history with p. 104, and Scott went on looking dumbfounded at the familiar blue book, out of its element here in Mrs. Ade's living room.

"I mean, whatever you wanted to do with her, we can do together," she said.

He pivoted from the book to analyze Mrs. Ade instead. Had she somehow found out that much? Could she know him that extraordinarily? Then he did simplify, and did understand. "You're talking about our going to bed together."

She flushed—unless the wine at last hit her face. No, it was a pure blush.

* * * *

Her bedroom was small and they had to sit on the bed itself, where they held hands, in a logical prelude.

Mrs. Ade, with a wry smile, said, "I can't mind my own business, or my manners, when it comes to you." Then not smiling she said, "I want to be undressed for you, completely, to give you in real life exactly what you had in the book. Please don't be too polite or too shy to look at me without my clothes." Standing, she shimmied the angora sweater upward and off, tossing her hair back into position before folding the sweater and storing it inside a bureau drawer. A thoughtful housekeeper, she hangered the skirt in the closet—alongside her purple and yellow dresses, and a few others. In her slip, in profile, she checked over at him. "Are you watching?"

"Does staring count?"

Although she had her audience and her stage, she performed no striptease—did not perform at all—and routinely unhooking, routinely stepping out of, she built a tidy nylon stack on the nightstand. Finished, she turned, positioning herself in front of Scott, in a general imitation of the stance on p. 104. For him, the little room could scarcely contain its expansively naked owner.

He said, "Your body's sensational."

"For my age?"

"For any age."

Her hazel eyes flashed their dominant emerald, a color of gratification. "You don't see your librarian anymore?"

"I see my librarian. She's a woman."

"Look at me anywhere you want."

With Mrs. Ade leaning, looming, over him, anywhere and everywhere is what Scott saw.

"Touch me here. And here. Now here. Kiss me here. Kiss me here." She started undressing him, with difficulty. "Help me, would you, darling? I'm trembling." When he was stripped—

and lying back on the bed—she asked, "May I have my turn?" and placed her hands, flat, on his chest, moving them slowly in outward circles, as if soaping his body. "My god," she said, crossing over his abdominal muscles, "how can you be this firm? We ought to make a plaster mold, to show future generations. Don't laugh. Michelangelo's David is no finer than this. Yes, do laugh. It makes these ridges stand out more. My god, they really are hard as sculptor's stone—" Her voice broke, with a combustible huskiness, and bent over him, her entire appearance was correspondingly aflame: her glowing face, her bright hair, her emanating heat. "Say my name, please."

"Cecilia . . ."

She lifted away her hands, and bending deeper, touched him with only her nipples. "Is this what you wanted from the girl in the book? Darling? You deserve it, the real, real pleasure. Now use your mouth instead of your fingers."

He was swimming in her softness, rhythmically bringing up his head for air.

"Will you kiss me?"

"Yes."

Lowering herself down beside him, she asked, "On the lips?"

Her lipstick had been blotted away, left on a wine glass. Scott could trace, as if under a jeweler's loupe, the tiny blossom lines on those lips, the patterned surface of the tongue. He put his mouth to hers—in defiance of Oedipal platitudes—hearing, simultaneously, her response, a gasp, as they kissed and breathed deeper into each other.

She whispered, from her mouth directly into his, "Let's do what you wanted to do with that girl in the photo."

"Never mind the book."

"Tell me about her."

"Forget the book. Forget her."

"We can do whatever you imagined."

"I don't want what I imagined." Scott sensed his own body in motion, moving off, away from the bed, gathering a helpless momentum, akin to a noodle-headed tourist in a canoe being swept gradually toward 300-foot Misty Falls.

"Scott," she said, "look at us. I'm not black-and-white like the picture. We can do and feel what you daydreamed about."

The current had him in its grip, steering to the fatal, watery plunge. He asked, "How old are you, Cecilia?"

"What?"

"Or in 1929 how old were you?"

"In 1929?" She dug her fingers into his hair, tugging, yanking on him so strongly that their foreheads knocked. "Sixteen. Does it make me too old for you?"

"Maybe too young. The girl in the book is two years older than you."

"Sweetheart," she asked, confused, urgent, "what?"

"I misled you. I mislead everybody. Why am I that way? I let you believe you were saving a poor sex-starved boy, but with the girl in the picture I was starving for something else."

"Dear heaven, I frightened you off, and I meant to be careful. Let's try again. We'll turn off the lights."

"It's impossible. My thoughts got scattered elsewhere. Very sorry."

"I can act different."

"I don't want you to be different. You're terrific."

"I spoiled it."

"*Stop*. I do my own spoiling, believe me. Brace yourself for a jolt. I know who this page 104 woman is. She has a name, Victoria. We wrote each other love letters every damn day. She wasn't my sexual fantasy. She was my fantasy wife."

* * * *

Retrenching into courtesy, he put on his clothes in the living room, allowing Mrs. Ade to dress alone.

Waiting for her to reappear, Scott went to the bookcase to evaluate a librarian's library. There was a standard set—cheap paper, eight-point type—of Plato, Aristotle, Lucretius, and other Greek and Latin dust-catchers. Two Bibles, one annotated. Cellini's *Autobiography.* Montaigne's *Essays*. Pascal's *Thoughts*. Rousseau's *Confessions*. There was a superseded Funk & Wagnalls, bearing a DISCARDED stamp, and the same with Webster's Unabridged. A few predictable Russian novels. There was a frayed lineup of aged college textbooks (*Anthology of Elizabethan Prose and Poetry* and such ilk), several of which the Bakkan parents had once imposed on their son. Within the bookcase two groupings, to judge by their ruffled condition, received most of Mrs. Ade's attention. The first was a cluster by those French bad boys Baudelaire and Rimbaud, in translation and the original. The second, and largest, section was a string of bulky paperback romances, with titles like *Stardust Memories, A Maiden's Heart, Fairest of the Fair.*

Mrs. Ade came to the bedroom doorway. She had brushed her hair into a fresh gloss, had on new makeup and wore the violet-into-purple dress. "Leaving now?" she asked, seeing him by the front door.

They exchanged semi-goodbyes.

She called, "Don't forget your book."

His hand remained on the brass doorknob, an engraved gem that a wise carpenter had reused when the house was modernized. If not a wise carpenter, then a Baxter Neef. "Return it to the library, please."

"The book was yours to keep."

"I appreciate the offer, and the gesture. For a multitude of reasons I couldn't stand to have the book around me at home. But thanks again for offering it, the book, and thanks for planning this out for us tonight. It speaks well of . . . your sympathies."

"No thanks necessary, none. We'll meet each other in the library. That won't change between us."

"We'll pretend it won't."

Leaning against her bedroom doorjamb (despite her large size, a lost child in a picture frame of her own) she attempted smiling and a half-fist went up under her chin, to support its drooping arc.

Were those tears on her lashes? When Scott went to investigate, Mrs. Ade said, "Stay back. You don't have to come over here." On the contrary, of course.

She tried to fend off his concerns. "Give me a minute to settle down. I just found out we had it switched," she said. "The wrong person needed instructions. The wrong person was desperate."

Reaching for her hand—still curled under her chin—a nobler move came to Scott and with a flourish worthy of a Gallic paramour he wrenched apart her bodice, the purple buttons popping off in several directions of the compass.

Naked in bed again, Cecilia Ade, interestingly, was as shy as a virgin, a legitimate *Maiden's Heart.*

She informed him, insisting on eye contact, "No other man has been in this bed."

Twenty-two

In the morning he awoke early, feeling regulated puffs of breath on his shoulder. In sleep Mrs. Ade was breathing like a happy baby.

She made them a waffle breakfast with strawberries on the side. "Shall I plan a dinner for you tonight? I want to."

"My family depends on each other for dinner at home. My grandfather's health—well, he hasn't any."

"Will you come over afterward?"

"Gladly, except we shouldn't sleep together again."

"Oh?"

"It won't be easy, not easy at all, but to teach myself a lesson I have a new rule of no more sex without love. Harder yet, I have a rule of no more love without love."

"I'll respect that. Very reluctantly. May I have two wishes myself? First, please keep coming here, until you tire of me, and then stop immediately. Second, I'd like to call you 'darling' and other sugary names. It's sticky, but they won't give you any bruises."

They drank a bottle of wine every night, the empties crowding into a box under the kitchen sink. Scott teased her, "I'm a boozer. You finally went and corrupted me."

"Have I done that? Ouch, dear, I have . . ." They lay on the bed—their normal place by evening's end—where they could best talk, given their fuzzy condition. Although Scott's vow of celibacy remained unbroken they did, literally, often sleep together. The convenience was irresistible. The hour would grow late, their conversation interrupted by fatigue, and automatically, off would come their clothes and under the covers they would go, usually exchanging a quick goodnight kiss. No, they always did.

Mrs. Ade said, "Are my eyes wet again? What's wrong with me? I never drink and get moody. I never used to drink much, period, before you. Until your birthday next week I even supply liquor illegally. In short, I'm a criminal. And I daydream at work. Constantly. I ought to fire myself. And I know, how I know, that now I'd never be satisfied with a man like Eddie. I remember that poetry line you quoted and ask myself the same question the poet asked way back in the year 1600. Can I be satisfied with any other man after you? Sweetheart, it seems you corrupted *me*, not the reverse."

"Eddie was your husband. Eddie Ade. Wins a prize for euphony. Why then did you marry him?"

"I have our wedding picture, somewhere, if you're interested."

"I'm not good at judging people by photographs."

"He's not a bad-looking guy. Could be I fell for his biceps. He has big ones."

"And he probably fell for your breasts. You've got big ones. Darwinism doing its lusty duty."

Mrs. Ade had only to tip her head slightly to see Scott, already by her side. "Do you think about my breasts?"

"Only one per day, alternately, for purposes of moderation. Today it's the . . . right."

She feigned a punch at his chin. "Now you make me giggle. I go from extreme to extreme. Let's empty this bottle. Oops, we have. With Eddie, I was never swept into anything, not into love, anyhow. That's clear in hindsight. I got warmer and warmer feelings about being married, about being half of a couple. That idea still warms me up. I don't think it's the wine."

"An urge for family."

"We never reached that far. Man and woman, we tried that part, but nothing else. Eddie later remarried, incidentally. For his sake I hope he found real love with his new wife."

"Why do you use that adjective? Love comma real."

"I shouldn't. Love shouldn't require qualifiers like 'real' or 'deep' or whatever. She rested her cheek on his chest. "You always bring me back to the truth on this topic."

"With me, even my truth is a lie."

"I like your voice with my ear held here," she said quietly.

"And, well, dearest one, it's always the same with you. You underestimate yourself. But you won't believe me."

"We could open another bottle."

"No, darling. Kiss me goodnight."

On Saturdays they would open and finish that second bottle of wine, in recognition of the traditional night for the extra social effort. Outside, in the towns, the entertainment venues bustled. Scott and Mrs. Ade could never be seen together at these places or parties.

"Don't you miss spending tonight with people your age?" she asked him.

"Do you?"

"No. I wondered whether you might need a break from me."

"Are you recommending that I take the night off, rest up from this labor?"

"What *labor*?" she mocked, with a wave indicating how they lounged on the couch, shoulders against opposite armrests, knees up, toes touching at the middle cushion.

"The work of my night shift here with you."

She kicked her feet against his—her bare feet against his socks. She kicked again.

"That tickles," he said.

"How can that tickle? It's supposed to hurt." She tried harder, kicking into a flurry, ending when she ran out of breath.

He said, "You're strong."

"I'm panting. The miler isn't. I liked watching you run, by the way, truly liked it."

"A toast to that."

"Now you're here in front of me, touchable. A toast to that especially."

"A toast to touching."

"What do you tell your parents, in the mornings, when you show up. Some vague and ingenious story?"

"I explain I spent the night getting drunk and touching my librarian."

A sip of atomized Chardonnay escaped from Mrs. Ade's mouth. She wiped her chin.

Scott said, "With a friend, I say."

"No details?"

"My parents have grown leery of details. Ignorance is their bliss, or indifference is. They've had far too many shocks from me lately."

"And I guess an older woman and a young man, in their love nest, is shocking. We should issue a bulletin: 'Attention. The librarian is not being touched, after all!' Would anybody believe us? No. We might as well do that touching." Reaching forward, she pulled off his socks by the toes. "Put your feet up against mine." Pressing bare soles to bare soles, legs bent, they pushed, building a force and counterforce.

"No baloney, you're strong," he said.

"Push harder then."

"Your toes really grip."

"Be tough back. Come on."

"Your face's turning red."

"Harder!"

"No, you're quivering already."

"Push . . . your hardest."

"No, we'll lose the balance. It'll hurt you."

"Do . . . all your . . . strength."

"I'm hurting you."

"Overpower . . . me. Come on . . . please."

When her legs collapsed the knees flew apart and Scott's feet landed on each side of her head, under her hair. Moist hotness from her cheeks passed across his arches and they both took a breather within this horizontal perspective.

"We're touching," said Mrs. Ade.

Every light in the living room was on, six in total, three ceiling lights and three floor lamps. That was Mrs. Ade's choice. Whenever Scott visited she never cracked the drapes and never answered the telephone.

Mrs. Ade chanted the nursery game "This Little Piggy Went to Market." Rather than count Scott's toes with her fingers, she used her tongue. The little piggy that squealed "*weee-weee* all the way home" she seized with her teeth.

"That," said Scott, "is touching."

"And this?" A toe went into her mouth.

"Definitely touching. And definitely seducing. And most definitely succeeding."

"Uh-oh, I'm going out of bounds, disregarding our rules. My fingers are creeping up above your knees. I'll remind myself I'm not Victoria. I'm Cecilia. Look, my fingers are back where they belong. Darn it, I made you stop smiling and I like your smile very, very much. Why did I use her name?"

"I can smile. *Voilà*."

"You do notice me throwing myself at you, don't you?"

"You're too intelligent to need to throw yourself at anyone," he said. "And too fetching."

"Too smart am I? Too attractive? Of your two compliments, the former outdoes even the latter. Watch how foolish I can be." Mrs. Ade wiggled up, sat on his lap, leaned down to wrap her arms around his neck, her hair, hanging forward, covering his. "I'm using my intelligence to speculate on love. Love, your most favorite topic."

"This is why they serve wine to lovers," said Scott. "Inhaling you is like drinking another intoxicating glass of it. Forget perfume."

"We'll write out a list of intelligent questions about love. Is loving another person only boredom with being stuck inside your own skin? Is love the highest act of human dedication or is love the highest form of egoism?"

"We're both plastered."

"Tell you what . . ." She brought her lips nearer—not by his ear, instead over his mouth. "For tonight give me a pinch, a sliver, of any kind of love from you, which kind I don't care. The worst of the lot is okay with me. Will you love me a little tonight? I want a speck of what you feel for her. Love her more than me, agreed. But just tonight I want *my* piece—a bitty, shitty piece—all for myself. Can you love me a little?"

"Yes." By speaking, Scott's lips had to brush against hers.

"Shut your trap." She buried a smothering kiss on his mouth and teeth. "You can't quite refuse a yearning soul, can you. No, I won't force you into 'a little' of anything, my darling hero, my darling absolutist. However observe how dopey I can act, at my age, perfectly like any gushy bobbysoxer chasing after her heartthrob. You should stop scratching your head over the great puzzle of why that old lady Victoria wrote you those letters."

* * * *

Elaine Bakkan served the family their dinner. Five sat at the table, with five plates. This arithmetic at least remained the same.

Joyce was hesitating over how much she should take from what dish. "I can't always make up my mind," she told her father.

"Me either," said Furman, "but I do it."

"A child is more confused, you know," said Joyce.

Scott wagged a scolding finger at her. "Are you calling me a child?" His sister did not laugh.

Four of the Bakkans ate the food.

"Can I have a small black puppy?" asked Joyce. Her face, bent over a bowl, is screened by her blonde strawflower hair.

Her mother answered, "Small puppies, inevitably, grow up

into bigger dogs. A cat possibly. Would you like a cat?" Elaine Lemay Bakkan had forgotten her lipstick tonight, and appears more attractive without any, her lips providing a pastel highlight of their own.

"How about a small black cat that you could teach to bark," said Scott.

No smile sneaks in around that spoon in Joyce's mouth. Nobody else seems amused either. Nowadays Scott was accustomed to being ignored, both he and his grandfather losing their visible shapes, two travelers departing on journeys without likely returns, and whose family must rehearse their absence in order to survive without them. For Leland, the destination was known, for Scott, uncharted.

An illustration of the family's disengagement came when Leland spoke up about the cabin in Bakkan Canyon where he and his wife, Wanda, first lived. Not merely giving a description of the whitewashed, tar-papered shack, he thinks he can find it again. Furman returns him polite interest. When—unexpectedly, as he now walks with miserable difficulty—his grandfather asked if Scotty would take him into the mountains, no one cautions against this venture. What was left to guard against? More pain than agony? More injury than death?

Afterward a remarkable day occurred when Leland did locate the meadowland where he and his Wanda had their cabin. Using Scott's arm for support, the grandfather winces along a path that wound by a thicket of blackberry brambles, into the shade, under trees, through clumps of sword ferns and along a demure brook. "We ate those blackberries back there," he said.

The cabin had vanished, not a board in evidence, with the outhouse pit filled in, flush to the ground. "Fine," claimed Leland, sitting with his back against a redwood's trunk, peering out into the pasture where the cabin had been. "It's preferable to kicking at a pile of rotten wood." He pointed. "There's the hillside. Here's the meadow, smelling like it was haying time on a farm. And the creek . . . and its tune."

"Brings back memories, does it?"

"I can feel an axe in my hands. I can feel myself splitting shakes." His eyes shut. He seemed frail beyond the sense of frailty, his head more a skull, the sharp bones of his face hurting his skin. "We put shakes on the inside walls to make the cabin tighter. We took our share of joking from other folks about those walls, but the shakes were free for the making, and she couldn't tolerate a draft, Wanda. She never held up under any chill or dampness. She picnicked whenever the weather allowed and we ate outdoors more than anybody I ever knew."

The creek went slurping over boulders. Water skippers skated in harbors behind logs. A honey bee wandered into the shade and hurried back to the sunshine.

"She," said Leland, "came here to the stream twice a day for our fresh cooking water. Usually she wore her favorite color, yellow. More than once I watched her hunting through the meadow, wearing her yellow dress, hitching it above the weeds, searching for wildflowers to pick and bring in for a bouquet."

"I can picture that myself," Scott said. "Wildflowers on a plank table inside a rustic cabin."

After a silence, Leland abruptly cursed. "I'm a jackass."

"What, what?"

"This isn't the meadow. See that bald granite hillside across from us? There was no bald granite. And I turned things backwards in my head. The creek was on the other side of the clearing, not over here. I'm a jackass."

"No harm done."

Leland pulled on the fingers of both hands, exercising them, and rubbed a hip. "We're trespassing, I reckon. Let's leave." He struggled to stand, and eased back against the redwood. "I'll rest a while longer."

Scott looked away, out of politeness. He saw: a lacy wood rose, wild ginger on the embankment, cloud shadows, a chalky stone with seashell fossils, three distinct high-water marks, dimples in the water, a wind-torn redwood limb sunk in the mud—what loggers call a widow-maker.

Furman said, "I can't unbend."

"What'll I do?" asked Scott.

Little to do but carry his grandfather to the car, cradled in his arms, in the manner a sleepy child is taken to bed. Back by the blackberries they went, leaving behind the false meadow. Scott thought that Leland might comment, "It was me toting you, once upon a time," but instead he said, "Warm day for a heavy load."

There was no load. Those few pathetic pounds summarized the sad state of affairs.

In the car Scott said, "We'll go to the hospital."

"Not the hospital." Leland lay on the rear seat, in his permanent coil.

"The doctor's office then."

"No, head on home."

The Ford dropped down from the hills. "I liked our trips together," said Leland. Fortunately, his tired voice was directed to the front. "I liked remembering these old mountains." They approached the flatlands, with the Soquel River canyon widening, the houses starting to cluster. "I always believed we fit in close. You and me."

Once along the main roads Scott stabbed the throttle and the Ford leapt homeward. Leland said, somewhere along the route, "Don't waste any pity. Nobody's picking on me. We all end up at the same spot, and young fellow, you'll get there yourself."

Within the week grandfather Leland, on his own, arranged admittance to the hospital. Too many mechanics of life had failed him. At the appointed hour (ten o'clock on a cool Saturday morning) Furman and Scott, son and grandson, hauled Leland from his bed to the car. Elaine handled the one suitcase. From a chair, Joyce observed. Conversation was limited to the single-sentence essentials of keys, light switches, toothpaste, the clock. Underway, in the car, they had the traffic to occupy them, and at the hospital, they had the admission papers.

Ultimately the family had to part from Leland in his room, where he lay swallowed up by white bedcovers and a white pillow, his blue eyes the only significant color, tubes already in both his arms.

Scott paused at the doorway, signaling V-for-victory. He was out of originality.

Back at the house, Joyce, after an afternoon of dark muttering, said she "wanted to do something for Leland."

Her father patted her on the shoulder, understandingly. "We can visit him tomorrow."

"But I hate the hospital."

Furman left his hand on her shoulder.

Joyce asked, "*So*? What can we do to fix stuff? And I *mean* it."

Later that night, going to bed, she opened the door to Scott's bedroom, checking inside, from habit more than hope, for she had doubtlessly heard his Ford leave hours before.

Part IV

"You want to test who the biggest liar is?"

<u>Twenty-three</u>

Tonight they did without the wine, nearly. They drank one glass each, on Scott's arrival, and no more, perhaps due to a whiff of unpredictability in the air. Cecilia Ade waited on the sofa for Scott to join her. He keeps forgetting to sit.

She tells him about Mr. Stempelton, her friendly retiree neighbor, who "out of nowhere" scowled over the hedge this morning. "I'm supposing he won't be mowing my lawn anymore, the way he always does as a favor. My reputation may finally be lost."

"Will that cause problems for you?"

"Not enough to give you up."

"I'll mow your lawn, plus I'll do Mr. Neighbor's lawn and win him over."

"Few secrets survive in a small town." Mrs. Ade tapped the couch beside her. When he sat down, she quickly held his hand in her lap, an act she would seldom forgo, and certainly not tonight. Once Mrs. Ade had explained how it was the tethering effect that appealed to her as much as the intimacy. She asked, "Are you tense about something?"

"Family worries, I guess. Or not a guess."

"Tell me."

"You can live without hearing any of my family's sad convoluted stories. You have Mr. Stempelton to deal with."

"Don't make light of this. We don't care about my neighbor and you know it. Tell me please what this is about."

"Let me say no. Give me permission to say no."

"If you want to ignore me you can say no. If you want to hurt me."

Scott recognizes the honesty of her fragility. To signal an appreciation he squeezed the hand that was squeezing his. "So all right. To begin, my grandfather has a month, maybe two, before he shrivels away altogether and dies. But he's probably dealing with that fact better than the rest of us. Joyce, my sister, concerns me the most."

Mrs. Ade said, helpfully, "It's difficult for a child to understand death, with that permanent separation. I lost my mother as a teenager which had a huge effect on me and Joyce is much younger."

"Cecilia, my fear is not about Joyce the child but Joyce the woman."

Mrs. Ade blinked her curiosity.

"Let me try not to be mysterious here, or anyhow, no more mysterious than Spencer Lemay, the uncle you heard me tell tales about, with his disappearance in Germany during the war, and his German woman waiting there for him. Her name is Silke Wolke. I never told you that before. The name by itself sounds easy enough to fall in love with, according to my uncle. Everything about her was simple to fall in love with to hear him explain it. I once considered traveling to Augsburg, Germany, and to stand in front of her, this woman from Spencer's papers and poems. But that'll never happen. Some parts of the past should stay back there, at least parts of my uncle's past."

Mrs. Ade waited, politeness managing, barely, to throttle that curiosity of hers.

"For years I assumed my mother rejected any claim of Spencer being killed in the war just because she hoped her brother was still alive. She did have a fair argument. No body was ever found. For practical purposes the guy had already survived everything a war can throw at a soldier. Myself, I thought he had been vaporized into thin air by a German landmine. Or an itchy-fingered American P-51 pilot—running out of real targets by April of 1945—had spotted this loner scout out in the brush and mowed him into mincemeat. But now I know my mother was right. Every hard bit of evidence shouts out that Spencer never died in combat. He was a genuine magician at staying alive on the battlefield."

"You think he *is alive* somewhere?"

"Not alive. My mother might still cling to that idea by her fingernails. I believe otherwise. I know otherwise."

"What do you know?"

"What I know you probably don't want me to say, judging by that face of yours."

"Do say it."

"I want to spare you the ending."

"Don't spare me from anything."

"All right. I can see my uncle, understand? Clearly. Step-by-step. I see him finding a pretty little lake hidden off in the pretty German woods. A very scenic spot to most people's minds. And possibly his. Without any hesitation he chucks himself into the deep water."

"Scott?"

"Down he sinks. A whirlpool of ripples, and then nothing."

"I do not like you thinking such things. It's wrong."

"Not wrong, not false."

"But it's wrong. I mean wrong for you to picture such scenes."

"Probably he tied weights to his boots, not wanting any messy evidence left floating behind for others to clean up, neither a bodily mess nor a judgmental one. For the same reason he would skip the standard rifle-in-the-mouth method."

"Scott, please."

"Oh, chances are I underestimate his suicide ingenuity. His impressive foolishness was matched by his impressive creativity, we have to realize. Or is there a causal equation between those two? Dead, however cleverly done, is still dead, nonetheless."

"But my god, why believe this?"

"As my mother constantly informs me, nobody will ever decode Spencer Lemay as well as I can. Why would he march like a demon across all of Europe just to commit suicide two days away from Silke Wolke? Once that stumped me. Not anymore. Now, Cecilia, I see my uncle putting sense into the story. To him, life is not a fate of waiting for when the end will come, on some unknown day, the way others wait, but of recognizing the best end. He picked his best end. Spencer wanted not to chance losing tomorrow what he had already won for certain yesterday. I suppose putting himself in Germany was his way of putting himself closest to that yesterday."

"Darling, you've made me all shaky. Can you feel me?"

"Because I might be the same, do the same? True, Spencer is my uncle, a spiritual brother in too many ways, and I inherited his famous box. But I'm only a lazy halfway martyr, I think. My question is, Who else in my family could ever make Spencer's choice? My mother, conceivably. My father, never. And for my special sister, who insists on curing her world of every ache and pain, have mercy, the answer is yes."

Ceclia Ade had minutes before already taken both Scott's hands into her own.

* * * *

The next morning—nine o'clock—and still in bed they try coming awake, the sun already lighting the drawn curtains, the neighborhood outside establishing its daytime noises—cars, dogs, muffled voices. "Shouldn't we get up?" wondered Scott.

"Not yet."

Later, he repeated, "Why aren't we getting up?"

"First I'm making a plan."

The phone rang, unanswered.

Mrs. Ade groaned, "Probably the library."

"I like it when you're being devious," said Scott.

"We're not leaving this bed until I settle the matter." She propped herself up on a pillow. "And don't interrupt me, please."

"I won't then."

Her colleen-color hair, mussed and spiked from sleep, emphasized her facial expression—which looked enormously solemn, if not close to being teary yet again. "I need you to prove yourself to me," she said, "for you to do a difficult thing for me, and to show how serious I am, I want you to stay away from here, from my house, and me, until it's done. Only you understand how hard those words are to speak. Let me finish while I can. I want you to drive a stake through Victoria's heart. Go visit her. Yes, all the way to Illinois. Send a letter, to prepare her, but leave before she can reply and object or change your mind. Meet her in the flesh and hear her voice. See how old she is. Find out how ordinary she can be. Destroy any fantasy of her, if you're the man your uncle Spencer wasn't. Then come back here to me, or come back, and not to me. It's a risk I take. We've been rivals, Victoria and I, and maybe I *required* her, to make you interested in me, as much as I wish otherwise. Whatever your choice, unless you end up as a survivor, I lose you, anyway, sweetheart."

"Cecilia, you're the heart that's sweet."

Twenty-four

The letter was mailed before he let himself think on it.

"It's a vacation," he told his parents, his insincerity deflecting any questions. "It's experiencing America."

Into his travel bags Scott packed the combinations of clothes to fulfill most social circumstances. At the bank he withdrew 500 dollars. Mr. Stalich was not present. He cleaned, washed, buffed the '51 Ford, bought new rear tires, replaced the water pump because of a wobble in the fan. He filled the gas tank, stored six quarts of motor oil in the trunk with his toolbox. He trimmed his hair and his nails. On a dawn damp with fog, he left.

Turn, wheels, turn.

As he crested the Santa Cruz Mountains that coastal fog stays behind, sunshine waits down in the Santa Clara Valley, and Scott sucked in a determined breath, a miler turned into a literal cross-country runner. He pushed ahead, past San Jose, along the East

Bay shoreline into Oakland, from the bay waters to the delta lands, on into the vast Central Valley, not pausing, on through Sacramento, up among the Mother Lode foothills, climbing steeply to the snow line and another mountain crest. There, at Donner Summit atop the Sierra Nevadas, he gave the Ford a breather.

A plunging descent down the eastern escarpment and he was in Reno, paying a king's ransom for gas at thirty-eight cents per gallon. In an attempt to recover that extravagance he lost five quarters in a chromed slot machine. Onward again. River-swallowing desert pockets, known as salt sinks, dominated the landscape, with barren mountains for a backdrop. Crossing into scrub rangeland he reached Winnemucca just as twilight could enhance the town's neon Midway—a junior sibling of Reno— where he ate a hamburger, and shaking off his road weariness kept the Ford at sixty, lights on now, mufflers crooning in the dark. In the shallow valleys the headlights ignited a gelatin glow inside the eyes of jackrabbits, and in the hilly passes separating the level stretches, ghostly owls glided across his path. At Elko he decided to rest. In this cow town with twenty-four-hour casinos, he found a dim street for parking, fell asleep on the front seat, his body buzzing from road vibration. At some post-midnight hour a persistent rapping on the car window awoke him. It was a hard-working whore at the wrong Ford. "Go back to sleep," she excused herself. Instead he drove the remainder of the night toward Utah.

Sunrise came while traversing the majestic desolation of the salt flats. Dawn bloods mixed with sterile whites. In Salt Lake City he bought fuel for the Ford, fueled himself with pancakes, observed inland seagulls sailing, reminiscent of his Santa Cruz beaches. Behind the city he headed up the Wasatch massif that led to an intermountain plateau and Wyoming. Fort Bridger, Medicine Bow, Laramie, Cheyenne, these names reactivated boyhood books about whiskery mountain men, Shoshone and Blackfoot Indians, and escape into anarchy. Atop the continental divide Scott realized that with a careless short doze at the wheel his parents would wonder what his car, and his body, had been doing in the far Rockies.

A gradual downward glide carried him two hundred monotonous miles from the high plains into the undulations and sluggish rivers of western Nebraska. Night again. Periodic bug blots decorated the windshield. He ate cold soup and warm salad in Grand Island, later napping off the road by cottonwood trees and farm fields with the scents of California's San Joaquin Valley in the thick air. For breakfast of the third day he was in Iowa, his last hurdle. Acres of cornstalks accompanied him. He thought of homesteaders and sod houses, their descendants today living in the satisfying cliché of a white clapboard house, green roof, shade trees, a barn nearby. This is where Overton belonged, among his farmer kin. Scott kept the Ford flying, only stopping for gas, not to rest. More and more he consulted his map and wristwatch. By afternoon, in the river town of Davenport, the state of Iowa was behind him, and there, across the fabled Mississippi, could be seen the Illinois shore.

Although his marathon race might be ending Scott does not hurry to the finish. At Huck Finn's Cabins he paid the bemused toothless manager two dollars for two hours, and Scott hosed the Ford clean and swept out the cracker crumbs. Using a cabin's bathroom he showered, shampooed, shaved. "From Californy," noted the man, a possible look-alike of Huck Finn at seventy, "and goin' whereabouts? Nope, never heard of New Hope in Illinoiz."

On the bridge's span over the Mississippi he gave less tribute than he should have to the grand mass drifting underneath, bracing himself instead for the touch of Ria's Illinois. He swung south. The land was rural: rises and declines, woodlots along the muddy creeks, with cornfields, pastures, and fat livestock. The afternoon had gone into a fade. In the town of Monmouth he drank a vanilla milkshake, slowly, slowly. Driving again, on went the headlights, and the road narrowed. Few other cars came along. He passed little Roseville (associated by suffix with home) and Scott knew from his map catechism that the next village would be hers. He crossed the La Moine River, shortly entering McDonough County, and at that, he swerved into a turnout and halted to brush his teeth, standing beside a billboard advertising DeKalb Seed. Crickets never slackened their talented racket.

Scott read the approaching sign marker before he could distinguish any individual letters, interpreting its spatial arrangement: NEW HOPE. Then the place was there, with an auto repair shop, a pair of vintage service stations, a church, some kind of grocery shop, all closed. Bumping over railroad tracks he made a right turn, following references once innocently revealed in Ria's letters, and two blocks up he recognized what had to be her house, on the corner, two-storied, facing north, and he drove past, turning right again and across the tracks again, where the grain elevators stood. Here also was the village square, or what remained of it from glory days. Circling, he returned to her Lincoln Street, and opposite her house shut off the Ford. He patted the dashboard—a voyage well done.

The night sheltered Scott, as did the blacker shadows under a canopy of maple trees. From this hideout he scrutinized across the street the house's lighted windows and entry, where the door has been set open behind its screen, because of the Indian summer's warmth or in anticipation of a visitor.

After driving close to 2,000 miles he decides to wait before walking the last 100 feet. It was too late in the evening for polite confrontations. "In the morning," he promised.

For tonight he will put himself to sleep with how, once upon a lifetime, ages ago, he had imagined this first meeting with Ria. The night is the same as tonight. Scott sits in the car the same. Presently, over across the street, a figure fills the open doorway, a girl in a pale summer dress. The screen door swings out, closes silently, and she glides across the porch, advancing to its outer edge, halts, in immovable silhouette, as if determined to be a perpetual figurine unless a distant traveler arrives with the reason for her to move again.

When Scott steps from the Ford she makes a single involuntary sound, without speaking further, or shifting. Crossing the pavement he could believe himself aboard a floating ship rather than on solid land, unsteady without his sea legs, and he pauses at the veranda stairs to find his balance and look up at her. The house lights from behind ignite her in a masterstroke of radiance, an aureola flaring around her hair and her dress, the glare tracing in demure chiaroscuro the body that Scott has already learned intimately. He suffers a constriction, like a wind-up toy whose resistless heart's spring has been cranked so tight it cramps. Her face tilts, illuminated in the glow, and the revelation of it torments him with joy, another of those emotional oxymora that only his love can decipher.

Hey, Leland, whaddya think about my vocabulary. Impressed? Are you still alive in that hospital bed, Grandpa?

Twenty-five

When the chill and the prairie sunrise roused Scott, he drove to a service station, filled the Ford's tank, washed his face in the restroom, changing into a fresh shirt. On a side street he parked by the local grammar school.

While he nibbled two apples down to their cores the children began arriving, on foot, in buses, with mothers in cars. Heard through his closed windows the separate excited young voices unified into a squeaky babble. Out on the playground future athletes spun a few turns on the climbing bars, their hands polishing the pipe and unintentionally maintaining the shine begun by their parents. The old school had many more wear marks on it—shortcut paths through the lawn, scarred benches, scuffed walls and doors—put there by Ria and other passing lives.

A bell rang, children fled inside, and Scott steered the Ford back to Lincoln Street. Without pretending to find total control, he is nevertheless satisfied with his unagitated heart rate, has the presence to count the trees in the front yard (seven), the number of steps up to the porch (five), the seconds that tick away (twelve) after he knocks and until the door swings open.

Into this doorway tentatively leans an elderly woman, the age of a grandmother, whose facial cast, subtly, is translatable to p. 104, fig. 84. He introduced himself, followed by his supposition. "Are you Ria's mother?"

Against the screen door her left hand rocked with a rhythmic flutter, possibly Parkinson's disease, possibly fright.

"Do you know who I am?" he asked. "Scott Bakkan. My letter from California arrived, I hope?" She appeared undecided on how safe it might be to let him inside. Scott spread on his best boyish smile. "I'm harmless, Mrs. Frazer."

The house was a time capsule of 1895 architecture, with tall ceilings, wide moldings, double-sashed windows, patterned rugs on oak floors. Its period furnishings also fit that era: overstuffed sofa and companion settee, massive oak armoire, beveled-glass oak hutch with a display of heirloom china, bookcases without a solitary paperback raising its flashy head. Overall, quietness.

Mrs. Frazer had food waiting for him, a "little breakfast supplement" she said, an obvious indication that this guest had been expected. From a quaint refrigerator, older even than Overton's, she took out a plate of fruit holding chilled wedges of melons—green melons and red—peach slices, and a bunch of plump grapes. On the rim of the plate she lined up a row of oatmeal cookies, home-baked. Bringing him a glass of orange juice she said, "You must be exhausted after such a journey, Mr. Bakkan. I can't conceive traveling that far, most especially by myself."

Her hand trembled setting down his glass and in a natural reaction he reached out to steady it with his own. The shaking did not stop. "Call me Scott, and don't be afraid of me," he said, after which they exchanged a frank look. She had her daughter's eye, but not Ria's eyes.

"I have a neurological affliction. Excuse my spilling it. Except, yes, I'm afraid."

"Of me?"

"More of what we've done *to* you."

"*To* me? I'm not blameless. My reason for coming the long way is to erase clean a sort of dirty slate. Ria and I can explain ourselves, apologize to each other for the confusions, and put an end to things."

Her head lowered, began a negative left-to-right swing, almost another palsy.

"Are you crying, Mrs. Frazer? You are. Why does this happen. Why do I make women cry. I'm the Typhoid Mary of hurt feelings."

"I'm ashamed."

"Ashamed?"

"I prayed, genuinely prayed, that I could, bravely, explain to you our circumstances. You earned that. But I'm not a brave person. Now here you are and I'm still not brave. I don't know how to speak, how to explain. I have only shame for my answers."

"Are we here in the house alone?"

"Yes, we are, Mr. Bakkan."

"Your husband's at his office?"

"My husband passed away years ago."

"Years ago. Then sad to find that out. I always thought of him—from his book—as a sturdy man who would practice medicine until age ninety."

"As a rule, doctors don't live long lives, and his was conceivably made shorter by our family hardships."

"He must have been a doctor out of the ordinary, to edit an academic text from a rural medical practice."

"Martin delighted in keeping up contacts at his old medical school in Chicago and regularly published in professional journals. Ria inherited his dedication." Mrs. Frazer locked her quaking fingers into a pyramid, a practical defense she must have devised against the tremors. "About Ria. Excuse me please . . . excuse . . . me."

"More tears. What's up exactly? Here, here, use my napkin. Why not tell me when to meet her today, and we'll stop at that."

"Mr. Bakkan, Mr. Bakkan."

"Call me Scott, just Scott. Now what are these tears?"

She blotted her face extensively, before asking, "Will you

indulge me in a request? Will you read a newspaper clipping first, before I try making a confession?" She shifted a formal photo album on the table in front of them, turning open the cover and retrieving the top item, a square of newspaper, which fluttered in her hand like a scrap of paper on a gusty day.

On the margin was inked the date May 9, 1934. "This is an obituary," said Scott.

"Yes, Ria's."

Yes, Ria's. Dr. Victoria Frazer, age 25, only child of Dr. and Mrs. Martin Frazer of New Hope, died from complications of the recent birth of a daughter.

"Reading the newspaper will convince you it's true," said Mrs. Frazer. "You would doubt me otherwise and I absolutely don't blame you. No, Mr. Bakkan, I wouldn't blame you for not trusting us at all."

"Excuse me, Mrs. Frazer," said Scott, "for correcting you, but there's been a muddling up of names, somehow, someway. This isn't the same Ria as mine."

"I wish it weren't. How I wish that."

"Stop with the crying. We'll figure out the mistake in a minute. Please calm down with the crying."

"Mr. Bakkan, Mr. Bakkan. No mistake."

"Listen. All these tears are pointless."

"Mr. Bakkan, Mr. Bakkan."

"Listen carefully. My Ria and I have been talking together, recently, in our letters."

"Oh dear, oh dear."

"Have I fallen down a rabbit hole somewhere? Are we off inside somebody's alternate world? I tell you, Ria and I have been exchanging letters. I *repeat*: I've been talking with her."

"Oh dear, oh dear."

"I hear myself almost shouting at you and that makes me feel bad. And I see that those tears on your face are real and that makes me feel bad, too, and it shakes me up, because I don't understand any of this. Mrs. Frazer, I don't understand."

"Oh, Mr. Bakkan."

Scott closed his eyes, or rather put the flat of his hand across his eyes, as if that would help him concentrate, or perhaps he only wanted to avoid that neatly trimmed newspaper clipping now dropped back into the old album. He said, "A picture of Ria was in your husband's anatomy textbook. Page 104. Age eighteen. Do you know what photograph I'm talking about, what textbook?"

Coughing from the teary sniffles that had found their way down her throat, Mrs. Frazer nodded her head.

"Is she the same Ria in this obituary?"

"Yes."

"What the hell then. You're telling me, proving to me, that Ria is dead."

"Yes."

Scott removed his hand from his eyes in order to look straight at Mrs. Frazer. "I want you to stop crying now. Please blot your face, take a breath or two."

"Thank you. Thank you."

"Deep breath again. Ready? Explain this obituary to me."

"Yes, Mr. Bakkan, yes." However no words came.

"Talk now."

"Yes, Mr. Bakkan, yes. I'll tell you more than anyone else has ever heard before, anyone, because you have the most right to hear it. Our Ria, your Ria, started interning upstate at the same hospital where Martin, my husband, once had, when suddenly she came home to have this baby. The episode hit us like a big big bombshell. Our Ria was pregnant? She wrote ahead, saying that we didn't know the father and we never would. The official birth certificate lists the father as unknown, although we believed Ria would, in time, give the whole story, secrecy not being Ria. But a secret it had to stay. The baby delivered normally and Ria took the baby with her to the bedroom upstairs, where the next day, in the afternoon, she called for me. I could barely hear her, she was already so very weak and covered with sweat. You've heard of childbed fever? Puerperal fever is the more technical term. They have better drugs to treat it nowadays. Ria, being a doctor herself, understood what had happened, and described a factual diagnosis after I telephoned Martin and we waited for him to hurry home. Likely part of the placenta had been left behind, she said, and that piece triggered an infection. My husband rushed her to the hospital, and that day, and that night, were horrible, with the doctors standing around helpless and poor Martin there with them. The infection had attacked her entire system with a massive shock. She was unconscious before midnight and dead before morning."

"You didn't, Mrs. Frazer, didn't send those letters to me."

"No."

"Don't take me wrong," said Scott, "but I'm desperate for a nap. My eyelids want to droop. I guess it's this news and those days spent in my car."

She led him upstairs to a spare bedroom along a central hallway. The album under Scott's arm contained those family photos of Ria that he once would have ransomed with his soul, and he laid the treasure tenderly beside him on the bed. Yet, at this moment, what he most would choose to see was *The Human Body*. That faithful companion of his had to be someplace in this house. Instead he simply formulates her image in his mind, as often done before, and sets about trying to swell Ria's maternal belly, trying to apply deadly sweat beads on her cheeks and a mortal glaze on her yearning eyes.

* * * *

For an evening meal Mrs. Frazer had prepared skillet-fried chicken breast, baked potato, vegetables from her garden, homemade bread, homemade pie with apples from a tree in the backyard, and she served it all with the attention of a Bakkan dinner. After eating, as he helped clear dishes, Scott said, "I've done the math, adding from the year 1934, which is my own birth year. I do this crazy math and I turn my sanity upside down and inside out. Was it Ria's daughter who wrote me those letters and decided to use her mother's name?"

Mrs. Frazer, about to carry away a bowl of sour cream, had to sit down promptly again at the dining table.

"Now don't fall apart on me again," said Scott. "If you start with the crying, I'm lost. And I'm already lost enough."

"Oh, oh."

"Just talk, Mrs. Frazer."

"Oh, oh,"

"Let the words come out. Why on earth did she use her mother's name?"

"Use her mother's name, yes and no." It was a foregone legal conclusion, she said, for the Frazers to adopt the baby when Ria died. Ria's daughter became their replacement daughter, "by default, and what a blessing, that saved us, Martin and me. He named the baby Victoria in memory of its mother and as a result we scarcely had to skip a single day without having a Ria in the same house."

"Well, well, Mrs. Frazer. I'm caught in the middle of a madhouse mess."

"I know, Mr. Bakkan."

He revisited his recent history, and deduced, "The daughter opened my first package assuming it was, I suppose, addressed to her. Correct?"

"Correct. Ria was in her senior year at the university, in

Urbana, but when this past spring I had myself a bout of bad health, my stroke, she returned and spent that semester at home until I recovered. Thankfully, she's back at school where she belongs instead of babysitting me."

"When she signed those letters to me, the name, literally, was her own and her mother's."

"Correct, correct. And, Mr. Bakkan, I allowed myself to telephone Ria already—during your nap—and she offers to come and express her regrets, in person, for the hardships she caused. I believe she'd like the opportunity. For weeks around here this summer she was . . . very stern with herself, very stern."

"No, please no, we'll avoid any meetings designed for regrets. The drama has cleared up sufficiently for me, at last, unless another surprise is waiting."

"None. I do ask you forgive Ria."

"I'm not resentful. No more than with my own self. Whatever our motives were, good or foolish, we both wasted too much emotion already."

"Wasted? Mr. Bakkan, Mr. Bakkan, that word is such a wrong one. Please realize that before you wrote here, Ria knew her mother only by the photographs in the album you have upstairs and by whatever Martin and I told her, which was limited. We didn't forbid the topic but it pained too much. With no memories of her own she had nothing genuine. I honestly believe it was impossible for her to care about her mother in any authentic way. You changed this. You came, pouring your attention into our other Ria, making her—dear heaven, yes—making her real." Mrs. Frazer stiffened her hands around the bowl, bracing herself. "She never showed me your letters. I only had to watch her face. And imagine what, Mr. Bakkan. I didn't want you to stop writing either. I encouraged her to answer. I did. How awful to admit that in front of you. But letter by letter, watching Ria read them, I could feel my daughter in the house again."

"Where are those letters now?"

"At first your letters surprised us so much," she said, overleaping his question, "that we couldn't wake up from the surprise and stop ourselves. We jumped to take advantage of you. I must repeat that again and again, how we took advantage of you. I went to the extreme of wishing, without an ounce of common sense, without an *ounce,* that somehow you could be the nice helpful man who would bring happiness to both of my Rias. Each one deserved you. Ria could see her mother being loved by someone, like a flesh-and-blood woman is loved, and mother and daughter were partners in it. The impossible was happening in our house . . . Ria smiling for her mother or with her mother or . . . or however this should be described."

With darkness, Scott accepted Mrs. Frazer's urgings to spend the night and rest himself before his California return. He hauled in his luggage from the Ford. After a hot soaking in the clawfoot tub that had once held Ria's body, he retired to the bedroom, where a ceiling light, from an earlier era of modest wattage, cast down its subdued wash.

Obviously he had found his mission in life, or a mission found him, no matter how far away Scott traveled. His purpose was to rescue the lonely, the aging, the dying, and trickiest of all, the dead. Few could match his skills with the latter. For his uncle Spencer he did the Lazarus stunt by pulling a fistful of poetry out of a cardboard box. For Ria he managed it with a barrage of postal letters, and he had proof that his creations were dimensional enough, solid enough, to convince other people besides himself. Congratulations, maestro.

Scott sat on the bed beside the album. To demonstrate his control over p. 104 he should not bother to open it. Yet would the more honest proof be to look at dead Ria?

Downstairs he heard the front door thunk and subsequent calls of greeting, one voice Mrs. Frazer's, the unknown voice, a young woman's. The sounds lowered, trailing off in the direction of the kitchen, where tableware clatter suggested a snack in preparation. In due course footsteps climbed the stairs and passed lightly by Scott's room. At the end of the hallway the other bedroom door opened and closed. From inside, a squeaky dresser drawer slid out and back, twice. Scott balled a fist and punched the mattress under him. Here was another loose end to tie up, another unraveled thread to knot. How even to categorize the person over there tonight: Ria in her bed? Ria in Ria's bed?

* * * *

He opened the album to Victoria Frazer as baby. As their first born—their only born—the proud parents had documented Ria exceptionally well for the period: baby fresh from the hospital swaddled like a papoose, baby at one week propped up in a bassinet, baby in mother's arms, baby in father's arms, baby at one month, baby with (presumably) grandparents, baby at three months, baby, baby, generic baby. The standard sequence continued into toddler shots, progressive birthday scenes, holidays, outings, pets, school, interleaved with report cards, piano recital programs, samples of questionable art, and sundry evidence of evolving childhood.

Scott paused, taking stock of his emotional condition. He felt stable at the core. Ria was a cute kid, and while a melancholy did press its weight on him, that natural pang and twinge had an appropriate place, when reviewing the sadly brief span of a dead girl and bidding her goodbye.

"Cecilia," he said aloud, "this is working out as we planned, lucky us."

He paged forward again. Here is a seventh grade report card, where teacher Mrs. Eloise Andersen meticulously looped in ink: "May I keep Victoria in my class for ever and ever?" Here is Ria with an impish grin and her outspread hands blocking the rest of her face. Here is Ria in the room down the hall, lying on her bed surrounded by books, her shoes off and bare toes up, a frown protesting the interruption. Here is her fourteenth birthday picture. Ria sits behind her cake with its lit candles, ready to attempt her obligatory part, leaning ahead, the hair swung forward, framing her face, the eyes upward to accommodate the camera. Crouching around her is a gaggle of mugging adolescents. No one else, nothing else, in the photograph matters other than Ria's eyes.

With the next pictures, the same. Each separate one demands recognition from Scott. Slowly, he turned pages, and they turned him. In Ria's graduation portrait from high school, the identical twin of Fully Pubescent Female, Age 18, looks inescapably at Scott, demonstrating finally what he had always suspected, that clothes would never have covered the nakedness of page 104, figure 84. Four years later, in another graduation portrait pasted opposite her baccalaureate diploma, Ria's hair is shorter, her face paler, her lips more separated with the shadow between them deeper. Her expression tells him: "I studied hard in college to learn answers. But nobody else asked me your questions."

He has to reply back: "Ria, are you saying that, after all, you're not merely my cerebral will-o'-the-wisp? That I didn't invent the Victoria Frazer behind the paper face? Because I vow, Ria, when I see you in this album, it has nothing to do with abstractions. I'm not Keats, rhyming the maidens he found on an ancient Grecian urn. His poem may be fine praise of timeless beauty and art, but only a verbal shadow molded around the actual stone. I have the opposite, the substance around the shadow."

Twenty-six

Scott must have slept, because he wakes up. Elemental logic is a friend when blue eyes show weary reds.

Already the sun floods his room. Downstairs he apologized to Mrs. Frazer for oversleeping, and she hardly let him finish, sympathizing, "You're way behind on rest," busily toasting slices of yesterday's home-baked bread and setting down a selection of jams, with a plump banana. "If you don't object, your breakfast is on the light side to save your appetite for a large picnic lunch at the lake. Ria's mother went there frequently. I thought you might enjoy some short sightseeing."

"Is this heavenly jam your own?"

"A neighbor makes it. Ria came home from school last night and I asked her to serve as tour guide, if that's agreeable." Mrs. Frazer rapped on a window at the rear of the kitchen. "She's out in the backyard, checking the garden for me." She rapped again. "We'll bring her inside for an introduction. Ria told me emphatically she needed to drive back tonight in order not to miss more classes, but an afternoon at the lake should give you two a good visit."

"My compliments to your neighbor."

At Ria's entrance—the back porch door snugging shut behind her—a lengthy mutual examination was avoided by letting formality engage its gears. Scott stood up from the table. Mrs. Frazer presented their names. Ria came forward with a courteous smile. At first appearance she was not a copy of her mother. While Scott dipped his head in a slight bow, Ria (it seemed) flexed her knees in a perceptible curtsy. They even exchanged a firm handshake.

Mrs. Frazer proceeded to pack and inventory their lunch: Ham with Mustard Glaze ("mix brown sugar, dry mustard, fruit juice; stud ham with cloves, spoon with glaze"), boiled eggs, Cheese Stuffed Apples ("blend softened cream cheese with touch of white wine"), Molasses Corn Muffins, whole pickles, whole tomatoes, celery sticks, crackers, leftover apple pie, freshly baked Cocoa Ripple Ring Loaf ("sprinkle instant cocoa powder and crushed walnuts directly into batter"), lemonade and ice in a thermos.

"That'll probably do," said Ria, squeezing her grandmother's shoulder, "probably do for at least six people." She addressed her as "Nan."

Scott told Mrs. Frazer, "You ought to meet my mother. The

two of you are stellar kitchen personalities."

* * * *

The Ford at last had a Ria sitting in it, as Scott drove to the village square again, by the elementary school again, past the house once occupied by Mrs. Frazer's own parents—all this viewing and reviewing important local spots where p. 104 had spent her years. A few miles out of town was Spring Lake, gathered within a crease in the low undulating watershed, held back by a rocked spillway. Other than an older man walking his piebald puppy the park area had no other human figures, only its vacant launching ramp and a rickety rental stand for rowboats, closed until the weekend.

"I know a picnic table right at the water's edge," said Ria.

They carried their baskets to the table and went on to explore the lake before eating. Huge maples lined the way, the branches a canopy of spectacular florid dyes on October leaves, and under this kaleidoscope of magenta, burnt orange, bleached green, flame yellow, Ria remarked, without any preamble, "Nan says you don't wish to hear any apology for my letters. That's generous of you, very generous. Excuse me if I just did apologize anyway."

"I have my own apologizing to do."

Back at the picnic table they set out the food, with Scott pouring the lemonade, Ria arranging the plates and utensils. Down at their feet early afternoon sunshine flittered on the lake. Wavelets along its shore—a baby Santa Cruz surf—dragged gently against roots and sand. Ria said, "This is the strangest sensation, us sitting here. You over there. Me over here. We exist but we don't. We're together but we aren't. It's like we're inside each other's hallucination."

"And at a picnic at that."

"Do you agree? Have you ever felt more awkward?"

"100-percent not."

They served themselves and busily ate for a time. "When Nan phoned me yesterday," said Ria, "she hinted that you wanted me to come home. You didn't say any such thing, did you."

"No."

"I suspected as much. Shame on her."

"What was her motive?"

"She likes you a lot. By instinct. And to be blunt about it, I believe Nan wishes we come together as a pair, the two of us, or that maybe we already are together. Where one Ria finds happiness, so does the other, is the idea. My whole life my grandmother and grandfather would mix me with my mother—not mix us *up*, understand, but *mix* us. Half of me was my mother when they called me 'Ria' and the other half was the new Ria. For that reason Nan will never grasp why I wouldn't dare to love you, or how the idea frightens me into shreds, because I couldn't bring myself to look into your face day after day and wonder which Ria you were seeing. When I read those letters of yours, I constantly reminded myself it was my mother's picture you had in your mind, when you wrote the words."

"I won't say you're wrong. Turns out I have serious trouble

forgetting your mother. Even dead I have trouble with her. I'm embarrassed to admit how my tongue sticks when I try calling you *Ria*. I need to practice more."

"Don't be embarrassed. I grew up with the same problem myself. Think back to everywhere we've been today, including here. Think about our house. My mother wasn't the only little girl raised there. She wasn't the only Ria who hunted for Easter eggs at the park. She wasn't the only Frazer girl who went to that school we saw this morning. Everywhere, I tagged along behind her, and my circle followed inside her circle. We took music lessons from the same fussy bald piano teacher. For all practical reasons we had the same parents. We heard Peter Rabbit stories read in the same pseudo-British accent by the same dear motherly woman. The same gentle fatherly man liked to brush our hair on Sundays. We ate the same foods—these stuffed apples, for instance. We got the same double goodnight hug. Why, think about it, I duplicate my mother so perfectly I automatically answer her private mail for her, right?"

"And answer it well," said Scott. "About the stuffed apples, they're tasty. I was skeptical and now I'm won over." They sampled the other food. "You study pre-med to take your mother's place as the next Dr. Frazer?"

"No. I major in psychology. As the joke goes, that's the subject where all the neurotic students hope to learn enough to cure themselves. When I was younger I did expect to do the expected and become a doctor. Then I watched my grandfather. He treated about twenty patients a day, one of those possibly deathly ill, most not, but whichever, he had to give each a fair share of his day's energy. He had to show them his total interest, he told me, because that's an ingredient of good medicine. I admired my grandfather's discipline but knew I could never spread myself around like that. My method would be to take the incurable few and splurge on those and have nothing left over for the ones who are just normally sick."

The glazed ham and the corn muffins made an especially flavorful combination, their curious mustard-molasses contrast stimulating the surprised taste buds. Ria put the thermos and a dessert selection into the smallest basket, suggesting they finish the meal out on the lake, in a rowboat.

"I've never rowed a boat before," warned Scott.

Ria had done it often. They only needed to tip a boat off the dock, toss in the oars that had been stored underneath, shove clear, and she would row. "I'll bring by two dollars when Mr. Metzer has the stand open. He's the World War I veteran who rules the place from a wheelchair. His usual greeting to me is, 'Your ma was a darlin', too.' Then he scowls to show that I'd better believe him."

As claimed, she could handle a boat, and without a splash of the oars sent it scooting to the middle of the lake, where they ate their apple pie and crunchy sugar loaf and drifted to the whims of a quirky breeze. When they leaned back, savoring the sweets, the impression of floating between sky and water brought a pleasant vertigo, and they debated whether the blurry bar of clouds overhead was passing them, or their boat was passing the clouds.

"Sorry, that I'm not as pretty as my mother," said Ria, "which is one difference between us at least. Anyway I'm not a good candidate for romance, or certainly not for marriage."

"No?"

"Like us in this rowboat, romance for me goes adrift without any known destination. I might, by chance, bump into somebody and bounce straight backward again. Action, reaction."

"Must be a law of social physics."

"Here's what happens. No, you don't want to hear about it. You do? You do. So, I notice a young man's profile behind the window of a car speeding past, and immediately his face haunts me, or even more, the fact that the car is leaving me behind, haunts me. Who is he? I have an urge to chase after him and get a second peek. Or on the street I might notice a particular sweep of masculine hair. A sight that minor. Or a dozen deep syllables heard penetrating through other voices. A sound that simple. I speculate on these moments. I go home, get in bed, toss and turn through the night, fretting about fate. I'm infatuated with this tease of possibilities. It's the potential that I fall for!"

Scott treated himself to another chunk of Cocoa Ripple Ring. "Ever talk to one of these passing possibilities?"

"My relationships turn into a process of mutual deflation. Therefore I'll end up an old maid, though still tossing and turning at night. The best rule is just plain to give up chasing those love ghosts altogether.”

“You could try my solution. Fall in love with perfect words in books. If about a woman in a book, then a woman made unchangeable by the language.”

“Thanks for the tip. Did my mother’s book accomplish that without the words?”

Scott said, “You ought to study psychology.”

Ria picked up the oars and began stroking, slowly, moving the boat only to counter the drift. Above them the clouds also braked. “What would you’ve said to my mother, if she’d been at the house yesterday?”

“Probably ‘Hello, Dr. Frazer.’ I’d have been respectful.”

“But after that. If she sat here right now, where I am, what would you ask her?”

“Nothing melodramatic.”

“If she were suddenly right here and you could ask her only one question before she vanished again?”

“You’re raising the stakes.”

“One question. One chance.”

Scott poured himself a partial cup of lemonade, drinking it, before saying, “Then I’d ask her if anyone had ever kissed away that shadow between her lips.”

“Oh dear,” said Ria. “Oh, you have a way with final questions, don’t you?” She picked up the thermos to pour her own drink.

“I’d like to try rowing,” decided Scott. “We’ll aim for that cove up ahead and try the shade for a while. Our last topic is somehow making me sweat."

She balanced the boat. "Changing seats can be sort of tricky. When we switch remember to keep our weight as much in the middle as possible. Ready . . . set . . . go." Crossing in the same narrow space they scraped shoulders, the boat lurched, and they reacted by grabbing hands as the green thermos with its silver top jettisoned in a parabolic arc, to plop into the water. They sat in their new places until the rocking diminished. Ria shouted out, "Thermos overboard! Can you save it?"

"I'd throw the life preserver," he said, "if we had one. Let me try reaching without tipping the boat." The thermos began to sink, green disappearing down into green. "Too late. I can just make out its silver head. Oops . . . gone. Who gets to report the bad news to your grandmother back home?"

"Reporting one cask of lemonade lost at sea, sir."

Scott positioned the oars. After a jagged course into the cove, he said, "You resisted snickering over my rowing. I value that." The boat grounded on a shelf in the shallows, bobbing there as if at anchor. Tree limbs, reaching out over the water from all points along the cove, obscured the sky, and when an occasional leaf dropped, its color on the lake appeared as an unnaturally bright reflection of the color above. Inside this dimmer and protected enclosure, Scott and Ria stayed silent, listening to the accentuated sounds of water on soil, water against boat, water against water. Although Scott and Ria sat on facing seats, scant inches between them—between bent knees to bent knees—the closeness did not lead them into any conversation.

At last Ria said, "About that shadow and her lips. I did lots of checking, and from what I could find out, you were the only boyfriend she ever had. In the meantime, she was dedicated to her career. She must have been excellent at waiting."

Scott extended and extended his reluctance to ask a question. By dropping a relaxed hand into the water, his fingers became separate floating parts of the lake's flux. Then the question did come. "I wonder how to explain . . . you."

"Where I came from. Who my actual dad is. When I was an older kid and wondered myself about it, I could see the subject was hopeless for my grandparents. I stopped asking. Later, when I figured out the best answer, practically the only answer, I kept it to myself, because I didn't like hearing it either."

"Let's drop it. Let's not ruin our picnic."

"I've never told anyone, never."

"Then don't tell me."

"I always wished, truly, for one other person to know. This isn't what a polite hostess does, but afterward, after you leave, we won't have difficulties keeping our secret, with you in California, me back here."

"I don't want you to be unhappy today."

"Ah, I won't be unhappy. This isn't new business for me. Just the sharing is new, and maybe you're already guessing . . ."

"Maybe."

". . . that my daddy had to be a rapist. Half of my genes come from a thug."

Scott raised his hand from the water, noting how the drops fell back from his fingers, fast into fewer, until a last droplet clung to the tip of his ring finger. He shook it free. Ria thanked him for listening. She asked, "Have I, added up, thanked you too many times in one day?" The sun had noticeably lowered its angle, and since more skilled at it, Ria rowed homeward across the lake.

"So let me thank you instead, for doing all the hard sailor work," said Scott, leaning back for the ride.

* * * *

Mrs. Frazer considered the lost thermos bottle a funny story. She had dinner preparations well underway and the picnic food went straight into the refrigerator. After they ate Ria checked the clock and sighed, deciding it was too late to leave for school until morning. To help fill the remainder of the evening Scott and Ria tried a moonlight tour of the garden, where the chilled air clouded their breathing as they hurried around a rectangular plot marked by twine and stakes, peering at broken rows of vegetables. "We're seeing the end of things here," pointed out Ria. "It's not attractive anymore with the season about over."

"The garden as metaphor," said Scott.

She nodded, turning toward him. "Garden as metaphor. You have the exact quote to support that ready on your tongue, I'm sure, a gem from Emerson or Whitman, yet you haven't quoted any great authors for me since you arrived, or any ordinary ones."

"I'm quitting cold turkey."

"What a waste."

"The general public would disagree."

Hunched in their coats, before stepping into the house again they glanced back at the yard and the moon. She asked, "Do you Californians own winter mittens? And I wonder, do you miss California?"

"Let me think. No more than California misses me."

Inside, welcoming the warmth, they settled into the plush upholstery of the parlor sofas, as Mrs. Frazer exited with an early goodnight, promising Ria "your favorite breakfast before you drive back." At that, Scott and Ria were left alone in an extremely still house.

"I can't offer you any lemonade," said Ria, "but how about some tea?"

"The memory of our lemonade will last me."

"No tea then."

"I insist you're through spoiling the guest. Your day's work is done."

More quietness, and Ria said, "I could offer you some decent chitchat, except . . ."

"Right. Except we don't want to hear it."

"Right. No small talk. Preferably no talk than small talk. Wait here a couple of seconds?" She went upstairs, coming back with a folded white envelope. "This is for you to keep." Unfolding the envelope, Scott counted five lengthy strands of dark hair, which he believed, with a lurch, he should recognize.

"They belong to your real Victoria," said Ria. "Real hair. Years ago I discovered a drawer where Nan had put away a small cache of my mother's personal items, including her hairbrush. Down in the bristles I saw these hairs, twisting every which way, and I carefully, carefully, teased them out with a bobby pin. No, no, I won't take them back—they mean more to you than me. Now you can touch her as much as her daughter ever has. I'll be leaving before eight o'clock in the morning. If I don't see you, a last thanks for your long trip here, and a last thanks on behalf of my mother. I feel we three have settled quite a bit between us. Could we shake hands again"—they did—"and I'll repeat what Nan keeps repeating to me, that you're a likable fellow, Mr. Bakkan."

Twenty-seven

The neighbor who made the jams also kept chickens and a rooster, and when it crowed Scott had his eyes open, facing across his pillow at the window, where last night's moonlight was fading on the curtains. He stayed in bed to watch that moonglow be replaced by dawn. Then the bedroom and bathroom doors down the hall opened and closed, in circular sequence, a pattern he repeated himself after rising and dressing.

Back in his room he made the bed and lay on it again. From downstairs Mrs. Frazer called out, softly, "Breakfast's ready . . ."

Scott and Ria met in the hallway. "Good morning," they greeted each other. An amusing action was that they formally shook hands, for the third time in less than twenty-four hours.

"I wanted to say goodbye before you left," said Scott, "but it came out as good morning."

Mrs. Frazer's voice floated up louder: "Breakfast. Ready!"

Ria told Scott, "Good morning isn't wrong. I decided to leave later this afternoon. Less hectic for me that way."

"Then an appropriate good morning."

"Good morning."

"And again good morning again."

"Say now," asked Ria, "do you want to step into my bedroom? Said the spider to the fly."

Mrs. Frazer had moved to the foot of the stairs. Cocking her head she listened, hesitant, before putting a hand beside her mouth, megaphone style. "Hello! Hello! Does anybody up there hear this?"

* * * *

With the door closed behind them, Ria's room was sealed shut, full of silvery grays and pale ochres and smelling like freshly shampooed hair. They stood barely inside the bedroom without any momentum to go farther.

Ria said, with a shake, or a sideways whip of her damp hair, "To barrel ahead about this announcement, when I finished my bath this morning I came out still unclean. Next, just now, I told you another little lie. And I don't like not feeling clean. Anyway the truth is, well, the truth is, I won't be driving back to campus this afternoon either."

"You have classes this afternoon?"

"I'm ignoring them."

"Ignoring them?" asked Scott.

"Ignoring them. Good morning again."

"And good afternoon. But why ignoring them?"

"Because I don't like feeling unclean this way. I despise it."

"Maybe I can help you," said Scott. "You ought to practice lying more. Build it up like any other skill. Practice, practice, practice, no different from training to run a race. I myself can tell lies without even making a sound."

"For instance?"

"For instance, the classic lie of omission. What if I could tell you about a bubble of warmth inside me from hearing that you'll stay here this afternoon. But I don't."

"I see. But you have no idea how big my own silent lies are. The biggest."

"From what I know about you, I can't believe it."

"That's why they're big."

"You enjoy criticizing yourself. It's an endearing trait."

"You think I'm lying about my lying?"

"I suspect not many people are as honest as you. I remember you yesterday at the lake."

"Seems you think I can't tell a big lie."

"Ria, not up in my league, never in my league."

"Bragging, are we. You want to test who the biggest liar is? Listen, friend, right now when I cutely claimed about just deciding to stay here this afternoon, that was a lie."

"It was a lie?"

"I probably *never* intended on going back to campus today. It was a lie because I doubt I'll go back tomorrow. I doubt I'll go back the day after tomorrow. It looks like I won't leave this house that I sometimes hate until you do."

"Well now."

"Well now."

"What if I stay . . . a month?"

"I guess I'll stay a month."

"Now you are really lying."

"Think so? You decided I couldn't say a big lie but now you can't be certain which it is, can you, a lie or the truth, and whether to believe me or not."

"I just lied about my bubble of warmth inside," Scott said.

"You did?"

"I have the bubble, except the truth is, since you want honesty, not a cheerful or pleasant bubbly bubble. It reminds me of that bile that used to scald my chest during the last 200 yards of a hard mile race. I didn't like the pain then, and don't like it now."

"And you won't tell me why it hurts."

"No, because I'm the superior silent liar. Admitting a weakness is a worse weakness."

"Okay, Mr. Bakkan," she said, "if you want big silent lies, here's one."

"Don't say it. Let's stop with these confessions. Let's quit."

"I lied, by not informing you first thing yesterday that I have your letters at my dorm, in a drawer by my bed, my *bed,* an easy reach away."

"You do?"

"I do."

"I brought your letters with me across eight states. I think it's eight."

"I take your letters out of that drawer and hold them more than eight times a week."

"No, you don't."

"I do."

"Is that 'I do' a lie or the truth?"

"The truth, the ridiculous truth."

"Guess what. I could repeat, almost verbatim, the heart of all thirty-three of your letters, probably in chronological order. Does that surprise you?"

"I know about your memory, but it does surprise me."

From out in the hallway, interrupting, Mrs. Frazer's voice was heard, apologetically loud, excessively clipped, anxious to get to the message. "Hello! Everybody. To notify. Just notifying. Breakfast *not* ready. Not until later. My mistake. Sorry and goodbye!"

"Good grief," said Scott, "now we have your grandmother spinning lies."

Twenty-eight

"I need to sit," said Ria, moving in a rush to her bed, where she plopped down with a graceless irritated flounce, her cotton dress sticking in a rumpled clump above bare knees. The morning sun now fills the east windows completely, brightening the bedroom, in disharmony with the tight darkened breathing of Scott and Ria.

"Did you shampoo your hair this morning?" asked Scott.

"Yes. Why are you sniffing?"

"The better to smell you, Little Red Riding Hood. And you smell tastier even than whatever delicious food Grandmother cooked down in the kitchen and is fibbing about. And for the first time I can describe that hair color, your hair color, and most things about you, your complexion, your height, your whole body."

"You were with me all yesterday."

"I was looking and not seeing."

"What does that mean?"

"Are the words in the letters all yours?"

"Yes, yes. Only a sentence or two in the first letter came from my mother's diary, those about her eighteenth birthday—they were perfect to what I wanted to say—and using her words made my pretending to be her feel legitimate, or in the beginning I fooled myself into believing that excuse. But I know you don't want to hear another apology."

"We never needed apologies."

"You're still looking at me?"

"Trying not to see you. I'm trying not to know you, not really."

"Scott Bakkan, don't I want you to see me?"

"Listen. I want this conversation to stop but it won't. Just listen. If truth is what everyone needs, here it is. I came to your house for an ending, not a dreamster's fairy-tale beginning where the dead queen's daughter shows up with the same name and a crown already on her head. A conclusion is what Scott Bakkan requires. Every story, to follow the rules, demands its *finis*. Ria, what if you do rival your mother, either clothes on or clothes off. What if, in the flesh, you match the letters you sent. What comes after?"

"What comes after."

"When I learned about your mother's death, after the shock a whisper of relief spoke up, advising me how helpful this information was. Now I had Ria from page 104 locked away in a handy box, a secure box, where she could never get out and change herself, and if in the future I needed to peek inside the box, during any spare minute I had, I could."

"I understand."

"You're not crying, are you?"

"No. I don't cry when I'm sad. I grind my teeth. You probably hear my teeth grinding right now."

"Good, because finding tissues for crying women, when I don't have any, has tuckered me out."

Ria fidgeted on the bed. Presently she said, "If you promise to look at me, I'll tell you my biggest lie. My biggest lie because I lied to myself and not only to you."

"I might not survive your biggest lie. Is that fair to me?"

"But I want to tell it. I want to hear it told. If you watch me I can believe that I have a witness."

He did, in every sense, open his eyes, and the room seemed to shimmer, causing him to blink. Ria's hair with its drying ringlets was brown, the palest of browns, as was her skin, which appeared darker contrasted against a white dress patterned with solid vermilion diamonds, the dress still lodged above the knees, where her own focus had become fixed—and not at Scott.

"Mother," said Ria. "My mother. I never had much emotion about her. A kid's curiosity, some of that, and a daughter's fuzzy nostalgia for a missing mother. All that changed when one day you brought her to life. Oh, god, it was a great exciting novelty for a week or two or three, discovering my mother because you had discovered her, and you falling in love with her as a living woman. That didn't last. While you and Nan worked hard at making her alive, the daughter, the other Victoria, began wishing she would stay buried. Scott, I had no intention of sharing you. You belonged to me. I got *mad* at my mother for using *my* name. Hear that? Mean, aren't I? I should have thanked my mother for motivating you to write—because how lucky that the old book, with page 104, somehow found its way out to California—but I didn't grant her the credit, couldn't. Couldn't. Instead I went on pretending to be her and writing you back, and lying and lying, and resenting and resenting. Even now, hearing you talk about her, I want to reach back, if only I could, and rip out her handful of diary words from my letter. They spoil—she spoils—my partnership with you."

"Ria, is anything in your letters a lie? Any of it?"

"You know there isn't."

"Then I believe you. I'm afraid I believe you. But inside a wider view maybe we were all living a lie without speaking lies. My generation goof-up about your mother was a kind of untruth."

"No. You saw my mother and you loved the person you saw in the photograph. That was real. The tingle of your words was all genuine from first to last. I felt that tingle in my own body, although sometimes it was more a sting, more a sweet pain, because you were impossible for me. Absolutely I could feel your love myself, and silly as it sounds, I fell in love with your love. I never expected actually to meet you, Scott, not with the age separation I thought you chose to ignore from afar, ignore for the sake of your darling page 104, and would always keep at a distance, you carefully off far away in California. My sneaky consolation was that I could at least have you by being a secret substitute. But I never for once believed we would come together and I never even took the trouble to hope it might happen."

"And now here this Scott is in your bedroom."

Twenty-nine

From her perch on the bed, facing now back up at Scott, Ria said, "We have a copy of *The Human Body* here in the house. I never opened it as a child, but after your first letter I undressed in front of a mirror—that one, that full-length mirror in the corner over there—and wondered what Scott Bakkan would think about me, if I had been a page in his book. I'm not beautiful, you agree? Sshhh, wait, wait. No lies, remember. If you lie once, I can't believe anything you say. So again, I'm not beautiful, agree?"

"Beautiful. What the devil does an opinion like that represent. What logic can it have?"

"No fancy lies either, please."

"What fancy lies?"

"You know. Your cowardly politeness. Answer the question."

"All right. What most people describe as beautiful, you're not."

"Fine. You can walk over and sit on the bed."

"I don't want to sit on the bed."

"Maybe you shouldn't, but please come and sit by me."

"Ria, it could be wrong. We both are too ready to bamboozle ourselves into something or other."

"It could be wrong."

The bed was soft, invitingly soft, fit for a Ria or "a Princess and the Pea test," said Scott. "I'm full of folktale allusions today."

"Here we sit," Ria said. "See how courageous we are?"

"I don't feel courageous."

"I'm such a virgin, in every category imaginable—you wouldn't believe it. Put your hand on me. How about on the knee there? I see that my knees are uncovered."

"I won't do any touching. Already I feel our trickery starting. I feel that urge people have to give their lonely selves a treat."

"Am I the only brave one?"

Since the back of a hand is more sensitive than the front, Scott tipped his over and glided it up the slope of Ria's leg. "You must have shaved this morning. So did I."

"Which is the smoothest?"

"On your shin versus my chin, we tie. But behind, on this polished curve that for some dumb reason is called a calf, you win. My cheek has no chance against your soleus and your gastrocnemius."

"Where'd you learn the anatomy lingo?"

"A runner's preoccupation with the body. Look at this. Your knee. Sure, everyone's knee gets high marks for engineering, and functions super for a hinge. Yet aesthetically, normally, the knee is a loser. Believe me, check a thousand sets of knees and you see bony, lumpy, bumpy knobs. Yours are the thousand-and-first. You have beautiful knees."

"Well sir, I'll take beauty wherever you find it, young man. I assume that you wouldn't care enough to lie about anything so humble as a knee."

"No, no lying. Notice how your knee snuggles symmetrically into the palm of my hand when I cup it. It would be a pleasure to watch these legs in action, running around a track."

"That was my dream, for months, to watch this S. Bakkan guy run. The idea of you in motion in a race thrills me with curiosity. Tomorrow I could buy you the proper shoes and there's a school athletic field about nine miles away."

* * * *

His left hand remains on Ria's right knee. Meanwhile the sun has risen toward the upper boundary of those bedroom windows, or more technically, the earth has rotated another twenty minutes eastward. Twittering birds are active outside.

"My hand's still on your knee," said Scott.

Ria told him, "I never mentioned it before, but I'm seven months older than you are. And I believe you usually prefer older women."

"Very observant. However my list of preferred women is definitely short."

"How short would that be?"

"I should remove my hand."

"Should you?"

"What do I know about anything. My hand would have moved by now, I suppose, if my hand wanted to move. Apparently the thing has a mind of its own. Apparently my hand has an attraction to beautiful knees. Apparently I have no idea what apparently means."

Ria, as if to comfort him, placed her right hand atop his left hand, there on her knee. "Will you ever forget my mother? Will you put her away in that box you planned for her and keep it shut tight, locked up forever? No lies."

"No lies," said Scott. "Besides, you know my answer."

"How do I know the answer?"

"Because yesterday, at the lake, you explained why you could never love me, or marry me at least. And because of that now you want me to remove my hand?"

But Ria had another request. She asked Scott to lift her legs and swing her over flat on the bed. Once there, she placed her head back, fanning her hair across a pillow even whiter than her dress. "Please," she said, "shift up here. Please look down into my face."

This shift Scott did, by positioning his palms on the pillow, one on each side of her head. Ria reached up to put a finger on his cheekbone, remarking, "It's somehow cheating to have blue eyes this blue."

"It's the Bakkan iris, from out of the fjords of Norway."

"Keep looking down. Let's not glance away. It's necessary."

"This must be why this spot is named a temple," said Scott, reaching out himself. "I get a shiver of solemnity by touching you there, along your hairline, on this circlet that we rub when we meditate. And this hair. When do girls first learn about the powers of their hair? I figure that mothers instruct their daughters, when around age thirteen, 'Shampoo your hair thoroughly, pumpkin dear, add in silkwood oils, with a tincture of myrrh, comb and brush until stardust hits every highlight, and then one day you simply give your hair a slight toss, or let it gather on your shoulders, or on the back of a car seat, or on a *pillow,* and any boy you wish for, you can have.' Did I guess it about right?"

"Mothers deserve every respect that they earn. I learned that lesson from you. Whoever earns Scott's respect has mine." Ria moved her upward hand higher, warning, "And now I'm going to use *your* hair," and grabbing a fistful of his hair, she tugged it forcefully downward. "Open your eyes wide. Come closer. Ria the daughter is going to search inside you for something critical. It frightens me, but anyhow I'm going ahead. I'm going to chance everything, everything, to find out."

"Well, you're frightening *me*. Find out what?"

"Find the person who wrote me the most important words I have ever read. These words I memorized the way you memorize. These words, two dozen words, I repeated to myself again and again and again, middle of the night, middle of the day, and at this instant, here, I keep repeating them."

"What words?"

"You'll remember them. You will, you will. Only, I must see the words in these blue eyes of yours right now."

"Tell me the words."

"You were writing, or speaking to me—speaking was how the letters always seemed—and you were talking about not wanting to end up as the only human being in your own life. And Scott, you said, 'Love is the only idealism in this world you can actually get your hands on, while . . .' Can you finish your own sentence?"

Scott said that he could.

"Finish it for me. I want to hear you and see you saying that sentence out loud."

"I'll verbally italicize it for you. *Love is the only idealism in this world you can actually get your hands on, while at the same time it puts hands on you.*"

"Are you the same Scott who told me that before, and who still believes what he told me?"

There are painful moments when lies plead to be used.

"You won't talk to me?" asked Ria.

There are moments when real thieves should claim real innocence.

"You don't want to talk," said Ria. Her face, showing the first heavy shades of concern, even of panic, agitated further his own helplessness, his own panic.

"More silence," said Ria.

"Silence because telling you hurts me. But tell I will. I borrowed those words from an uncle of mine."

"From an uncle?"

"An uncle, an uncle I steal from a lot. He's long dead. During the war."

"Oh." Ria absorbed this truncated information with a patient nod. "Your dead uncle. Sorry. And just when I could use him, your uncle."

At that Scott almost replies, "I already used him for you," but instead he is swallowing, is gagging, on a bitter discovery, the discovery that the man Ria seeks in this room is Spencer, not Scott. Or, more yet, between the two of them here on the bed, Ria herself is the Spencer. Or, more yet, this Ria is a woman who would have saved Spencer Lemay's life, if waiting for him in Augsburg, Germany, in place of Silke Wolke. What if, what the damnation if, his uncle might be a wiser one, at the end of the end, and the nephew a dim disbeliever? Was Scott the cardboard box of poison, and Spencer the antidote? "His name was—it is—Spencer Lemay. I want you to hear the sound of his name. I probably should honor his bones, wherever they are."

"Wherever they are?"

"Wherever they are. It takes unraveling an ancient family saga to explain Spencer Lemay. But I can guarantee you this much, Ria. If my uncle Spencer were the man on this bed, looking down the way I am, at your face, directly at your face, he would be devoting himself to you. That I can swear."

Ria lowered her hands to her sides, then crossed them at her chest, and closed her eyes, sighing in drowsy tones, "Someone understands this S. Bakkan more than S. Bakkan understands S. Bakkan."

"Someone. My uncle does?"

"I do, obviously. This Ria."

The sun is above the window. Ria's eyes are peacefully shut. He watches the brown hands on the white dress rising and falling, rising and falling. He studies her as only unaware sleepers can be studied, without reservations. "Ria," he says, "I may have lied earlier. Or it was a mistake, in fact, not a lie."

"What lie?" she murmurs.

"I'm looking at you now. And I see that the whole of you might be beautiful, head to toe. All of you maybe."

No response comes from Ria and those eyes stay firmly closed.

He asks, "Ria? Asleep?"

"No. Only sleepy thinking, old-fashioned daydreaming, with my eyes shut."

"And thinking about?"

"About what we'll do first. About whether we go down below for breakfast, or whether we kiss instead."

Scott checked at the windows, as off in the distance, in a broad sky, a ragged flock of birds sailed by, southward, beneath loose strands of clouds. "From what I judge, outside these windows, it's more lunchtime already than breakfast. We should show your grandmother some courtesy, and go to the kitchen."

Ria never unfolds her crossed hands, never opens her eyes, never raises her voice, never bothers even to smile. Her only movement is the delicate tip of a pink tongue that in preparation moistens her lips. She barely speaks, her voice as remote as those wispy brushstrokes of cirrus clouds lingering in the heavens, and as gentle, saying, "You're lying."